Autumn's Ghost

A Larry Macklin Mystery-Book 15

A. E. Howe

Books in the
Larry Macklin Mystery Series
(in order):

November's Past

December's Secrets

January's Betrayal

February's Regrets

March's Luck

April's Desires

May's Danger

June's Troubles

July's Trials

August's Heat

September's Fury

October's Fear

Spring's Promises

Summer's Rage

Autumn's Ghost

Winter's Chill

Valentine's Warning

St. Patrick's Cross

Memorial Day's Escape

Independence Day's Search

ISBN-13: 978-1-7346541-2-7

This book is a work of fiction. Names, characters, places and incidents are the product of the author's imagination or are used fictitiously. Any resemblance to actual events, locales, business establishments, persons or animals, living or dead, is entirely coincidental.

DEDICATION

This one is for all the rescue groups for animals both big and small. Thanks for all you do, especially when resources are limited and the need is great.

CHAPTER ONE

It was just past noon on a Friday in October. The last clouds of the season's first real cool front blew across the sky, leaving a crystal-blue expanse in their wake. My partner Pete Henley and I were sitting at a picnic table in front of one of our favorite lunch haunts—recently rebranded as Not Your Typical Taco.

"These really *aren't* your typical tacos," Pete said with a smile as he munched his way through a cheeseburger taco and a cup of curly fries. A barbeque taco waited to be his next victim.

"Aren't you watching your weight?" I chided him.

"Yeah, yeah. I'll take the barbeque one home for dinner," he said grudgingly.

"Have you seen Darlene this week?" I asked, taking a bite of my Greek taco and savoring the flavors.

"Chief Marks is too high and mighty to be hobnobbing with the likes of us." There was a hint of sadness in his voice. I knew that Pete missed my ex-partner as much as I did, though I couldn't help but be happy for her. Becoming Calhoun's chief of police was a good career move. The department was small, but it would still look good having "chief" on her résumé.

"I've waved to her a couple of times. She'll have more time once she gets settled in and weeds out some of the chaff in the department."

"I was always surprised that Chief Maxwell let some of them stay on," Pete mused.

"He liked to do most of the thinking in the department so he was mostly satisfied if his officers just said 'yes, sir' and did what they were told."

"I guess he could get away with micromanaging the few cases they actually had."

"And that's exactly why he let us take on anything that looked too involved," I agreed. "On the other hand, I've already noticed that Darlene has offered to investigate a couple of major crime cases, including that sexual assault at the Roads Best motel."

"She's welcome to it." Pete didn't mind murders or bloody vehicle accidents, but more than once I'd seen him flinch when the case involved sexual assault or rape. His wife and two daughters were his world, and I'd always assumed that was the reason such cases were particularly difficult for him to investigate.

"Weekend plans?"

Pete rolled his eyes. "Sunday we're going hiking."

"To a restaurant?"

"Ha, ha, smartass. We're going to Bear Creek Educational Forest. Sarah went there a couple of years ago with Kim on a school trip. She's been leaning on me, like everyone else—" He gave me the squint-eye. "—about getting in shape."

"It's because we care," I said with a smile.

In truth, he had been doing much better with his diet and exercise, especially after the SWAT team commander had read Pete the riot act about his health. Pete was the department's firearms instructor and the SWAT team's ace sniper, and he dearly loved both positions. When Lieutenant Barron had told him that they were instituting physical requirements for the SWAT team, Pete went into a three-day pout before pulling up his big-boy pants and getting serious about taking off some weight and increasing his aerobic fitness.

"Just you wait. This is only your first year of marriage. Give it a few years and you'll have a semi-truck-size spare tire around *your* waist."

"Never," I scoffed, though I had to admit that my weight was fluctuating more than it used to.

"You on call?" Pete asked.

"Yes, so keep your fingers crossed for a quiet weekend around here."

"I have absolute confidence that you can handle anything that comes up," he said, putting his second taco back in the bag with a few remaining fries.

As if on cue, my phone rang with a call from dispatch. Deputy Matti Sanderson had answered a call at 1912 Dodmoe Avenue concerning an unresponsive male, which she was now reporting as a possible homicide. I responded that I was five minutes from the scene and on my way.

Pete had been making strange faces while I talked on the phone. As soon as I hung up, he started babbling. "No way! Not that place. Cripes!" His eyes were wide. Seeing my lack of reaction, he said, "It's the Lynch house!" His voice was as high as a ten-year-old's.

"Damn it, you're right."

Pete had grown up only a couple of blocks from the place, while I'd been raised in a neighborhood about two miles away. Still, I knew the house. Everyone in town did. It was Adams County's most famous haunted house. I gathered up what was left of my lunch and tossed it into a trashcan on the way to my car.

"You're really going over there?" Pete asked.

"What do you want me to do, call up dispatch and tell them to send someone else?" I laughed.

"I would!" Pete yelled, following me.

"Come on," I said derisively as I climbed into my unmarked car.

"I've got stories," Pete said darkly as I started the engine.

I grinned and shook my head as I drove away, but there was something deep in the pit of my stomach that said I wasn't going to like what I found at the Lynch house. All the old stories of the murders rose up from the depths of my childhood—1930s, whole family killed by the oldest son, a bloody axe, a court case ending in a hung jury, and a boy found hanging in his cell before a second trial could be convened. By all accounts, it wasn't until World War II that the murders had stopped being the number one topic of conversation in the county.

As I neared the old house, I saw Deputy Sanderson's car parked out front. She was leaning against the hood, looking at her phone, but she made a beeline for me as soon as I parked at the curb.

"You aren't gonna believe this mess," she said. The tone of her voice caused me to reconsider Pete's concerns. She didn't sound scared, necessarily, but definitely a little freaked out. And she was one of our most rock-steady deputies.

"That bad?"

"Creepy. The victim has deep penetration wounds to his back." By the sound of her voice, she was making an effort to sound clinical.

"Deep wounds?"

"I was trying to be circumspect, but screw it. He looks like he was hacked to death," she said bluntly.

Like the Lynches, I thought, forcing back an inappropriate chuckle.

I stared at the building. It was a large, two-story farmhouse with a wide, wrap-around porch. It had originally been the main house for a farm that grew more than two hundred acres of shade tobacco. After the murders, all the land had been sold except for the house and the three acres surrounding it. Now it sat fifty yards from the road with houses on either side, a far cry from its farming days. I wondered who owned the house now. It had been empty for as long as I could remember, but it had always been well maintained. Even the yard was always trimmed and neat, though I did notice that it lacked any personal touches.

When we got to the porch, I could see splatters and pools of blood. Clearly, someone had taken a beating.

"The body is over here," Sanderson said, pointing to the north corner of the porch. I looked over to see two feet sticking out from behind an old wicker loveseat that was lying on its back. There were broad smears of blood on the loveseat, stark against the white paint.

"No one lives here, right?"

"Yep. According to the neighbor who called it in, the place is owned by a grandson of the Lynches, but he's never here."

"Which neighbor?"

She pointed to a two-story brick house next door. "She could see the body from her second-story window."

I walked gingerly around the loveseat to get a better look. "Did you call Shantel?" Shantel Williams was the head of our crime scene unit and also in charge of the evidence room.

"She and Marcus are on the way."

The dead man was lying face down with his head and one arm hanging off of the porch. The old plaid shirt he was wearing was coated in blood. Half a dozen deep cuts scarred the middle of his back.

"I take it you knocked on the door?"

"*And* walked around the house. All the doors and windows look secure."

I nodded. The last thing I wanted was to find out that our killer had been hiding in the house all along.

"Have you called Darzi's office?" Dr. Darzi was our coroner, but since Adams County was too small to employ him full time, he worked out of a hospital in Tallahassee. Though with the number of murders we'd had over the last couple of years, I was beginning to wonder if we should reassess the situation.

"No. I thought I'd leave it to you."

"Thanks, Sandy. You're all heart," I said, retracing my

path to the porch steps while I made sure that I didn't tread on any of the blood evidence. "We should wait out by the cars."

"It's creepy, the guy getting killed here," Sanderson said once we were back in the yard. "And like that. I mean with an axe."

I'd seen Matti Sanderson work some pretty grisly car accidents and never show any emotion other than professional detachment, so I was a little surprised at her reaction. I looked back at the house and had to admit that it had a farm Gothic aura that made me think of grisly murders with pitchforks, chainsaws and, of course, axes. On top of that, it *was* October.

I hit speed dial for the morgue. It took me a couple of minutes to get through the phone tree and reach Dr. Darzi. "I need the A-Team," I told him.

"Linda *is* the A-Team today. I'd love to come out and explore the countryside and your own special brand of rural homicide, but I'm afraid I have a demonstration to present to a group of pathology students in one hour."

"Linda will be fine. But are you sure you want to pass up on what looks to be a genuine axe murder?"

"Sounds delightful and macabre at the same time. I'll be sorry to miss it, but I will look forward to reviewing footage of the crime scene, and I promise to personally perform the autopsy."

"Did you ever see the TV show *Psych*?"

"Woody is my favorite fictional pathologist," Darzi said and I could hear the smile in his voice.

"Yeah, well, you're beginning to sound like him."

I hung up to the sound of his laughter. Five minutes later, Linda texted me for directions. Before I could hit "send," Shantel pulled up beside us in the crime scene van, Marcus Brown riding shotgun beside her.

"I didn't come back to work in Adams County just to go into some freaky haunted house in my first week," Marcus said, a frown on his dark face as he stared at the house.

"Listen to you," Shantel chided him, then said in her best church-lady voice, "If you have God in your heart, there isn't anything to fear from the devil." She was already pulling equipment out of the back of the van.

"A whole family was slaughtered in there," Marcus said with a shudder.

"Honey, our *job* is to go into houses where people have been killed." Shantel handed him a video camera, then grabbed another camera bag for herself.

"This is different." His serious tone contrasted with his usual happy-go-lucky manner. "I've heard stories about this place. A friend told me he saw lights floating in the windows."

"If it makes you feel any better, the body is on the porch. Right now there's no reason you have to go inside," I told him.

"That's something," Marcus muttered as he followed Shantel up to the house to document the scene.

I turned to Sanderson. "If you'll stay here and make sure we don't have any gawkers, I'll go talk to the neighbor who saw the body."

"Sure. Things have been quiet all day. Probably got another hour before the Friday afternoon calls start coming in."

"Just let me know if dispatch needs you. Did the neighbor say if she heard anything?"

"Not to me." She shrugged. "Her name's Lucy Holder."

I left her scrolling through her phone and headed next door. I barely had a chance to knock before the door was opened by a woman in her late thirties who looked like she spent a lot of time experimenting with make-up in front of the mirror.

"Is he dead?" she asked as soon as I introduced myself.

"It would appear so." I was there to get information, not give it out. "When did you notice the victim?"

"I really thought he was just drunk this morning when I saw him sprawled out on the porch. That's why I waited a bit to call it in. I've reported vagrants over there a dozen times in the last month. I keep an eye on the place because of its… reputation, you know. And now that it's almost Halloween… it's always bad over there this time of year. Y'all *could* be a little quicker getting here when I call." This speech came out of her mouth with the speed and cadence of a machine gun.

"So you saw the man there this morning?"

"Exactly. 'Cause I always look out of my window when I get up to see if I need to report any bums sleeping over there, or any damage that kids have done during the night. There have been a few break-ins over the years. I really wish that Hinson would sell the property to someone or, better yet, tear the house down and sell us the land. We've tried to buy it a couple of times, but he insists on the appraised value with the house. Not that I think he really wants to sell…" She stopped talking and looked at me, a bit confused. "I'm talking too much, aren't I?"

"I understand you being a little nervous." I tried never to stop a witness or suspect when they were talking. I'd been pleasantly surprised by how many bad actors would reveal themselves if I just let them ramble a bit.

"I guess that's it. I mean, seeing a dead guy. That's not something that happens every day. Did he overdose or what?"

"We'll let the coroner determine the cause of death," I answered, telling the absolute truth even though the state of the body gave pretty heavy odds that it hadn't been an accidental death. "Have you seen this man here before?" It was a bit of a trick question as the view from her house would have made it hard to see much of the body.

"I don't know. There are a lot of bushes between the houses. I couldn't see him very well. All I could tell is that there was someone lying on the porch. Honestly, I couldn't even tell for sure if it was a man or woman."

"Did you hear anything odd this morning or last night?" I asked, wondering if the victim had made any noise when he was attacked.

"No. Not really. We still have our air on." She rolled her eyes elaborately. "Tim is awful. He's like an oven at night. I turn the air up during the day, but as soon as he gets home he puts it down to, like, sixty-eight. Costs us a fortune during the summer…" She stopped herself. "There I go again. You don't care about our electric bill."

"Was your husband home last night?"

"He works in Tallahassee and got home about six."

"I'll want to talk to him too. Can you think of anything else odd or different that's happened in the last week?"

"Not really. Most of the people who live around here stick to themselves. I tried knocking on doors when we moved in five years ago. Everyone was polite enough but… you know."

"Any strangers or strange cars?"

"I don't look out of my windows that often. Oh, I know I came off as a snoop, telling you about the Lynch house, but it *is* a magnet for kids and weirdos."

"Any weirdos in particular?"

"There've been a couple of homeless people who, you know, had mental issues that we've had run-ins with, but nothing recently."

"Did you involve law enforcement with the homeless people?"

"First thing we do is call and report them, though it's usually a waste of time. Don't get me wrong, I know that your deputies can only do what the law allows. I've heard that speech a dozen times. It's just frustrating. I don't have anything against the homeless or the mentally challenged, but I mean, that house isn't supposed to be a homeless shelter, is it?"

"No, it's not," I agreed, knowing that even a small town like Calhoun had its share of people down on their luck.

"So it's for their own good. Right?"

I just nodded, not wanting to encourage more ranting about the homeless. I asked a few more questions and gave her my card, then headed back to the crime scene.

CHAPTER TWO

A black-and-white Ford Escape bearing City of Calhoun Police decals was parked behind my car. I looked around and saw Matti Sanderson talking with Chief Darlene Marks, who'd been my partner at the sheriff's office until a couple of months ago.

"You know that the city police are our sworn enemies," I said, walking up to them.

"Hey half pint, this is my jurisdiction too," Darlene reminded me.

"By two blocks." I pointed toward the city limits.

"A foot is as good as a mile."

"I might just let you have this one."

"There was a murder here years ago, right?" Darlene had been raised in Tampa and hadn't come to Calhoun until she graduated from the law enforcement academy.

"Whole family was killed," I told her.

"Not the whole family," Sanderson piped up. "The brother did it and was waiting in jail for his second trial when he was found hanging in his cell."

"You sound like an authority on the subject." I was a little surprised. Sanderson was always focused on the job and seldom talked about herself or any of her interests.

"I've read everything I could find on the murders. I guess I find it interesting. I can read about an old crime like that and use some of what I know about police work to try to understand what happened, but it's not like I'm still at work. There's some distance from the blood and guts."

"I think someone is going to make it to CID someday," Darlene said, giving her an elbow bump.

"I *would* like to do a little more than guard crime scenes and write tickets."

"They haven't filled my old job," Darlene said, looking at me pointedly. I raised my hands in surrender.

"Don't look at me. I'm just a grunt myself."

"Your dad's the sheriff," Darlene reminded me.

"Which means I get to hear him moan and groan about the budget all the time. The truth is, I don't think he's going to fill your spot in criminal investigations until he gets some of the federal money they still owe us in reimbursement for the costs of Hurricane Marcy."

"I'm not in a big hurry." Sanderson looked embarrassed by the focus on her job advancement and quickly changed the subject. "Do you think this is some kind of copycat thing?"

"Seems farfetched to me. The house and murders *are* well known around here, but the man's clothes and the property's history with the homeless would lead me to think it's a crime of opportunity. Maybe an argument or a fight over money, food, alcohol or drugs," I said with a shrug.

"And the first lesson is: don't make your mind up before you see the evidence," Darlene added.

"Or, better yet, recognize that you're going to come to any case with preconceived notions about the victim and the circumstances. By being aware of your bias, you can make sure you don't fall into the trap of trying to make the evidence fit your theory instead of the other way around."

"We should teach a class, Poindexter," Darlene told me with a laugh.

"You started this," I reminded her.

"You two never should have been allowed to be partners," Sanderson said, shaking her head.

"And here we are again." Darlene grinned.

"I'd turn it over to you if I could. Pete isn't going to want to get anywhere near this one, the big wuss."

"I'll talk with your dad. I think we can both work on it. But I don't think you should let Pete off too easily."

"We can agree on that."

The coroner's van pulled up and Linda hopped out, followed by a man who looked like he'd been sent from central casting to fill the role of a lumberjack. He had a full beard on a head twice the size of mine, and the rest of his body was in proportion.

"What have you got for us today?" Linda asked, not bothering to grab any equipment from the van. She was familiar enough with the routine to know that she'd probably have to wait awhile for Shantel and Marcus to finish documenting the scene. "Oh, yeah, this is our newest intern, Andre." She waved back at the man plodding behind her.

I looked back and forth between Linda and the lumberjack, trying to decide if his name really was Andre. He and I locked eyes for a moment before he shook his head and smiled.

"Go ahead, laugh. According to my folks, they didn't know I was going to be a giant when they named me," he said with a distinctive Canadian accent.

"No jokes from me," I said, then filled them in on what they needed to know before getting hands-on with the deceased.

"It's a *murder* house!" Darlene said, using her most sinister tone of voice.

"Well, yeah, there's a dead body lying on the front porch," Linda joked.

We let Sanderson tell them the full story.

"So it's a *real* murder house," Linda said, sounding impressed. "We had one in my home town. A woman poisoned three of her family members before she was caught. Said that they weren't happy, so she thought she'd put them out of their misery. Turned out, she had a hefty insurance policy on each one of them. We used to dare each other to ring the doorbell on Halloween. The owners seemed to take it in stride. Which is amazing, since it must have been annoying as all hell."

Linda and Andre headed back to the van to get the stretcher and the rest of their equipment, while Sanderson took off to respond to a call from dispatch.

"Let's take a walk around the house," I told Darlene. "We haven't found the murder weapon."

As we walked up to the house, I told Darlene everything I'd noticed about the victim.

"I might recognize him. We've been visiting the homeless camps recently, trying to get a handle on any predators that might be lurking among the sheep."

There were a few spots throughout Calhoun where the homeless tended to congregate. One camp had about a dozen semi-regular shelters made up of tents, cardboard boxes and tarps. The local churches had come together a few years earlier to form a joint food bank that also served hot meals when they could, and helped to coordinate emergency shelters when there were storms or extreme temperatures.

"Are you going to break them up?" I asked. Both the sheriff's office and the police had busted up the camps from time to time, but the homeless just relocated to new digs.

"No, not right now. But we've been getting lots of calls for service lately. Fights, overdoses, theft, that sort of thing. I thought by showing our presence, we might get more cooperation with catching the bad actors... or at least scare them away."

"Think this could be spillover from some of the stuff that's been happening in the camps?"

"Maybe. We've seen some nasty attacks in the last two months. One resulted in an old guy landing in the ICU in Tallahassee with a severe concussion. The perp for that one is still on the loose. That's one of the cases we'd like to get more cooperation on. Talking to some of the folks, I got the idea they know who did it. Unfortunately, the victim wasn't very popular."

"Speaking of the ICU, how are you and Hondo getting along?"

Alejandro Valdez, known by everyone as Hondo, was one of the county's EMTs. He and Darlene had been an item for over a year. I knew it was an odd time to be catching up on our personal lives, but I hadn't had much of a chance to talk with Darlene since she'd become chief.

"We haven't been seeing much of each other. It's strange. He never seemed to have a problem with me being a sheriff's deputy. I don't know if it's me being chief that's made him step back, or if it's because I've been busy settling into the new job."

"I'm sorry. I think Hondo's a great guy." I'd already heard through the grapevine that their relationship seemed to have cooled, but I was disappointed to have it confirmed.

"Me too," Darlene said with less than her usual bravado. Eager to distract me, she pointed to an old shed sitting about fifty feet from the back of the house. "Let's check that out."

As we approached, I listened and watched for any movement. Crepe myrtles surrounded the wooden structure and moss grew thick on a couple of the windows. It was dirty, but looked sound, the perfect dive for someone wanting to live under the radar. I wasn't surprised to find that the ground outside the door was well trodden.

"Someone's used this regularly," Darlene said.

"Hello!" I called out in my official, no-bullshit voice. "If anyone's inside, we'd like to speak with you."

There was no response. Beside me, I saw Darlene slide her right hand back and undo the snap on the retention strap over the top of her Glock. I stood to one side and opened the door, prepared for someone to come dashing out of the shed. When nothing happened, I shrugged and took out the small flashlight that I always carried with me. Flicking it on, I shined it around the interior of the shed.

The light revealed an assortment of rusty yard tools, along with cans, bottles and bags of weed killer, ant poison, fertilizer and every other chemical sold at a garden center in the last thirty years. Stepping in, I saw an old cot with a hunter-orange sleeping bag lying on top of it. There was a cup from the Fast Mart on the floor next to the cot that still had liquid in it.

"Someone's been sleeping in here," I said.

"Thanks for the news flash, Captain Obvious," Darlene replied good-naturedly while bending down to peer under the cot. "You'll want to get Shantel and Marcus to come in here. There's a bag that looks interesting, plus a couple of plastic grocery bags with food in them."

"So you want to be part of the investigation, but it's our techs doing all the work," I said.

"Each of my cops knows how to collect fingerprints and take pictures, but that's the sum total of our evidence collection capabilities."

"I'm crying a river of tears. Just remember that you abandoned me."

We left the shed and finished circling the house. By the time we got to the front again, Shantel and Marcus were heading for their van.

"We're done documenting everything with the body," Shantel told me.

"That's what you think. We just found what could be the victim's campsite in a shed outback."

"Putting me back to work already. And after I found a perfect bloody print for you."

Shantel walked toward me, scrolling through the images on her digital camera. My hopes rose at the thought of a solid piece of evidence right out of the gate. As I wondered if it would be a print from a shoe or a hand, she turned the camera's screen to me. Centered in a small pool of blood was the perfect outline of a cat's paw.

"Ha, ha," I said dryly.

Always a perfectionist, Shantel had even taken a couple of shots with a ruler next to the print for size comparison. "Kitten from the look of it," she said with a grin.

"Hey, you never know. This print might match up to a neighbor's cat and they'll know they let it out of the house at a certain time, which will help establish the time of the murder and catch our killer." I tried to sound upbeat.

"Stranger things have happened," Darlene said, rolling her eyes.

"Y'all are up," I told Linda and Andre, who'd been watching us, anxious to get started. I couldn't imagine manhandling corpses for a living. It was bad enough seeing what I had to see, let alone having to be hands-on with them, all day every day.

"Not to tell you your business, but I'd say you're going to need to consult with a blood spatter expert," Shantel said as she and Marcus headed for the shed.

"You aren't wrong." I thought of all the blood I'd seen when I went on the porch to look at the body. I knew of a guy at the Florida Department of Law Enforcement who was top notch. I made a note to give him a call as soon as I got back to the office.

Darlene's radio squawked and I could tell by the way the conversation started that she was going to be busy for a while, so I glanced across the street. There were two houses that would have a decent view of the Lynch house from their front windows. I looked at my watch and saw that it was after four. Hoping someone was home, I picked the house on the left, a modest little mid-century that had probably been built in the early '60s.

My knock was answered in a timely manner by a dapper older gentleman wearing a sweater and slacks. His smile told me that I wouldn't have any trouble getting him to talk.

"What happened over there?" he asked, not even giving me a chance to introduce myself.

"A deceased male was found on the porch."

"Dead. You can say dead man. I'm not one of those

sensitive types. Three tours of 'Nam pretty much wiped out the niceties. But not my manners. I'm Howard Tippets." He stuck out his hand.

I was still trying to picture this hundred-and-forty-pound elderly man stomping through the jungles of Vietnam and was slow to respond. The second time he pushed his hand toward me, I took it and felt the grip of the younger man he'd been.

"I'm Deputy Larry Macklin."

"Macklin. That's the name of our… yeah, you're his son. I'm a friend of Albert Griffin. He's mentioned you a few times. Come on in." He turned and was halfway down the hall before I was through the door.

"I'd like to ask you a couple of questions."

"Ask away. Want some coffee?"

"No. I'm fine."

"Suit yourself. We can sit in the kitchen. Hip's been bothering me. The orthopedic doctor's been after me for a couple of years to get it replaced."

He led me into his tidy kitchen and waited for me to sit. I didn't want to be there that long, but after he mentioned his hip I didn't feel right making him stand so down I went into one of the kitchen chairs.

"Now tell me all about it." His eyes were clear and focused.

"A neighbor reported a man lying on the porch, and when our deputy arrived she discovered that he was decea… dead."

"She's a looker."

"What?"

"The woman deputy. Cute as can be. I've always had a thing for a woman in uniform," Tippets said with a broad smile.

"Have you seen anyone across the street in the last week?" I decided to ignore his remarks about Sanderson.

"She married?" He wasn't having it.

"Mr. Tippets, I can't act as a matchmaker for you and

one of our deputies."

"No need to get snooty, son. I was just asking."

"About the house across the street?"

Tippets sighed. "There are folks that come around. I've seen some picture-takers over the last couple of months. Talked to a pair of them for a while. He was a filmmaker and she was his camera… person, I guess you'd say. They loved all the grisly details about the house. She had a nice set of boobs."

"When was this?" I asked, pretending I hadn't heard the comment about the woman's breasts.

"A week ago. Something like that. Vicky. That was her name. I got her number, but it didn't work. Think she mixed up one of the digits."

I bet she didn't mix them up by accident, I thought as I took out my pad and made some notes.

"Did you get her last name?"

"She was pretty coy. Said she'd give it to me on our first date." He laughed.

"What about the man?"

"I don't swing that way."

"Did you get his name?" I had a hard time hiding my frustration with his constant innuendos.

"It was something odd. I don't remember. He's filming some silly ghost show about the Lynch house. He gave me his card, but I threw it away."

"Have you noticed any homeless people in the neighborhood?"

"My eyesight isn't what it used to be. I was a sniper in 'Nam. Barely got the job 'cause I was so scrawny."

Your eyes are good enough to be checking out Sanderson from across the street, I thought, but didn't press him on it. "Does anyone else live here?"

"Not since my wife passed away five years ago. Now she was a beauty, hot as a firecracker in her day." He saw my expression. "I know what you're thinking. I'm a randy old man. You're damn right and I'm proud of it. My wife and I were active, if you know what I mean, right up until she got sick. Not like some of my friends living in a sexless, dead marriage. Veronica and I had fun. That was another lesson I learned over in 'Nam. Life is a gift. Ronny and I never wasted a day, and if she's looking down today, she's cheering me on."

"I didn't mean to imply anything," I said, properly chastised. However, I did think a few warning signs should have been posted around his property to warn any unsuspecting women who might wander too close to the old letch.

"It's all right."

I listened to a couple of grisly war stories before making my way to the door. I wanted to get back to the house before they moved the body. That would be my first chance to get a good look at the victim's face and to search the body for ID.

On my way across the street, I thought about what Tippets had said about the filmmaker and his camerawoman. Could someone gawking at the Lynch house have gotten into an argument with our victim?

CHAPTER THREE

Darlene's car was gone, so her crisis must have evolved into a big enough fracas to demand her personal attention. But Linda was waiting impatiently on the porch, waving her hand at me.

"I thought you'd want to be here when we moved the body," she scolded.

"Just interviewing a witness," I explained.

"So we should wait around while you do your work?" Linda shook her head in mock irritation.

"Admit it. This is nothing but a day in the country to you."

"Shhhhhh! Don't tell Dr. Darzi. I always pretend like I'm irritated when he assigns me to one of your victims."

"You make it sound like we have a lot."

"Let's just say you aren't lagging behind in the statistics."

Andre was standing near the body, his expression bemused. They had already bagged the victim's hands and feet, and laid an open body bag beside it.

"We're going to roll the body onto the bag so his head and back wounds won't pick up any dirt from the porch," Linda explained to Andre.

Once the man's face was revealed, everyone's attention

was drawn to an indentation on his forehead that was surrounded by abrasions.

"A blow like that could have killed him," Linda said, more to herself than to any of us.

This changed my way of thinking significantly. There was a big difference between a victim who was killed by blows from behind and one who was hit while facing his attacker.

Looking past the head wound, I took in the rest of the man's features. His face was weather-worn, a common trait of someone who'd spent years on the streets. He looked to be in his late thirties, neatly shaven and clean. If it hadn't been for the sunburned face and his ragged clothing, I wouldn't have immediately taken him for a homeless man.

I squatted down and looked at his bagged hands. The nails were long but clean, as was the skin. I put on gloves before searching his pockets, where I found thirty-two dollars and a wallet containing a state ID card and a few other odds and ends.

The man's name was Gregory Wells and he was thirty-seven years old. I bagged the wallet and let them finish wrapping up the body for transport to the morgue.

"What's your best guess for time of death?" I asked Linda.

"From the body's temperature, and assuming that the victim has been lying outside since his death, I'd say between ten last night and one this morning. But that's just a guess."

Linda and Andre gingerly lifted the body and carried it down the stairs to a waiting stretcher. As they rolled it away, Shantel and Marcus came back to start taking blood samples. There was a bunch of evidence to catalog. With dozens of spots, streaks and pools spread across the porch, the wall and on the furniture, it was impossible to tell if all of the blood belonged to the victim, or if some might have been left by the killer. If we could find blood that didn't type out as the victim's, then we could have it DNA-tested with the hope that it would lead to the perpetrator.

Working with Shantel and Marcus made my job easier.

Not only were they technically good at their job, but they were often able to come up with things that I'd overlooked. I left them to it, walking down the front steps where I saw Pete talking to Linda by the coroner's van.

"So you decided to brave the scary haunted house," I said in my best smartass voice.

"Go ahead and laugh, my friend. I tell you, that house is bad voodoo." Pete nodded toward the Lynch house.

"It was for Gregory Wells. I'll give you that."

"I'll leave you boys to argue it out. Autopsy most likely won't happen before Monday," Linda said.

"I thought we ordered the premium service," I groused.

"Yeah, but you're paying for basic."

After Linda and Andre had left, Pete and I walked up to the house. On the way, I told him everything I knew so far. Pete exchanged greetings with Marcus when we got to the porch.

"That's a lot of blood," Pete whistled.

"I'm going to call Nick Foster at FDLE."

"Short of someone with a national reputation, he's the best I know," Marcus said. He'd recently returned from a stint working for FDLE where he'd eventually realized that he preferred life in Adams County. "The good thing about all this blood is that an expert like Nick ought to be able to give you a pretty good idea of how things went down."

"What do you think?" I asked him.

Shantel and Marcus each had their strong suits. Shantel was sharp and would come out and tell me right away if she thought I was making a mistake. When I'd first become an investigator, it had been Shantel who'd, more often than not, helped me choose the right evidence to collect and focus on. Marcus, on the other hand, had to be coaxed for his opinion. When he finally gave it, it was usually insightful and built on years of observing crime scenes and the investigations they'd triggered.

"With the blood by the door, and the trail of it leading to the puddle near where the body was found, I'd say he was hit in the face there," Marcus said, pointing to a spot by the door about fifteen feet from the edge of the porch. "Then I think he stumbled and fell over, with the attacker hitting him along the way. Not that I'm an expert."

"I figure the killer must have been between Wells and the front steps, otherwise it would have made sense for him to move toward the steps to escape instead of the edge of the porch," I said.

Pete nodded. "Makes sense. So was Wells waiting on the porch for this person, who then walked up to him and started wailing on him with a hatchet? Or was Wells facing the door and the person said something or made a noise that caused Wells to turn, at which point the hatchet job started?"

"Maybe Nick will be able to tell," Marcus said. "All I can say for sure is that the victim was between the killer and the house. You can see a light outline of Wells's body where it shielded the house from the spatter when he was hit in the face."

"I wonder what the original murders were like." Pete sounded thoughtful.

"You aren't suggesting that there's a link? That was more than eighty years ago," I scoffed.

"A copycat? Someone obsessed with the murders?"

"Seems farfetched," I said, though I couldn't help thinking of the man across the street and the folks he'd met who were interested in the Lynch murders.

"Same type of weapon is all I'm sayin'."

"Everybody in town knows about those murders." Marcus had gone back to collecting samples, but was clearly still paying attention.

"I'll talk to Albert Griffin. He'll be able to fill in all the background." Mr. Griffin was a historian with an encyclopedic knowledge of the county… and a vast collection of past issues of Calhoun's now-defunct local paper.

"I know the murders have been included in a few anthologies of true crime cases. I think they'd get even more attention if Daniel Lynch hadn't been arrested," Marcus suggested.

My text alert went off and I saw a message from Shantel: *At the shed. Pictures and video done if you want to search it.*

Shantel was walking around the outside of the shed, taking more pictures, when Pete and I joined her. "I found a couple of possible tracks," she said, placing a ruler next to a partial print in the dirt. "There are evidence bags and gloves in my box." She nodded her head toward a plastic toolbox by the door of the shed.

We gloved up and grabbed some bags before going inside. Remembering what Darlene had seen, I got down on my hands and knees and reached under the cot while Pete held the flashlight. I pulled out an old green knapsack first.

"What the hell?" was my first response when I saw the wires and tools in the bag. The more items I pulled out, the odder the cache seemed.

"A junk collector," Pete muttered, examining a circuit board that looked like it had come from a radio or some sort of electronic toy.

"Here's a solder gun. He seems to have been making something." The items in the knapsack made me think of tinfoil hats and radios designed to communicate with aliens. "I don't recognize some of this stuff." I held up a black plastic thingy with input and output ports marked on it. There were also two mysterious boxes held together with duct tape.

"It's not from this world." Pete imitated the eerie sound of a Theremin.

After emptying the bag, I couldn't see how any of the items would help us identify the person who had killed Wells. But it was too early in the investigation to make those judgments, so I set the bag aside to be cataloged.

Reaching back under the cot, I pulled out a grocery bag loaded with crackers, cookies and several small bags of cat treats.

"Wells apparently had a soft spot for cats," Pete

observed.

He had his own weakness for felines; not that I could point fingers. More than three years ago, I'd taken in a stray that had been living behind the sheriff's office. "They're so cute when they're kittens."

"Then they grow up and judge you for not feeding them at five on a Sunday morning," Pete sighed.

"Two more bags to go," I said, pulling out another bag of groceries and an old duffel bag. Inside were a change of clothes, a couple of books, two old cell phones that didn't look like they'd worked for years, a few bags of potato chips and a can of Red Bull.

"The man was living the life." Pete's voice echoed with an unusual sadness.

"Mental illness or addiction. We'll know more after a background check and the autopsy."

"Do you think this was a homeless-on-homeless crime?" Shantel asked as we helped her put everything into evidence bags.

"The weapon seems right. Those types of murders often involve knives, blunt objects or something like a hatchet," I said.

We took another walk around the property, looking for any evidence that might have been missed. We were lucky that the owner obviously had a lawn service to keep the place looking neat. Collecting evidence at an abandoned house could be next to impossible.

A month earlier Julio Ortiz, one of our newest investigators, had been working on a shooting at a drug house. We'd all gone over and pitched in to help him separate any real evidence from all the trash in the house. The drug dealer had been shot with a 12-gauge loaded with birdshot, which wouldn't have been too bad except that the muzzle had been only six inches from his left side. Blood, skin and birdshot had been spread all over a room that looked like everyone in the county had decided to dump their trash there that week.

Adding to the nightmare was all the flotsam from a year's worth of drug addicts shooting up inside the house. All we could do was pick up what was on top of the trash pile and looked most likely to be important to the current investigation. Luckily for all concerned, the dealer pulled through and, not surprisingly, was willing to talk for hours about the person who had shot him. Of course, what he'd mostly talked about was what a lowlife scum the addict had been for shooting his connection.

"Here!" Pete yelled from a back corner of the yard, bringing me out of my memories.

Pete was standing over a clear footpath that led from the yard, crossing behind the backdoor neighbor's house to a side street.

"I haven't talked to this neighbor yet. Let's walk the path and see if anyone's home," I suggested.

As we walked, I kept an eye on the neighbor's house. There were spots where anyone walking along the path could be seen from several of the windows of the two-story brick house.

"Wonder if they've ever had a problem with the homeless?" Pete mused, pulling out his radio and calling dispatch to see if they had any record of calls for service from the house on the south side of the Lynch house.

"The owner's name is Haris Khan and he's made a dozen complaints. Couple of burglaries, a yard theft, a prowler and several nuisance calls," the dispatcher replied.

"You heard the man," Pete said to me after signing off.

"Great. The homeowner will be really glad to talk with me."

"Send Darlene. Most of the calls were routed to the police."

"Citizens seldom make the distinction. Let's go knock on the door."

The Federal-style house looked like it should have been sitting on the banks of the James River instead of in our little North Florida town. There was an almost-new Mercedes convertible and a Lexus SUV in the driveway.

"At least the crooks that robbed them weren't picking on the poor," I said. It was always sad when the meth-heads stole a poor family's ten-year-old TV or their only running car.

"Ten bucks says we get the 'I pay your salary' routine," Pete mumbled as we mounted the steps of the small tiled porch that did not invite you to sit down and chat awhile. In fact, the only space on the porch where you could have put a chair was taken up by a pair of life-size concrete bears standing on their hind legs and a couple of ferns.

"Look! They have statues of you," I told Pete.

"Funny boy. Ring the damn bell and let's get this over with." I'd noticed in the past that Pete didn't like folks who put on airs.

I rang the bell, which was loud enough to be heard out by the curb. I half expected a butler to answer, but instead we were greeted by a very petite Indian woman wearing a blue-and-gold embroidered dress and gold jewelry that sparkled in the fading light.

"Yes, may I help you?" she said, with just a hint of an accent.

"I'm Deputy Larry Macklin with the sheriff's office. A man was found dead next door. We'd like to ask you a few questions," I blurted.

"I did notice the cars. Come in," she said, stepping aside. "I assume you will want to talk with my husband too. Follow me to the library."

The hallway looked like it was straight out of Old England, the walls hung with paintings of men and women riding to the hounds and classical battle scenes. The woman opened a pair of eight-foot-high oak doors and gestured for us to enter the library.

"If you'll wait in here, I'll be right back," she said, closing the doors behind her.

"Are we going to have to call him 'my lord' or 'baron' or something?" Pete joked.

The room wasn't as big as the expensive decorations in the hall would have led me to expect. However, no shortcuts had been taken with the furnishings, all high-end antiques. The centerpiece was a massive mahogany desk that took up a quarter of the room.

I was reading the papers that were laid out on the desk and had just deduced that the owner of the house was a doctor when the door opened and Haris Khan and his wife came into the room. Khan was tall and lanky, wearing a polo shirt and slacks. He extended his hand.

"Haris Khan. My wife informs me that a man has died next door."

I nodded and introduced myself and Pete.

Khan surprised me by smiling and nodding. "Macklin. Yes, I know you." He wagged his finger at me like he was chastising a naughty child. "My good friend Dr. Darzi talks about you."

"He does?" I was a bit surprised to find out that Darzi had told anyone about me.

"He says that you bring him the most interesting cases."

"You're a doctor?"

"I'm a neurosurgeon and I also do consulting work. Darzi was one year behind me at medical school before we entered our specialties. What happened to the man next door?"

"I'd rather…" I'd started to say that I wanted to wait for the autopsy, but I realized that there wasn't any point in putting it off. "From the look of the wounds, he was assaulted with an axe or hatchet."

The result of my blunt answer could be seen in the Khans' expressions. Mrs. Khan's mouth opened and closed and her husband changed from having a casual academic interest to being a concerned homeowner and family man.

"The man was murdered? Do you have any idea who the assailant was?"

"Not at this time."

"We've had trouble in the past with vagrants. That house

should be torn down." Khan's voice had an edge to it.

"Have you seen anyone hanging about in the past week?"

"The last time I reported one of them was a couple of months ago. But I've seen one or two in the neighborhood. I expect you will have patrols in the area?" This last line was delivered in a tone that suggested it was a hair's breadth from being an order, not a request. I honestly had not considered the need, but I understood their viewpoint.

"I will notify our patrol officers and they'll be keeping a closer eye on things." I pulled out one of my cards. "Feel free to call me if you see anyone in the neighborhood who doesn't live here."

He took the card. "I will."

"Do you have security cameras?"

"Of course. We put some in when we built the house and had more installed after one of our cars was broken into last year."

"We'll need the footage for the past week."

"Our cameras keep two months' worth of video stored on a hard drive. I can have a copy made for you."

"What have your schedules been for the past two days?" Pete asked, causing Khan to look over at him as though noticing him for the first time.

"I worked both days. Yesterday I got home quite late. Midnight. I had to consult on an accident victim. Naveena?" He turned to his wife.

"I went to work both days. Got home at six. Maybe a little later."

"And did either of you see or hear anything unusual?" I asked.

"Not I. Naveena?"

"No."

"I haven't read the reports related to the crimes that you called in. Was your property recovered or anyone prosecuted for the crimes?" I asked.

"They did catch one of the men. He'd taken some jewelry that Naveena had left in the Lexus. The man tried to sell it at a pawnshop in Tallahassee. This was…" He looked at his wife.

"Almost a year ago, about a month before the hurricane." Hurricane Marcy had struck in late September.

"Was there a trial?" Pete asked.

"He pleaded guilty and spent a couple of months in jail." Khan waved his hand. "The man was in his forties, a deadbeat."

We asked a few more questions before shaking hands and receiving Khan's promise that he'd drop the camera footage off at the sheriff's office the next day. My mind was already trying to figure out who I was going to con into doing the mind-numbing business of reviewing a week's worth of footage from two or three cameras.

CHAPTER FOUR

Darlene was back by the time we returned from speaking with the Khans.

"Deal with your pressing business?" I asked.

"There's some… politics involved in being the chief of police," Darlene allowed.

"I thought it was good to be king," Pete ribbed her.

"If only I was," Darlene said wistfully. "Shantel brought me up to speed on the hobo horror."

"Is that going to be the name of the movie?" I asked.

"It's at least a working title." Darlene smiled.

"You shouldn't be so disrespectful," Pete kidded.

"You're joking, but you're also right. I need to learn to hold the humor in check. 'Cause no one has a sense of humor anymore, and I'd be shit-canned from my job if some of my jokes got out to the general public."

"*I* think you're funny," I assured her.

"Why does that make me feel worse? All joking aside, what do you think happened?"

"I was going to ask you," I responded.

"An attack like that screams personal. Someone he knew. Someone who felt wronged."

"Makes sense," I said. "I don't think he's been getting

around in high society from the look of his clothes, so his social circle is probably going to be confined to the homeless camps and hangouts."

"I've made a few contacts through our recent outreach efforts, and have at least one gal who's given me some pretty good tips. I can check with them and see if any of them knew the deceased and if there was anyone in particular who had a problem with him."

"Have you ever known a homeless person who didn't have some enemies?" Pete asked.

"Oddly, no. Poverty, alcohol, drugs, mental illness and bad hygiene don't make for happy campers." Darlene's voice held more than a little melancholy and I understood how she felt. For me, the homeless had always felt like the embodiment of *There but for the grace of God go I.*

"Finding his friends and enemies is definitely the first step," I said.

"Mid-morning is the best time to catch folks in the camps. Around ten o'clock is when they're waking up," Darlene advised.

"Except for that guy in a green coat who works the morning commuters." Pete shook his head. "I was flashing my blues for a light crew a couple of years ago while they repaired a line. I watched that guy from like seven to nine work the folks coming into town. At least fifty cars stopped for him. At a dollar or more a car, plus the afternoon commute and no taxes taken out, I figured he was making more working four hours than I was in eight."

"Not really a stable career path," I said, shaking my head.

"Like I said, we've been making it a major initiative to clean up the camps in town. I can take you around to them," Darlene offered.

We helped Shantel and Marcus finish up with the crime scene before we stretched tape around the porch, hoping it would keep people away. In reality, it would probably just attract nosy kids. If we had enough personnel, I'd have requested that a deputy be posted to the house. But that wasn't going to happen.

Pete and I canvassed the other houses in the immediate vicinity, but no one was home at most of them and the others were older folks who'd seen and heard nothing.

"It's after six. I'm gonna run by the office then head home," I told Pete. Darlene had gone off to deal with another small-town crisis.

"Good luck this weekend," he said with a shake of his head that clearly read: *Better you than me.*

"I'll get up with Darlene and check out the homeless camps. We should also try to find the guy's family."

"See what you can find out talking to his homeless homies, then if that doesn't provide any leads on the next of kin, we'll run a full background on him."

"No sense waiting. I can do that from my laptop." I hated to wait too long on next-of-kin notifications. The thought of a body lying in the morgue with no one to claim it always drove home the loneliness of death.

"Are you trying to make me feel guilty for not working this weekend?"

"No, really. I'm on call anyway."

"The weather should be great, and Sarah and I have our hiking trip on Sunday, so don't call me. Besides, I didn't see you coming in to help me with those multiple assaults last weekend."

"Come on, that was a kid's birthday party," I said, knowing that he wouldn't be able to let the comment slide.

"I've got pictures of the four, count them, *four* individuals that we had to arrest. Not one of them was under three hundred pounds." Pete wasn't a small man himself, but he'd had his hands full with the call. I'd heard the story from several of the patrol officers who'd been on the scene. The birthday boy was five and his father had shown up at the party three sheets to the wind and with his new wife in tow. Before it was over, the poor boy's mother and grandmother had squared off against the father and the new wife. Cake, presents and furniture had been thrown and windshields smashed.

"You did your duty. Go enjoy the weekend," I told him with a wave of my hand.

Back at the office, I checked the property appraiser's site and got a full name and address for the current owner of the Lynch house. Just a little more searching led me to a phone number. Three cheers for the power of the Internet.

"Alistair Hinson?" I asked.

"I don't want any," answered the grumpy voice on the other end of the line.

I bet you don't, I thought. Aloud, I said, "I'm not a salesman. I'm with the Adams County Sheriff's Office."

"Something happen at the house?" Alistair seemed instantly on edge.

"A man was murdered on the front porch." I decided not to sugarcoat it.

"Seriously?"

"You seemed to be expecting to hear that something had happened there."

"This isn't the first call I've gotten over the years. But I never expected..." He trailed off.

"We've taped up the house. We'd like to preserve the crime scene as best we can for the next week or so."

"Whatever you need to do. Was there any damage to the house?"

"There is a good deal of blood on the porch."

"Oh, hell. That's all I need." He paused for a moment before letting out a great sigh. "I know I sound heartless. Who was killed?"

"He was a homeless man named Gregory Wells."

"I've never heard of him. Of course, I haven't lived in Calhoun since I was a kid."

"You lived in the house?"

"Heavens no! My mother wouldn't even drive by the place. We had a house down by the First Baptist Church."

"So the Lynch house has been vacant for a while?"

"No one has lived there since... oh, I guess the mid-fifties. My grandfather rented it out until he died in 1955. That's also about the time that the stories about the place being haunted gained some mileage. My parents were always upset when the papers would run stories about the murders. Like clockwork, you could count on someone vandalizing the place."

"Why haven't you all sold the house?" This had nothing to do with the investigation, but I couldn't help being puzzled by why a family would own a house for more than sixty years just to let it sit empty.

"The long and short of it is that my father promised my mother that he'd never sell it. It was her uncle's family that had been killed and she inherited the property. She had a strong attachment to it, even though she never wanted to live there." He paused. "Sounds crazy, I know, but you'd have to know our family."

"And you own the house now."

"My dad died two years ago and the will stipulated that I could only sell the house, and I quote, 'if extreme financial hardship requires it.'"

"So he gave you an out?"

"And I won't lie and say that I've never thought about claiming it. The cost of maintaining that house has pushed me *very* close to extreme financial hardship. Especially when you consider that I have two daughters who are working on doctorates."

"I can imagine."

"Oh, there *is* one other way for me to be allowed to sell it. That condition is the exoneration of Daniel Lynch of the murder of his family."

"How is that possible? Any other perpetrator would have to be long dead by now."

"It doesn't say that they have to catch the person who did it. Simply that Daniel Lynch must be shown to be innocent, vindicating my mother's belief in the innocence of her cousin."

I whistled. "Those are very long odds."

"It doesn't matter. This ends with me. Even if I don't sell it, and I *have* considered it, my kids will be under no obligation. I think this has gone on long enough."

"Getting back to the current murder. I just want to be clear, no one should have been at the house or on the property, correct?"

"That's right."

"Could someone in your family have visited recently?"

"You think one of us was involved?"

"No. But when we're evaluating evidence, such as fingerprints, it's important to know who had a legitimate reason for being at the crime scene," I explained.

"I see. I can't imagine anyone going down there. My family lives here in Tennessee and my brother's family is out in Arizona. I'll check with him. I know his kids have gone by the house when they were on their way to Orlando a couple of times. Last time any of my family was there was... I guess... last fall after the hurricane. We had some minor damage."

"Who looks after the property?"

"I forgot about her. Of course. It's Samantha Rutledge. My father hired her to manage it thirty years ago."

"I'll talk to Sammy." Everyone in the sheriff's office knew Sammy. She had been a real estate agent for years and had managed a number of properties in the county. Whenever she had evicted someone, she'd requested to have a deputy on hand. She'd also used us for background checks and would give us a heads-up if she saw any illegal activity going on in one of the rentals. On top of that, most of the older deputies had used her to hunt for property or had rented from her back in the day. Now she was retired from the real estate business, but she still owned a number of rental homes.

"I'll tell her to give you a key to the house," Alistair assured me.

"I'd appreciate that." I could have easily gotten a warrant, but it was nice not to have to jump through the paperwork hoops. "I'll let you know if we find anything unusual or have any breakthroughs in the case."

I used the Internet to try to come up with any next of kin for the deceased, but Gregory Wells wasn't an unusual enough name to make it easy. I doubted that any of the possible leads would prove useful. I texted Linda at the morgue and told her I'd need Wells's fingerprints as soon as possible. With a homeless man, there were even odds that he'd been booked for some infraction of the law.

Cara called and I answered with, "I'm leaving now." A glance at my watch told me it was a quarter after six. "You know I'm on call this weekend, so I might not even make it home."

"Such is the life of the wife of a lawman," she said in a happy little sing-song voice. "We've got leftover pizza for dinner, so it's here whenever you want it."

I was lucky to have a wife who could go with the flow. I tried to put every bit of that acceptance and good nature back into our marriage. Recently, Cara had added to her responsibilities as office manager for our local small animal clinic by doing similar work on the side for the county's equine vet. It took up a chunk of her free time, but knowing that she enjoyed the work made me bite my tongue anytime I felt neglected.

All was quiet on the drive home. I had my radio on, but the only calls were for the patrol guys to handle the typical Friday night traffic, as well as a couple of guys who had already drunk up half their paychecks and were trying to duke it out in front of the Fast Mart. The fight would only concern me if one of them inflicted serious bodily harm on the other. Luckily, from the descriptions coming in over the radio, the combatants would be doing good to even make contact with one another.

"I remember hearing folks talk about that house last Halloween," Cara said when I told her about the body at the Lynch house.

We were done with dinner and were sitting out on the

small deck of our old doublewide, enjoying the cool, dry air and the sound of the wind in the trees. Our twenty acres were surrounded by larger plots of land, so we seldom heard anything but sounds from the road and the occasional distant neighbor. That evening, there was only the lonely bark of a dog and the croaking of frogs down in the swamp at the back corner of the property.

"From what I heard, the murders made quite a dent in the community's peace of mind. I know that's when the sheriff's office became more than a three-man operation. The county paid for two fancy new patrol cars, and they also chose the sites for the sheriff's office and jail. There are pictures of the groundbreaking on the wall outside Dad's office."

"In 1935, they still would have been dealing with the effects of the Depression."

"Exactly. So it was no small thing for the county to be tossing money around like that. Of course, there were still gangsters and rumrunners around, so a lot of the local police forces were manning up."

"Even out here in the sticks?"

"Florida was jumping with gangsters. Admittedly, the only way they'd have ended up in Adams County was if they got lost going from Chicago to Miami."

"Are you going to talk to Mr. Griffin about the old murders?"

"Who else? I'm sure he's got notes on the murders, as well as all the archived papers."

"But the murders were solved, right?"

"Everyone thought they were. They arrested the oldest son. Do you remember the Amityville house?"

"The horror movie?" Cara gave me a puzzled look.

"The real house was also the site of a famous murder case. The 'haunting,'" and I made air quotes with my fingers, "was either the result of the murders, or maybe what caused them in the first place."

"And…"

"The Lynch murders remind me of the Amityville murders, or at least what I remember about them."

"How?" Cara rested her head against the back of her chair and stared up at the stars. I leaned my own head back and looked up in time to see two meteors streak across the sky, earning a *Wow* from me and a *Cool* from Cara.

"The Amityville murders were also committed by the family's eldest son," I said, returning to my story after our astronomy interlude. "He used a rifle and managed to kill the whole family without causing much of a fuss. None of the neighbors heard anything. Though most folks were sure of the son's guilt, there remained a bit of doubt because of the crime scene. How do you kill six members of your family in the middle of the night without waking any of them up? It's the same with the Lynch killings. A fair number of people didn't think the boy could have killed his whole family with an axe, and the first trial ended in a hung jury. When the boy was found hanging in his cell before a second trial could be held, the sheriff closed the case."

"How old was the boy?"

"I don't remember. I'll find out when I talk to Mr. Griffin. Of course, all of this is just a wild tangent. I don't think Wells's murder has anything to do with the Lynch family murders."

Cara reached out and took my hand. "This is nice."

"Talking about murders?" I asked, raising my eyebrows.

"That wasn't exactly what I meant, though it does seem appropriate on a cool autumn evening out in the woods. I specifically meant the weather and the company. But you know what would make it better?"

"A beer?"

"Especially if one was brought to me," she said in a dozy voice.

"Your wish is my command," I said, squeezing her hand as I stood up.

When I came back out with her beer, she looked at my other empty hand. "I forgot you can't have one."

"Not worth the risk when I'm on call. All it would take is for something to happen and someone to smell beer on my breath." I almost had my butt back in the chair when my phone buzzed. "Keep your fingers crossed," I said, looking at the number. I didn't recognize it, but I was relieved that it wasn't dispatch or one of our patrol officers.

"Macklin," I answered.

"There's someone over there now!" an excited woman on the other end of the line exclaimed.

"Who is this?" I asked, even though I was pretty sure I knew the answer.

"Lucy Holder. I live next door to the murder house."

"You say there's someone there now?" I was already heading back inside to grab my keys, gun and duty belt.

"That's right. They're skulking around the side of the house. Should I call 911?"

"No, I'm on my way," I assured her. I didn't want a patrol car rolling up and scaring whoever it was away. I kissed Cara on the forehead and hurried out to my car while trying to calm Mrs. Holder down.

"Is your husband home?"

"No, he's at his mother's. Typical for him to be gone when this is going on," she grumbled.

"It'll be fine. I'm less than ten minutes away."

"Ten minutes!"

"Maybe less. Stay in your house with the doors locked. I'll come there as soon as I check out the Lynch house."

CHAPTER FIVE

I made it in eight. I parked half a block away, put on my belt, attached my Streamlight to the rail on my gun and quick-walked up to the house. I'd decided to use the light on my gun to search the property instead of a flashlight; if I ran into someone who was involved in the killing, I didn't want to be caught flatfooted.

Cautiously, I circled around the side of the house. I didn't see anything until I neared the backyard. There was a pale yellow light coming from the shed where we'd found Gregory Wells's personal items. As I crept closer, I could hear someone throwing things around inside and talking to himself…well, actually it was more like cursing. The shed door was partially open, so I moved around until I could see a figure hunched over, searching under the cot. I approached as quietly as I could. The figure, who was wearing an old black hoodie, cargo pants and sandals, never heard me as he focused all of his attention on rummaging under the bed.

"Well, hell's bells and damnation," he muttered, clearly frustrated at the failure of his efforts to locate something.

"Can I help you?" I said, keeping my gun lowered but ready.

He screamed a high-pitched little squeal and scurried

away from the door. "Who the pisspot are you?" the man asked, trying to regain some composure.

"I'm a deputy with the sheriff's office and you are trespassing on my crime scene," I informed him.

"*Your* crime scene? You aren't the one that was murdered," he said indignantly.

"That's true enough," I agreed. "But neither are you. And, on top of that, you aren't a deputy."

"How do I know *you* are? You aren't wearing no uniform."

I turned slightly so that he could see the star mounted on my belt.

"Get that darn light out of my eyes," he scolded, squinting and holding his hand up to block the glare. I hadn't really been shining it in his face, but I pointed my gun a little more to the right anyway. He looked at the star on my belt and back up to my face, repeating the action a couple of times.

"I guess you are who you say you are," he finally mumbled.

"And who are you?" I asked.

The man looked at me through a pair of milky eyes from under his dark and dusty hoodie. His smile pushed up his suntanned cheeks.

"That is an interesting question." He waggled his finger at me, as if expecting me to ask something else. But I'd gone round and round with the drunk and intoxicated so many times that I just frowned and waited.

"Am I my father's son or my sister's brother? Maybe I'm a friend or an enemy." All this deep thought seemed to tire him out. He half stumbled and caught himself on the cot.

"Do you have some identification?" I asked in my most officious voice.

He attempted to straighten up as though to put on a show of dignity, but his constant wobbling spoiled the effect.

"Somewhere." He patted at his pockets. Unfortunately, his cargo pants had at least ten pockets, so the process took a while. Eventually, he produced a biker's wallet with only a few inches of chain attached and handed it to me. Inside, I was surprised to find a valid driver's license in the name of Bartholomew Jamison Crenshaw, as well as a claim ticket for possessions stored at the Baptist men's shelter. I looked from the picture on the license to the old man in front of me and confirmed that they were one and the same. I took a picture of the license, then handed the wallet back to him.

"Now, what are you doing here?" I asked.

"He… he took my can opener. I loaned it to him for the one time, but he kept it. I told him I'd get it back. All I wanted was the can opener. Is that such a big deal?" This was said in a pleading tone more appropriate to wanting a lost child returned.

"Gregory Wells stole your can opener?"

"No, no, not at all. He borrowed it then didn't return it, even when I asked him for it back."

"What does this can opener look like?"

"Like a can opener." Crenshaw looked at me as though I were a chimpanzee in need of training.

"There are different types of can openers. Please describe the one you loaned to Mr. Wells." I knew that losing my patience would be counterproductive, but it was a strain.

"It was my brother's can opener," he said as though this should settle the matter of its appearance.

"Pretend like I haven't ever seen your brother's can opener and describe it."

"He was in the Army and gave it to me when he came back."

A light went on in my head. "Was it small? About an inch long with a cutting edge that folds out?" I held out my fingers to the approximate size of an Army-issued P38.

"Of course, it was my brother's." Crenshaw seemed relieved that I finally understood. He sank down on the cot and I caught him just in time to keep him from actually lying down. I knew enough to realize that once he settled on the cot, I'd have to get help to get him up again.

"So you came looking for your can opener. When was the last time you saw Gregory Wells?"

"Gory, that's what we called him."

"When was the last time you saw Gory?"

"What's today?"

"Did you see him today?"

"Maybe." His voice was fuzzy.

"Listen, I'm going to get you back to the shelter."

"Okay, sure."

I looked closely at his clothes. They were marked with any number of stains and odd spots, but nothing that looked like dried blood. And from the smell, I was pretty sure he hadn't changed clothes in at least a week. The odds of him having killed Wells seemed slim to none. Still, I wanted to talk to him when he was at his most cognizant. I was sure that "fully sober" wasn't an option, but there was probably a point during his normal ramblings when he was sharper than other times.

I called Reverend Tolliver at the Baptist shelter, who was an incredibly tolerant man. Every patrolman had his number on speed dial for the cases when it wasn't quite necessary to Section 8 someone and send them to the hospital for evaluation, yet they needed to be off the street. Tolliver happily agreed to take Crenshaw in and promised to keep an eye on him.

"Bart's a harmless old soul. I used to let him drive our church van occasionally, but he's past that now," the reverend told me.

"I need to talk to him when he can make sense."

"Twelve-thirty tomorrow. After a night's sleep and lunch. You'll have about two hours before he manages to beg, borrow or steal a bottle."

"I'll ask someone on patrol to bring him there and I'll see you tomorrow. Thanks, Reverend."

After I called dispatch for assistance, I was surprised when Matti Sanderson showed up at the house again. "Weren't you working this morning?" I asked her.

"I'm covering Derick's shift. His daughter is performing in a dance recital in Tallahassee."

I took her back to the shed where I'd left Crenshaw slumped on the cot.

"I know the Bartster," she said, shaking her head. "He must drink more than three normal alcoholics."

"Apparently he knew our victim and wanted him to return a can opener, of all things."

"I've never seen Bart get violent. Paralytic drunk, yes. Unable to remember where the sky is located, absolutely. But never mean. Not even when you're trying to wake him up or move him along."

"I'm not really pegging him as a suspect," I assured her. "But he knew the victim well enough to be mad at him, so I want to interview him when he can put two words together and make sense."

"Early afternoon is your window."

"That's what Reverend Tolliver said."

With much effort, we managed to get Bart onto his feet and out to Sanderson's patrol car.

"You're lucky that he's not a barfer," she told me once he was safely in the car.

"*I'm* lucky?"

"'Cause I'd never forgive you if I had to clean his rancid puke out of the back of my patrol car."

I had my own memories of that particularly horrid job. The back seats of the county's patrol cars had a molded plastic liner to make jobs like that easier, but still no one wanted to clean bodily fluids out of their car. Even after ten minutes with a hose and a liberal amount of bleach, somehow the odor still managed to be there when you got back in and drove away from the carwash.

Once Sanderson was gone, I headed for Lucy Holder's house. She opened the door before I'd even gotten up the porch steps.

"There's nothing to worry about," I told her. "It was a homeless man. A friend of the deceased."

"See what I mean? They wander around the place all the time." She clenched and unclenched her hands.

"Rest assured that we'll be keeping a close eye on the place for the next few weeks."

"I hate to say it, but if you'd been watching the place liked we've asked dozens of times already, there wouldn't have been a murder." It was obvious to me that she didn't hate saying it at all. She was just the type to complain about a million things and not understand why we didn't take *all* of her concerns seriously.

I offered a few more assurances, then headed back to my car. Midway, I decided to take one more turn around the Lynch house, just to be sure that Crenshaw hadn't pried open a door or a window. I was halfway around the back of the house when I thought I heard a baby crying. *That's odd*, I thought. *There aren't any homes* that *close to the Lynch house*. I stopped and listened.

I heard the soft crying again and this time I thought it was coming from the azalea hedge against the side of the house. Creeping forward, I heard more mewing sounds coming from the darkness under the bushes. I took the light off of my gun and shined it around, sure now that I was looking for a cat. I got down on my hands and knees and saw two large saucer-shaped blue eyes staring at me from the small round face of a white kitten about nine weeks old.

"Come here. I'm not going to hurt you," I told the little thing, holding out my hand. It looked back at me with the same expression I'd use if I saw a Kodiak bear in the wild— wonder, amazement and a healthy dose of fear. I tried crawling toward the kitten, which immediately turned and scuttled back from me.

"I'm not going to hurt you," I reassured it again.

It? I wondered if it was male or female. I broke off a piece of azalea bush and swished it back and forth. The kitten came hopping forward, curious, but as soon as I tried to draw it within arm's reach, it backed away with a suspicious glare. I tried to edge forward while moving the branch seductively in front of the kitten, but this only caused it to disappear through a hole in the wooden flashing that had been used to enclose the crawlspace under the house. Nothing I did enticed the kitten to come back out.

Sighing, I stood up and dusted myself off. My heart wanted to search for a way to get under the house, but I knew that was a job better left for daylight. Walking back to the car, I vowed to get some cat food as a lure and come back tomorrow. Suddenly I remembered the paw print that Shantel had found in Wells's blood. With a smile, I decided that I could justify the time I was going to spend catching the little rascal since it had left evidence at the scene of my murder investigation.

I got home by eleven o'clock to find Cara reading on the couch with Alvin, our Pug, curled up next to her. Ivy, the tabby cat that I'd rescued from the parking lot of the sheriff's office, stretched and came running over to me. Oddly, she stopped a foot away and gave me a cold stare.

"She knows I've been seeing another cat," I told Cara, then explained about the white kitten at the Lynch house.

"You're right, Ivy definitely knows," Cara agreed as Ivy went running to her lap. Cara petted her while the cat kept her butt focused in my direction.

"The kitten was cute. Strange blue eyes."

"Probably part Siamese."

"Could be, but it was all white."

I went to bed and made it through half the night before getting called out again.

CHAPTER SIX

On Saturday I slept past nine, which sounded good until I remembered I hadn't gotten back to bed until seven after spending most of the pre-dawn hours picking up the pieces of a domestic battery that had come close to attempted murder.

"You look like death warmed over," Cara greeted me as I crawled out of the bedroom.

"Thanks. You're beautiful too," I grumbled groggily, sitting down at the kitchen table where Cara put a bowl of cereal in front of me.

We sat in companionable silence for a while as Cara nursed a cup of coffee and I finished waking up.

"What are your plans for the day?" she asked when I got up to rinse off my bowl.

"I'd like to take about a three-hour nap, but instead I'm going over to Albert Griffin's to see what he's got on the Lynch murders."

"I'm headed out to Dr. Horvath's to check her supplies…" she said, letting her voice trail off in a way that I could easily interpret, even in my sleep-deprived state.

"Do you want to go to the Palmetto for dinner?"

"That would be nice. I don't feel like we're spending

much time together these days."

I took my cue, walking over and pulling her into a hug. "We are important, busy people. What do you expect?" I said with a smile in my voice.

"I know. It's not a big deal. Working for Dr. Horvath was my idea and I enjoy it. It's just…"

"Are you unhappy?"

"No. I like being busy and having the extra money."

"Do you have a problem with the demands of my job?"

"No…"

"Then don't go borrowing trouble," I said gently, holding her tight. "A friend once told me that if things are fine, then accept that. Don't make problems where there aren't any. Who knows what the future will bring. I might get fired tomorrow, in which case I'll be underfoot all the time. Or think about twenty years from now when I retire and you're trying to push me out to work in my woodshop."

"You don't have a woodshop." Cara gave me a playful punch in the chest.

"I will in twenty years."

Cara started laughing uncontrollably.

"What's so funny? Puttering in a woodshop is a perfectly acceptable pastime for an old man."

"I just…" She tried to gain control of herself, but she could still barely speak. "I'm sorry… But I just got an image of you as Geppetto… carving Pinocchio…" She lost it again and this time I couldn't help but join in.

"This is what comes from only three hours of sleep," I said, still chuckling and wiping tears from my eyes.

We took Alvin for a quick spin around the woods before I headed over to Mr. Griffin's. When I got ready to leave, I grabbed a can of Ivy's special-occasion cat food. She gave me the evil eye as I left the house with it tucked into my pocket.

I texted Pete before I left my driveway: *Heading over to Griffin's to get scoop on Lynch murders.*

Pete: *Really? Can I come?*

Me: *Thought you were going hiking?*
Pete: *Sunday. Today is wedding day.*
Me: *What???*
Pete: *Explain when I see you.*

I beat Pete to Mr. Griffin's house by less than two minutes. He pulled in behind me just as I was getting out of my car.

"I thought you weren't interested in the scary haunted house and its murders?" I kidded Pete as we walked up to the house.

"It's a love-hate thing. Besides, Jenny has one of her friends over at the house. The girl's getting married in a couple of months and Jenny is going to be a bridesmaid. Sarah and Kim have also gotten in on the wedding planning, so the estrogen levels in the house are at red level. You provided a legitimate escape plan."

"Glad to help," I said with a grin.

Mr. Griffin was sitting on the front porch of his old Victorian house, pecking at his laptop.

"I'm working on an article about our wartime governors for the Florida Historical Society," he said with the enthusiasm of a ten-year-old kid who'd just found a five-dollar bill. I knew I had to quickly steer him away from the subject or I'd spend an hour listening to him tell me everything about Florida's war history.

"That's great, but…"

"You want to talk about the Lynch murders." The older man smiled.

I don't know why it always surprised me when he did that. I should have known that he knew everything that went on in the county and was more than capable of putting two and two together.

"So you heard about what happened yesterday."

"The homeless are an interesting group of people. They're often willing to talk, but very seldom are their stories collected," he mused. I was afraid that this would lead to another tangent, but luckily Mr. Griffin was as interested in the Lynch story as I was. "The Lynch murders were a pivotal event in the development of law enforcement in Adams County. The investigation and the trial marked the county's turn from nineteenth century law enforcement to twentieth century methods."

"That's interesting," I said, not being completely honest. "But I'm really interested in the facts of the case."

Mr. Griffin raised his eyebrows. "You don't really think that yesterday's murder is connected, do you?"

"Obviously it can't be the same killer, or anyone who was involved in the original case. But I need to know enough to rule out a copycat killer... or maybe just someone with an unhealthy fascination with the old case."

"I don't know about unhealthy, but there are quite a few true-crime fans who are interested in the story. I think the main reason why is because the suspect died before he could be convicted. So while the case was solved, it's also *not* solved."

"Daniel Lynch was tried once, right?" Pete asked.

"Yes. It ended in a hung jury, which most people attributed to his lawyer getting several motherly types seated on the jury. Look, the best way to tell the story is from the beginning. Pull up a rocker." Mr. Griffin gestured toward several white rocking chairs arranged along the wide porch.

Pete and I pulled two over and I settled down, interested in spite of myself.

"There were two brothers who came down here from North Carolina around the turn of the last century. Thaddeus Lynch was about twenty and Simon was only sixteen. Their parents had died in a fire, so they took what little money they had and came down here to grow tobacco. They did well, especially Thaddeus. After a few years, he was farming five, six hundred acres. By the 1930s, Thad was able to weather the stock market crash and managed to keep his land free and clear of any bank mortgages. Simon, however, was cut from a different cloth and lost his hundred-acre farm in 1931."

"That must have been tough. His brother didn't help him out?" I asked.

"The talk was that Simon had asked for one too many favors. But don't despair for him and his family. He was a talented carpenter by all accounts and became the go-to man around here for anyone who wanted a house built. Which is exactly what his brother decided he wanted in 1934. Despite his financial and farming success, Thaddeus's family wasn't having it all roses and honey. His wife was a bit odd. In those days a lot of folks didn't talk much about mental illness, but from what I've read about her moods, she was most likely bipolar and used alcohol to medicate herself."

"I've seen plenty of that," Pete said.

Mr. Griffin nodded. "And it worked as well then as it does now. There were reports of her having very violent mood swings when she'd beat her children even beyond the accepted limits of the day. The oldest girl was out of school for a month because of a fractured jaw. The Lynch family claimed she'd fallen off the front porch and hit the concrete steps, but from what I've read, no one else believed that story."

"There wasn't any attempt to intervene?" I asked, knowing that those were very different times. A man's home was his castle and all that.

"According to most accounts, Simon tried to convince Thaddeus to have her taken away to the mental hospital in Chattahoochee. Which begs the moral question of what would have been better. Institutions, even the more progressive ones, were far from pleasant places to be and most likely wouldn't have done Mrs. Lynch any good. On the other hand, the fact that Thaddeus let his children live in a situation like that is unconscionable."

"And there weren't many other options at the time," Pete mused.

"Exactly. Thaddeus Lynch was well off, but only by local standards. He certainly couldn't afford a small staff to look after his wife."

"The whole situation must have been hard on everyone," I said.

"Even Thaddeus seemed to be going a little crazy himself toward the end. I'll revisit that in a moment. So here we are in 1934 and, for whatever reason, Thaddeus decides to build a new house on his land. Maybe he thought it might improve Mrs. Lynch's spells. He wouldn't be the first spouse who's tried to buy his partner out of depression and alcoholism. Simon agreed to build the house, which helped his own financial situation. As you know, it was to be quite large, with six bedrooms upstairs and six rooms down, including an imposing office, dining room and parlor, with a kitchen in the back.

"For almost a year, the mood in the family appeared to change. The brothers were getting along well and Mrs. Lynch looked, to the outside world at least, to be improving. The children had fewer fights with other kids and their grades improved."

"But..." I said, wondering where everything had gone off the rails.

"But indeed. Starting in March of 1935, ominous clouds began to gather," Mr. Griffin said darkly. I could tell he was enjoying reciting the story of the murders. "Thaddeus's family had been in the new house since New Year's Day. On March 17, the first event in the run up to the murders occurred. Thaddeus went down to the main barn around ten o'clock in a furious mood. Steven Dawkins the farm manager and four other men were working on an old steam tractor. Thaddeus told Dawkins that he needed to talk to him. The other men figured they'd go off somewhere out of hearing range, but no sooner were they out the barn door than Thaddeus accused Dawkins of stealing money from his office."

"Bet that went over well," Pete said.

"As well as you would expect. More words were exchanged until either Dawkins quit or Thaddeus fired him. Over the next couple of months, Thaddeus became more and more convinced that someone was stealing money out of his office in the new house. It was the ground-floor room at the back of the house on the north side."

"On the side next to the Holder house now," I said, more to myself than the others. "*Was* money being stolen?"

"Yes, no, maybe. Opinions vary, both then and now. Some people thought that Thaddeus was just losing his mind, while others believed that Mrs. Lynch or the children were responsible."

"What about someone from outside the household?"

"Thaddeus himself settled that once and for all. He installed bolts on all the doors and windows that couldn't be opened from the outside."

"The money still disappeared?"

"Yes."

"Why didn't he put it in a bank?" Pete asked.

"Don't forget that this was 1935. Trust in banks was still at an all-time low."

"So people think the stolen money had something to do with the murders?" I asked.

"That's one theory. Maybe the thief was about to be discovered and someone killed the family to cover it up," Mr. Griffin suggested.

"Could Lynch have imagined the whole thing?"

"That's the second theory—that the pressure of having a mad wife, along with the expense and effort of building the new house, had driven Thaddeus crazy. The third theory is that all of it was Mrs. Lynch's doing, both the stolen money and the murders."

"Since the son was eventually arrested for the murder, did they figure he did it as a way to cover up the fact that *he'd* been stealing the money?" I asked.

"And to keep from being punished by his father." Mr. Griffin nodded. "It's possible. Remember that his wife had broken the jaw of one of the girls and Thaddeus helped to hide the truth. I think it's safe to say that if the boy had been discovered to be the one stealing the money, then his father would have meted out a very harsh punishment, perhaps even banishment from the family."

"Kids have killed for similar reasons. How old were the children?"

"The youngest boy, Malcolm, was ten. Cynthia was fourteen and Daniel was sixteen." For the first time since he'd started to talk about the murders, Mr. Griffin sounded solemn. "A lot of the time when I'm talking about these older cases, I forget we're dealing with real people. But when you think of the children it's… gruesome."

"Murder is murder. Old or new," I said.

Mr. Griffin gave himself a little shake and got back into the story. "The murders happened on a Saturday. That morning, the kids got up and went about their individual chores."

"How do we know this?" I asked. The reliability of evidence always needed to be weighed carefully, and who was giving that evidence played a big part.

"This was all according to the family's cook, Deidra Hamilton. She came in every morning to fix breakfast for the family. Before Thaddeus started to report the missing money, she came and went on her own, but now she had to wait until someone let her in in the morning. She wasn't allowed to go anywhere in the house but the kitchen and pantry."

"She must have resented that."

Mr. Griffin shrugged his shoulders. "All we know about Deidra comes from the transcripts of the trial. Her testimony lasted two days. She was, in fact, the last to see the family when she served them dinner that evening."

"Did she notice anything strange?"

"No stranger than normal. She stated that Thaddeus seemed calmer than usual, which she attributed to there not being any thefts for over a week."

"How did she know if there'd been any thefts?" I asked.

"According to her, *everyone* knew when any of Thaddeus's money went missing. I'm sure this is true. From all accounts, he wasn't a man to keep his anger bottled up. At dinner that night, she claimed that everyone was… what was her word… at ease. No fights or harsh words. Even Mrs. Lynch was calm."

"When did the cook leave?"

"By all reports and her own testimony, she followed her routine, which was to clean up the dinner table, wash the dishes and make sure that she had everything she'd need for breakfast in the morning. She reported that they'd needed butter and eggs, which she added to the list for the milkman before leaving for the night at ten o'clock. Everything was quiet as she closed the door. As had been his habit since the bolts were installed, Thaddeus followed her to the back door and pushed the bolt home once the door was closed."

"She heard the bolt being closed?"

"Yes. Though we don't have to take her word for it since the bolt was definitely closed the next day when she came to fix breakfast."

"Did anyone else hear anything that night?"

"No. At that time, the house was almost a quarter of a mile from their nearest neighbor. No one heard or saw anything after Deidra left."

"Except the Lynch family and any outsider who might have murdered them."

"Precisely. So the next morning, Deidra shows up to find the milk, eggs and butter waiting on the stoop at the back door. The milkman claimed that he heard and saw nothing unusual when he delivered the items about half an hour before Deidra arrived. His schedule was double-checked and he'd been on time with his deliveries, leaving no extra minutes to spare for a quadruple homicide."

"Who found the bodies?"

"Deidra got frustrated trying to get into the house and finally walked over to a neighbor's. She'd been dropped off at the house by her husband, so she didn't have a car. Almost an hour passed by the time she got to the neighbor's and convinced him to return with her to the Lynch house.

When they got there the neighbor, Joe Hendricks, tried again to get someone to come to the door. Neither he nor Deidra wanted to break in, knowing what kind of temper Thaddeus had. They discussed going for either the sheriff or Simon Lynch."

"Wasn't there something about a dog?" Pete asked, completely caught up in the narrative.

"His name was Shep. There've been a lot of stories about the dog over the years. He became a big part of some of the ghost stories. Some said that he howled uncontrollably from that morning until he died a year later. Others say that the dog wouldn't let anyone into the house to check on the family. The truth is that Hendricks found the dog cowering under the house."

"The house is skirted now," I said, thinking about that ornery white kitten.

"Some folks say that the skirting was added because the dog kept hiding under the house. But I wouldn't bet on that. It was probably just to keep raccoons and other critters from tearing things up. Anyway, photographic evidence suggests that it wasn't put up until after World War II."

"So how did Hendricks and Deidra finally get into the house?" I asked.

"Deidra didn't. Hendricks climbed up on some wooden boxes stacked against the back of the house. He tried to open a window, but they were bolted too, so he broke it. Even if Deidra had wanted to go into the house, she was a large woman and couldn't climb up on the boxes."

"Couldn't he have just opened the front door from inside to let her in?" I said, confused.

"No. All the bolts on the doors were secured with padlocks."

"Wow!" This detail made it clear how deep Thaddeus Lynch's paranoia must have been.

"Hendricks found Mrs. Lynch's body right away, lying on the stairs. She was on her stomach with her head smashed in. She looked like she had been trying to go up the stairs and didn't get past the first step."

"What was she wearing?" I asked. Her clothes would have been a good indication of what time the murders had happened.

"She had on a nightgown and robe. At first Hendricks thought she might have had an accident, but this theory didn't hold up when he looked closer and saw the number of blows that had been delivered to the back of her head. He also noticed bloody footprints leading up the stairs. Bare feet. That was the point where his nerve broke and he left the house. He testified that he'd been in France during the Great War and this was the most chilling scene he'd ever witnessed. Within an hour, the sheriff, various deputies and a doctor had all been called to the scene."

"Back then, a lot of investigations were pretty shoddy, with the police letting every idiot in town walk through a crime scene. Can we really be sure about the details? Especially the part about the doors and windows all being locked from the inside?" Pete asked.

"Good question. The reason I'm confident about this is simple. The crimes were personal for the sheriff and the department. The sheriff was a cousin of Mrs. Lynch and one of the deputies, Drake, was Simon Lynch's son. I'm sure that the sheriff and his deputies wanted the killer to be a stranger. Every quote I've seen from the sheriff talking about the deaths and the boy's arrest are poignant with regret. He even reached out to several nationally known criminologists, as well as J. Edgar Hoover and Elliot Ness."

"Where was the boy found?" I said.

"When the sheriff and the doctor crawled through the window, they began a very thorough search of the house. The only victim on the ground floor was Mrs. Lynch. In the first bedroom upstairs they found the two younger children, dead from single blows to the head. Next, they looked in Daniel's room. His bed had been slept in, but they didn't see the boy. They found him next door in his parents' room. Mr. Lynch was sprawled on the bed with multiple axe wounds to his head and body, while the boy was curled up in a fetal position next to him."

My eyes widened. "I don't even know what to say about that. He was sixteen, right?"

"Yes, he'd turned sixteen two months earlier. Today we'd think that maybe he had a psychotic break, or suffered some sort of shock or trauma. At the time, the two schools of thought were that he was crazy as a bedbug, or that his mind had snapped when he discovered his murdered family."

"I have a million questions," I said. The Lynch case was crazier than I'd realized. I'd heard about the murders ever since I was a kid and we used to scare each other with ghost stories on Halloween. However, the version that was told in the schoolyard was pretty simple. The kid went crazy, killed his family and now haunts the town forever. But hearing the details and wearing my investigator's hat, I was surprised by the complexity of the case.

"Of course, the case is pretty simple if the kid did it," I muttered to myself.

"What?" Mr. Griffin said.

"I was just thinking that the case is pretty simple if the boy did it, but it becomes very complicated if he didn't."

"You hit the nail on the head. Everyone in town liked Daniel. He'd had a paper route when he was younger and he helped his father run the farm. Bright, energetic, caring— those were all words that were used repeatedly to describe him by the townsfolk."

"What did *he* say happened?" Pete asked.

"He said he slept through the night, got up before Deidra arrived and came downstairs because, quote, 'something wasn't right.' When he saw his mother's body, he said that he ran down and tried to help her. He knew she was dead as soon as he touched her, so he ran back upstairs to get his father. According to him, that was the last thing he remembered."

"Which makes sense if he went into shock," I said. "During traumatic events, victims and witnesses can enter into a sort of fugue state and do things they don't remember later."

"I've certainly seen it," Pete concurred. "The bloody footsteps on the stairs were the boy's?"

"Yep," Mr. Griffin confirmed.

"What about the murder weapon?" I asked.

"An axe. It was found by the kitchen door where it was usually kept. Oddly, it was a holdover from the house they'd lived in before moving to the new home. The new house had a gas stove, but when they moved the axe still came with them. They'd always kept it inside the kitchen door, so that's where it went in the new house, even though it served no purpose without the old woodstove."

"Was there evidence on the axe?" I asked, already guessing the answer.

"There were traces of blood and hair, but not much. The weapon had been washed off in the sink."

"Did they ever find any evidence that someone else had been in the house?"

"No. Oh, there were a few queer things that people have pointed to. Dirt in the hall by the staircase. A book that no one knew where it had come from. A rifle shell found in the kitchen. All items that might or might not have had anything to do with the murders."

"Did they check for fingerprints?" Pete asked.

"Yes. The sheriff desperately wanted to find another suspect. He got a state expert to come in and dust the entire house. While they found a few odd prints, almost all of them could be attributed to family members or people who were supposed to have access to the house."

"What was the trial like?" I said.

"Another reason this case stands out. Instead of the typical circus that high-profile murder trials usually were—"

"And still are," Pete interjected.

Mr. Griffin smiled. "Quite. But everyone described this one as solemn, with the accused looking more like a victim than a killer. The only one who seemed to take any joy in the affair was the prosecutor, who was lining himself up to run for governor. Though even he turned a bit morose when it was obvious that he wasn't on the side that was garnering the most sympathy. Some folks even suspected that he *wanted* a hung jury so that he couldn't be portrayed as the man who sent an innocent boy to sit in Old Sparky."

"So everyone thought he was innocent?" I asked.

"Pretty much everyone who knew the boy or who sat through the trial. Don't get me wrong, there were plenty of newspapers in the state that were printing the usual stories about the decadence of modern youth, and how the boy was a monster raised in the bosom of a loving family that he rose up and slaughtered. A few papers covered the 'crazy mother/crazy son' angle. However, the mood in the courtroom when the jury was sent to deliberate was summed up by a woman who told our newspaper that: 'All God-fearing folk should be praying that this boy is found innocent.' She got the next best thing. Eight jurors for guilty and four for innocent and none of them were going to budge. I can't blame them."

"Were they going to retry him?"

Mr. Griffin shook his head. "I don't think they had a clue what to do. The suicide was very convenient for the powers that be. The funeral was a zoo, with folks wailing and gnashing their teeth over the death of innocence while another group, smaller but very loud, was celebrating the death of a monster. I think the suicide played into both camps' theories. Those that thought he wasn't guilty figured that being accused of killing his parents and the trauma of the trial pushed him over the edge, while those who were sure he was a cold-blooded killer assumed that guilt caught up with him."

"*Was* it suicide?"

"I think it was. The sheriff took it hard. He fired the jailer and used it as a platform to build a new jail. The surprising thing was that he resigned as soon as it was finished. Said that he would have quit when Daniel died, but that he wanted to build the new jail as a legacy to the boy's memory."

A lightbulb went off in my head. "At the sheriff's office, there's a plaque in the hallway that says the jail is dedicated to the memory of Daniel Lynch who died… let me think…"

"In between heaven and hell," Pete finished.

"I get it now," I said.

"That plaque hung at the jail until it was torn down in the 1980s. I was there when the sheriff pried it off the wall so it could be preserved before the wrecking crew got there. In fact, Daniel's cousin was still alive at the time and there was talk of giving it to him."

"You mean Drake, the one who was a deputy at the time of the murders?"

"Yes. I interviewed him for an article in the paper and he said that he wanted the plaque on public display. He got choked up talking about the case. Said it was the worst experience of his career, because every instinct told him that the boy didn't do it, while every bit of evidence pointed toward him."

"You said that there are still a lot of people interested in the murders?" I asked.

"There are threads dedicated to it on all of the major true crime forums. Several books have sections devoted to the Lynch murders, and I know of three podcasts that have tackled it. I was even a guest on one of the podcasts last October," Mr. Griffin said with more than a little pride.

"I'm impressed," Pete said.

"Everyone's done a podcast by now," Mr. Griffin said modestly.

"Not me," I said. Then I remembered that Jessie Gilmore, a young woman who'd recently attached herself to me as a sometime-confidential informant, had asked me to talk to Pete about going on a missing persons podcast. "But Jessie did ask me if you'd be willing to go on the Missing Florida podcast to talk about Terri Miller."

"Really?" Pete looked at me. "And you're just now

mentioning this? That's a great idea!"

I knew that Pete was frustrated by the lack of movement on the five-year-old case, but I was more than a little surprised by his enthusiasm to do a podcast. *Then again, Pete loves to talk*, I reminded myself.

"Sorry. I'll give you her number."

"No need," Mr. Griffin said, pointing toward the driveway

CHAPTER SEVEN

A blue Dodge Dakota pulled into the driveway. Eddie Thompson, my old, once drug-addled CI, was riding shotgun while Jessie drove. They looked rather cozy. I wasn't that surprised. Earlier in the year, they had been acting out the typical I-don't-like-him-I-don't-like-her-either opening act of a Hollywood rom-com. Didn't all those couples wind up together in the end?

Eddie and Jessie saw us on the porch and came over. Eddie lived in the apartment over the garage. Mr. Griffin had let him move in more than a year ago when Eddie had been in hiding from the more nefarious members of his family. Since that time, Eddie had sobered up and formed a strange and endearing friendship with his landlord.

"Don't tell me you two are an item," I ribbed Eddie when they joined us.

"She just drove me home," Eddie grumbled. They both worked at the library. Eddie didn't like being teased about his relationships.

"Looked pretty friendly to me," Pete said cheerily and Eddie glared at him. He turned to Jessie. "Aren't you trying to get into the law enforcement academy?"

"I'm in!" A huge smile swept across her face and she

looked at me. "I couldn't wait to tell you! I got the letter yesterday!" It was not uncommon for Jessie's conversation to be punctuated with exclamation points. "I start in January!"

"Hanging out with a felon won't help your career," Pete said with a friendly nod toward Eddie, who proceeded to discreetly shoot him a bird.

"Eddie helped us out of a few scrapes," I admitted.

"So did Jessie and she's got a face that you can stand to look at." Pete couldn't resist poking Eddie. "She was a CI upgrade, for sure."

Jessie smiled widely and nudged Eddie in the ribs, who grumbled something about everybody picking on him.

"I'm glad you got into the academy. I think you'll make a great cop," I told Jessie sincerely. She had a passion for the career that I admired. Though I hoped she'd realize that she'd need to stop her habit of dying her hair, which today sported bright pink streaks in its usual brown.

"Are you working on the murder at the Lynch house?" Jessie asked me.

"We were just getting some background on the original murders from Mr. Griffin," I told her.

"That house is creepy as hell." Eddie visibly shuddered. "I was walking around with some… friends a couple years back and we ended up hanging out on the front porch. Something… happened."

Mrs. Holder must not have been looking out her window that night, I thought.

"How high were you?" Pete had a skeptical look on his face.

"You're scared of the place too," I reminded him.

"I'm not saying the place isn't spooky."

"Truth is, we were pretty mellow that night. Just alcohol. There were three of us sitting there talking and drinking when we heard a thud from inside the house. We got up and tried to look in, but couldn't see nothin'. Freaky. Really." Eddie was sincere, I didn't doubt that, but I knew from experience that his fear meter could redline without much excuse.

We talked for a few more minutes before I looked at my watch. "I need to go talk to a witness," I told them, standing up.

"I'll go with you." Pete followed me down the steps.

As we walked out to our cars, I watched Eddie and Jessie head back to Eddie's apartment and wondered if a relationship between them was a good idea. Eddie's sobriety was still barely a year old, and Jessie was an impressionable young woman who needed to concentrate on getting her career on track. I shrugged. Who was I to say what was good for either of them?

I called ahead and made sure that Bart Crenshaw was still at the Baptist shelter. Reverend Tolliver assured me that he'd even managed to eat a little bit of lunch.

"Don't let him go anywhere," I said as I drove the five blocks over to the church.

The church owned most of the city block and managed to keep it by virtue of the fact that they didn't have to pay taxes. Reverend Tolliver was a good man who meant well, but he had a hard and querulous side that didn't always serve him well when it came to building his congregation.

Pete and I parked near the older brick building that served as the church's outreach center. It was kept in good repair by the men and women it served. Reverend Tolliver was never hesitant to preach that idle hands were the devil's workshop. Every chance he got, he'd put a rake, a paintbrush or a hose into someone's hand.

We found Crenshaw sitting in the room that served as the dining hall. There were half a dozen tables set up with chairs around them. In the back of the building, we could hear dishes being washed in the kitchen as we walked over to the man, who didn't even look up.

"Bart. Do you remember me from last night?" I asked him.

He shook his head, looking down at the table.

"You were wandering around the Lynch house. In fact, you were ransacking the shed, looking for something."

"Ransacking?" he mumbled, still not making eye contact with me.

"Do you remember what you were looking for?"

"Looking?" he asked the table in front of him. "He's dead, isn't he?"

"Yes, Gregory Wells is dead. How well did you know him?" I decided to follow his lead in the conversation.

"I guess some. We camped close to each other. He's crazy, and I'm a fu…" He seemed to remember where he was and started over. "…stinking drunk. But we had each other's backs. At least until…"

"Until what?" Pete gently pushed him for an explanation.

"He stole my… can opener."

"That's what you were looking for last night," I prompted.

"Yep. I wanna find it."

"What's so special about a P38 can opener?" I asked, though I knew that the homeless, addicts and the mentally ill didn't always need a reason to become attached to small possessions. Really, that was true for anyone. Then I remembered. "You said it belonged to your brother?"

"That's right. My brother gave it to me. He carried it in Afghanistan."

"Did your brother get killed?" Pete asked.

"No, but he don't want to see me anymore. Called me a fu… drunk and not to come back. He's got a wife and kids. I want that can opener," he said with some grit in his voice.

"We might have picked it up when we searched the shack, or it might turn up in his pockets. If we find it and determine that it isn't evidence, we'll return it to you. I promise," I said solemnly.

Crenshaw turned and looked me in the eyes for the first time. "Really, you promise?"

"I do. Now, can you tell me when you last saw Gregory Wells alive?"

"Gory. I always called him Gory."

"Why?" Pete asked.

"'Cause that was his name, or at least part of his name. Greg-gory," he said, breaking the name into two words. "Especially 'cause the first time I saw him he was… you know, gory. All messed up 'cause some kids had kicked the shit out of him. Blood all over his face and all."

"So when was the last time you saw Gory?" I asked, trying to get back on track.

"The morning he gave me my phone back. He'd fixed it. Gory was real smart when he wasn't crazy."

This comment gave me several different avenues to pursue. I decided to stick to the timeline and come back to the other questions later. "Where was this?"

"Behind the Fast Mart."

"Which Fast Mart?" There were half a dozen of them scattered around the county.

"The one by the railroad tracks. I slept in the old house behind there."

"Did Gory stay there too."

"No, he moved to the shack behind the haunted house."

"When did he move there?"

"I guess a week or two ago. He saw one of the kids that beat him up over at the Fast Mart and thought they might beat him up again."

Both Pete and I got excited at this news. Here was a solid lead if we could track down the kid. "Did you see this person?" I asked.

"Nah."

"Did he describe him or any of the other kids that beat him up?"

"Said they were punks that he tried to buy drugs from. They took his money and kicked the shit out of him. What's new?"

"Think, is there anything else you can remember him saying about these kids? Their age maybe?"

"No."

"You said that too fast. Think about it for a minute," I told him.

He frowned at me. "I can't think of nothin'," he said after a short pause.

"Was there anyone else he talked to?"

"Maybe…"

"Like who?" Pete pressed.

"I guess that foreign guy at the Fast Mart. 'Cause he asked about Gory after he moved to the haunted house and stopped coming by the Fast Mart," Crenshaw said.

"You said all this happened about two weeks ago?"

"Yeah, maybe… or three. Kinda hard to figure out what day of the week things are. You know?"

No, I don't know what it's like to walk around in an alcoholic haze, unable to tell one day from the next, I thought with a shake of my head. What I did know was that a trip to the Fast Mart was in order. They would have surveillance camera footage, and while it probably wouldn't go back more than a week, if those kids hung out there regularly then there'd be a good chance of identifying them.

"Where did he get beat up?" I asked, hoping to get a few different locations where we could look for the kids.

"Don't know."

"Where did you first see him?"

"Oh yeah, I guess it was the Fast Mart near the library."

That Fast Mart saw more than its share of homeless because of its close proximity to the library. I knew that the library often had problems with the homeless. They didn't mind them coming in, but the librarians just didn't want them sleeping in the cubicles or taking a bath in the restroom sinks. I made another note to check with Eddie and see if he or anyone at the library recognized Wells's picture.

Crenshaw, for all of his fuzzy-headed answers, had provided us with a few good leads. We spent a little more time going down a few blind alleys with him before coming back to the subject of the can opener.

"Tell us what happened with the can opener," Pete asked.

"*My* can opener." Crenshaw wasn't budging on ownership.

"So how'd Wells get it?"

"I gave it to him. Not gave, loaned. I *loaned* it to him." He said all of this slowly and firmly as though he were explaining it to a child.

Pete and I just looked at Crenshaw, creating an uncomfortable silence for him to fill.

"Yeah, okay, my phone was busted and Gory said he could fix it. See? So I said sure, 'cause I wanted to get a call about a job, see? So I said I really need my phone and he said he'd fix it if I'd let him have my can opener. I thought he meant to use, not to have. So I said sure. I didn't think he could fix the phone anyway, though he did. I just meant for him to use the can opener."

"Did you all get in a fight over the can opener?" I asked.

Crenshaw stared down at the table.

"How bad was the argument?" Pete asked in his *I'm-a-friend* voice.

"Yelling. A bunch of that. I guess we threw stuff at each other. He sure liked that can opener too. Said I was trying to cheat him."

I shared a look with Pete. It was obvious that we both agreed Crenshaw was not likely to be our killer. There were a number of reasons that I couldn't see it. One was pure intuition. Crenshaw might hit someone once in anger and the blow could be deadly, but he was unlikely to keep striking the person. The second reason was solid evidence. Crenshaw's clothes didn't have any blood on them. From the blood all over the porch, I couldn't imagine the killer escaping with clean clothes.

"Did Gory say where he was from?" I asked. We still needed to find his next of kin.

"No. Didn't talk about his other life. We just hung out… before… the argument."

"He never mentioned a family?"

"No… Well, maybe. You know, in passing, but I don't remember nothin'."

"Did you think he came from around here or from up north or somewhere?"

"I guess around here," Crenshaw said, not sounding very sure about it.

We asked a few more questions about his whereabouts the night of the murder, which were answered with only vague locations and times. I assured him that I'd check on the can opener, then said, "Look, Bart. I don't want you going back to your usual haunts."

He looked at me like I'd told him I was placing him under arrest.

"Whoever killed Gory might think you're a witness since y'all spent time together," I warned.

"I got… things to do," he said, which I interpreted as: "I get my money for liquor at certain spots and drink it at my own special locations and I don't know how to do anything else."

"I'll talk to Reverend Tolliver." I took out a twenty-dollar bill and he reached for it instinctively. I pulled it back. "I'm going to give this to him. He'll see that you have something to wet your whistle."

"He'll never buy me my Mad Dog." Crenshaw shook his head sadly.

"If he won't buy it, then I will and I'll bring it by here. Bottom line, stay here."

Crenshaw softly thumped his hand down on the table in a show of frustration. "Guess I don't have a choice."

"No, you don't," Pete told him.

We started to walk away when we heard Crenshaw say to our backs, "When he wasn't crazy, he was a good guy. I'm gonna miss him."

I caught up with the reverend and explained the situation. "Keep him here with a steady but not overly indulgent supply of Mad Dog," I advised, handing him forty dollars.

"I've never given any of the men or women in our

mission liquor," Reverend Tolliver said, sounding appalled at the idea.

"He doesn't need the DTs right now. And if the lure of easy-to-come-by liquor keeps him here out of harm's way, then I would think that God would approve." I knew it wasn't fair of me to play the God card, but I did it anyway.

"I suspect that *you* could use some time in church," Reverend Tolliver said thoughtfully while taking the forty dollars.

"Amen, brother," Pete said, giving me a smile. I knew that Sarah was active in their church and managed to drag Pete there a couple of times a month, usually when there was a lunch after the service.

Before we parted ways at the mission, I called Darlene to fill her in and find out when she'd have time to show me around the best homeless camps in town.

"Can we do it on Monday?" she asked, sounding tired—a rare thing in a woman who could normally put the Energizer Bunny to shame.

"Sure. I've got a few other leads to follow up on." I told her about the kids that had beaten up our victim and left him scared to the point that he'd left a familiar camp and moved across town.

"Sounds promising. I'm trying to think who they might be. What do you think Wells meant by kids? Under eighteen? Or just younger than him?"

"No clue. Crenshaw never saw them, so he won't be of any help."

After hanging up, I asked Pete what his plans were for the rest of the day.

"I'm going to the office and work on… something. If Sarah asks, give me an alibi for at least another couple of hours." Pete held up his phone, showing a long list of text messages from Sarah and his two daughters.

"You love it," I told him, knowing it was true. Pete had his faults, but not one of them had to do with a lack of love for his family.

I told him I was heading over to the Lynch house to look around the crime scene one more time. But my real motive was to see if I could spot that kitten again. I shouldn't have been wasting my time, but I was a sucker for a cute face. I made sure I still had the can of wet food I'd stolen from Ivy's cupboard and headed for the Lynch house.

CHAPTER EIGHT

I got a text as I was pulling up to the Lynch house. It was from Dad: *Where are you?*

I probably should have questioned him more before responding with my location, but I'd received many texts from him like that and never heard another word, so I didn't think too much about it.

I found a plastic fork in the glovebox left over from some long-forgotten fast lunch. With it and the can of cat food firmly in hand, I started walking around the house. I stopped every couple of feet to see if I could spot any signs of the kitten while calling out, "Heeeree, kitty, kitty!" in a high-pitched voice that did nothing but make me feel foolish.

When I reached the spot where I'd seen the ball of fur dash through the hole, I got down on my hands and knees and opened the pop-top on the food can. Almost immediately, a little pink nose peaked out from the bushes. Regretting that I hadn't brought Cara along on the kitten hunt, I leaned forward and held out the spoon filled with a little bit of cat food. I saw the kitten's nose twitching as it caught a whiff of the stinky stuff. Slowly, its head emerged and I held as still as I could. The kitten slunk out closer to the spoon until it was able to take a few licks of food. The more it ate, the more relaxed it seemed to become and I crept a little closer. Finally, I thought I could reach out with my other hand and grab it, but no sooner had I moved into position than the kitten spooked and dashed back under the house.

After ten more minutes of trying to coax it out, I was frustrated enough to look for an alternative approach. I stood up and looked more closely at the skirting under the house, figuring that there had to be an access door somewhere. Sure enough, behind a large camellia about twenty feet from the kitten's bolt hole, I found a two-and-half-foot-square hinged plywood access panel. The hardware was rusty, but still functional, with only a latch and no padlock.

I noticed a couple of camellia branches that were broken off and lying by the access panel. At first I wondered if someone else had been there, but then decided that they had probably been broken or bitten off by an animal. Still, I made a note to warn Mr. Hinson about copper thieves. We'd had a couple of vacant homes recently hit by tweakers, who'd stripped all of the copper wire out of the walls, doing thousands of dollars' worth of damage in order to make a hundred dollars at the scrap yard.

I took out my phone and turned on the flashlight app, then peered under the house. It was dusty and dirty, but there weren't too many cobwebs. The house sat on brick pillars that were almost three feet high, giving me enough room to crawl around, though I wasn't very comfortable while I was doing it. I ducked under pipes and electrical conduits, watching the kitten stare at me from against the skirting as though I were a neighbor come to play a game. The next half hour bore out this assessment, as the kitten repeatedly let me get close enough to feed it, but never close enough to grab it.

On the fourth try, the little rascal ran past me toward the middle of the crawlspace. I turned to pounce on it, not noticing that one of the pillars was not in line with the rest until I swung my head around and slammed into the bricks. My vision went black and for a moment I thought I'd knocked myself out. I certainly had *something* loose in my head to be down there chasing the stupid kitten. After a moment, my vision cleared and I picked up the phone that I'd dropped, determined to play through the pounding in my head.

After a few more close calls, I was ready to give up. Then I watched as the kitten frolicked its way back out through its bolt hole and into the yard. Looking around quickly, I found a broken piece of board and carefully placed it against the hole, pushing some dirt against it to keep it in place.

Aha! I thought as I crawled back out from under the house. If the kitten couldn't dash away through its hole, then I might be able to get my hands on it. By this point there was no question about why I was going to all this trouble. It was a grudge match, pure and simple.

Back in the yard, I could see the white kitten jumping and leaping spastically at leaves while chasing imaginary insects. I started moving very slowly toward it, making every effort not to spook the wily critter. With only five feet to go, a waist-high black-and-white blur streaked by me and a thick whip of a tail almost knocked me down.

"Shit!" I yelled, watching Mauser, my dad's one-hundred-and-ninety-pound Great Dane, streak toward the one-pound kitten. I was pretty sure that Mauser wouldn't actually hurt it. The goofus had zero prey instinct. However, I'd been hit, stepped on and jumped on by the canine menace enough times to know that he didn't have to be trying to kill you to put a hurting on you.

"Where are you?" I heard Dad say as he rounded the house.

"Dad, damn it! Do you have to let your moose run wild? There are leash laws in this town," I said, frustrated both at him and at myself for not having seen this as a possibility when I got the text.

"What's the problem?" Dad asked, genuinely puzzled at my anger.

"I've been trying to catch a stray kitten for about an hour. All I needed was for your—"

"*That* kitten?" Dad asked, pointing toward Mauser.

I turned around to see Mauser down in a perfect puppy bow and the kitten dancing around his coconut-size head.

"You're kidding me!" I growled. The kitten, who'd been skittish at my approach, was playing with the ginormous couch wolf as though it couldn't imagine Mauser's two-inch canines doing it any harm.

Dad walked over to Mauser while the kitten, completely fixated on its own fierce attacks on the giant black nose, never even glanced up. Dad knelt down beside Mauser, who seemed completely smitten.

"I don't believe this," I said, shaking my head in frustration.

Dad reached out and started playing with the kitten, who was still focused on Mauser. The dog was making pathetic mewing sounds at his new best friend. I walked over with little concern of disturbing the *bonhomie*, and all three of us played with the kitten.

"What'd you want?" I asked Dad.

"I just wondered if there was anything I needed to know about the murder."

"You know that I've promised not to go around Johnson's back anymore." My lieutenant had laid down the law a few months back about me going directly to my dad whenever I wanted something, particularly something I thought that my direct supervisor wouldn't allow. Johnson had been right about me taking advantage of my special relationship, so I'd vowed to separate my dad from my boss. So far, I'd managed to stick to it.

"This isn't anything I wouldn't ask Pete or any of the other investigators. Knowing you're trying to maintain more separation, I thought I'd better check in on this one to make sure you don't go too far the other way. This house," he waved his hand behind him, "has a fan base. A murder here could become big news."

"So far I don't see anything that could get… political. Look, I better get this guy to the vet." I reached down and picked up the kitten, who was still batting at Mauser as I lifted him into the air. Mauser rose and followed me to my car, totally focused on the little ball of fur.

After assuring the Dane that I'd let him see his new friend again, I waved to Dad and headed for the veterinary clinic, grateful that this was one of the Saturdays it was open. It closed at two, giving me only half an hour to get there. I called Cara and asked her to give the clinic a heads-up that I'd be bringing the little tike in.

The kitten seemed content to ride in my lap, and I thought I'd make it a leisurely drive until I felt the first bite on my hand. When I came to a stop sign, I looked down and saw half a dozen fleas crawling on my hands. Cursing, I picked up my radio and told dispatch that I was en route to the vet clinic with an animal in need of medical attention. Flipping on the blue lights, I sped up and used the power of law enforcement to get to the clinic before I was completely bitten up by fleas.

I walked up to the front desk, holding the kitten at arm's length and hoping to keep as many fleas off of me as possible. Gayle, the receptionist, smiled at me.

"Cara said you were on your way with a little one."

"It's covered in fleas," I said, my lips curled a bit in revulsion. I knew that even after a hot bath, I'd still feel them crawling all over me.

Angie, one of the kennel techs, came out of the back and gently took the kitten from my hands.

"Dr. Barnhill is taking care of another patient right now, but we can get this little…" She turned the critter over and looked at the rear view. "…fellow cleaned up. My, you are a cutie. Look at those blue eyes!"

"He's a little rascal and he's taken up with that buffoon my dad calls a dog."

"Any friend of Mauser's is a friend of mine," Angie said.

"Traitor," I labeled her as she walked away.

Gayle sat back down at her computer. "Okay, let's get him checked in. What's his name?"

"I hadn't even thought about a name." I stood there looking stupid for a second, then said, "He was found at a haunted house… and he's white. How 'bout Ghost?"

"That's cute," she said, typing it in.

"Though the way he was acting, he's probably going to fall more into the poltergeist category," I said.

I left ten minutes later with their assurances that Ghost would be well taken care of and that Cara could come pick him up after hours if she wanted. I reported all of this to my wife, who was excited at the thought of adding another mouth to feed to our happy home. Before I hung up, I told her that we'd have to take Ivy aside and apologize in advance for all the trouble that was coming her way.

I was less than two miles from home and pondering what kind of domestic issues our new family member was going to cause when I saw red and blue lights up ahead. I turned up my radio and heard enough chatter between dispatch and Sergeant Will Toomey to realize that an accident with a fatality had occurred where the road crossed a creek. I flipped on my blue lights and pulled over near the bridge, figuring I could lend some assistance to Toomey.

When I got out of my car, I could see that the railing on the northbound side of the bridge had been ripped off when a semi slammed into it and drove off into the creek. I went over to the edge and saw Toomey climbing back up from the creek.

"There's a BMW pinned under the semi," he told me as I gave him a hand up the embankment.

"Any survivors?"

"Not in the car. The big rig driver is pinned in the truck. I might be able to free him with a crowbar, but he seems stable and the good news is, with the creek, there's no risk of fire. I think the best course is to wait for the fire rescue, which shouldn't be more than five minutes out."

As if on cue, we could hear sirens in the distance.

"We'll need to block off the road back to the last intersection. We're going to be here for hours. We'll also need to have the bridge checked out. I'm no engineer, but having a semi slam through the rails and rock back on the pillars can't be good for the structure."

"I'll coordinate the road closure," I volunteered. Toomey was the best vehicular homicide investigator we had and I was all for letting him do his thing. We were lucky that he'd been first on the scene.

A Florida Highway Patrol car pulled up behind us and I went to talk with the trooper about coordinating the road shutdown before we had any more accidents.

An hour later, we'd been joined by two more troopers and a couple of tow trucks. The injured trucker was already on his way to the hospital in Tallahassee with a crushed leg and a face that looked like someone had worked him over with a baseball bat. I stood on the bridge with the tow truck drivers, looking down at the semi turtled in the creek bed.

"You're gonna need a crane. We couldn't even budge that thing," one of the drivers said.

"Unhook the cab and take it out in two pieces," the second driver suggested sagely.

"I can't get close enough to the driver of the car," a young and limber state trooper called up from the creek bed. "I'm going to try to find the tag," he said, crawling under the trailer.

"Be careful, damn it! We don't need another casualty," his sergeant fretted.

We still had no idea who the driver of the BMW was, or if there had been anyone else in the car with him. The driver's side was just above water, so the driver's arm and the back of his head were visible. The rest of the car was under the trailer. While we couldn't dismiss the possibility that there had been one or more passengers, it was a certainty that no one in the car had survived.

"Got a partial plate." The young trooper's clothes were soaked as he climbed around the rig and back up the embankment to his patrol car. He handed his sergeant a piece of paper with four numbers on it before starting to put his duty belt back on.

"Forget it. Go back and get some dry clothes on," the sergeant told him before turning to me. "Do you want to take the lead on this?" he asked, holding out the paper.

I looked over at Toomey, who was measuring skid marks and taking pictures of the gouges in the tarmac.

"Sure." I figured it was our accident scene, and it shouldn't be that hard to come up with the registration. The trooper had even put the BMW's model number on the paper.

I called dispatch and got ahold of Marti. "Are you busy?"

"It's quiet for a Saturday. You know it won't start hopping until the sun goes down."

I gave him the information we had.

"Sounds like a hell of a wreck."

"It's bad. See if you can get me a phone number."

"Can do. I've got a break coming up anyway."

Ten minutes later, I had a name and a phone number. I dialed and got nothing. I looked back underneath the semi and wondered if a phone was ringing down there. I looked back at the paper. I was only fifteen minutes from the address on the vehicle registration.

I called Cara and told her that our dinner date was probably cancelled. She was a little disappointed, but happily distracted with the prospect of bringing Ghost home from the vet. I reminded her that she'd have to take a different route into town since the main road from our place was going to be blocked for hours.

Hanging up, I got Toomey's attention. "The car is registered to Tommy Romano at an address in that new subdivision on the north side of town. Summer Meadows."

"Tommy Romano sounds like a character in *The Sopranos*. I guess you already tried to call the number. The phone is probably down in the creek with the body with the semi on top of it." Toomey was clearly frustrated. "At this point, we'll just have to wait for a crane."

"That's going to take a while." I wished there was another way to get the tractor trailer out of the creek bed, but with seventy-five feet of swamp on both sides of the creek, it would be impossible to use a tow truck. They couldn't even get near it.

"We're going to lose a lot of information too," Toomey said.

"Information?"

"Stuff that the car's systems can give us. I still do all the old-style measuring of skid marks and all that, but a lot of what is used in court these days comes off of a car's electronic control units." He looked at me. "You really need to come back on the road with me for a while."

"I remember that Pete had a case a couple of years ago where he was able to prove that the driver was operating the car erratically using information from the car's ECU."

"There are at least two systems. The entertainment system covers the phone, radio and displays, then there's the telematics system which shows whether the car is accelerating, braking, if emergency braking is taking place, if seatbelts are fastened, which seats are occupied, and a whole lot more."

"You went to a seminar about that, right?" I asked, remembering that he'd been gone for a week earlier that year.

"It's amazing how much information your car is collecting. Unfortunately, the systems aren't in airplane-like black boxes that can withstand being submerged for any length of time. And there's also the body to consider."

"Yeah, they don't get any better being immersed in water." I recalled a couple of gruesome bodies that I'd had to deal with over the last few years. I looked at the paper in my hand. "I'm going to drive over to Summer Meadows and see what I can find out."

"Good idea."

CHAPTER NINE

According to the large billboard at the entrance to Summer Meadows, phase one of the subdivision was completely sold out, but there was still time to buy a lot in phase two. Prices for lots, which ranged from five to fifteen acres, started at a quarter of a million dollars. I didn't see Cara and myself moving in anytime soon.

Romano's house was a monstrous stone edifice with delusions of castledom. I parked near the front door in a wide, circular drive. By the time I got out of my car, an attractive brunette wearing jeans and a sweater was smiling down at me from the open front door.

"Can I help you?" the woman asked, looking a little surprised to have a visitor.

"I'm Deputy Larry Macklin with the sheriff's office. I need to ask you a few questions."

"I'm expecting my husband any minute, if you want to talk with both of us," she said, then gave me a strange look. "You said your name was Larry Macklin?"

"That's right." I held out my ID as I walked up the steps and across the portico to where she was standing.

"You don't recognize me?" she asked.

The question took me by surprise. "Should I?" I asked,

looking at her and trying to think back over all of the cases I'd worked, as well as all of the people I'd met while helping Dad campaign for sheriff. Nothing rang a bell.

"And I thought you had a thing for me. You always picked the seat right behind me in sixth grade." She pretended to be offended, but her eyes were smiling.

"Sherry? Is that you? Sorry… I can't remember your last name," I said, flustered and completely losing track of why I was there.

"O'Neal. I'm Sherry Romano now." She was still smiling, though I wasn't. The mention of her married name reminded me of why I was standing on her porch. I didn't think this was going to be the fond reunion she thought it was.

"I'm sorry," I stammered. No one liked to perform death notifications. I certainly didn't, but under normal circumstances I could deliver the bad news in an unemotional, professional manner. But finding out that the wife was an old acquaintance from elementary school threw me off my stride. "I don't know… Maybe this…" I stopped and regrouped. "There's been an accident. The driver was killed. I'm afraid the car was registered to a Tommy Romano at this address."

As soon as I said the name, I saw her knees buckle and I just managed to catch her before she hit the hard stones of the portico. I helped her inside the house and eased her into a chair not far from the front door. Sherry was shaking her head in disbelief as I backed away, leaving her slumped in the chair with tears in her eyes and her mouth working to find words.

"I… I… He just went into town. I'm sure you have the wrong person. Maybe… I don't know what… Please, what does he… I mean, are you sure it's him?"

"No. I can't say that we are. The circumstances of the accident are… unfortunate."

"I don't understand."

"The car is still trapped under a semi. We're bringing in a crane to help remove the truck and get to your husband's

BMW," I said as gently as I could, though I couldn't help the brutal images I was planting in her mind.

Sherry was crying softly. With no way to cut the pain, all I could do was stand beside her and pat her shoulder awkwardly.

"Is there any chance that someone else could have been in the car with him?" I asked after a few minutes.

"No. There was no one with him. I want to see him."

"They will need time to recover the body."

"Then I want to go there." She stood up, wiping at the tears in her eyes.

"I don't think that would be a good idea," I said, standing between her and the door.

"No. I must go to him," Sherry insisted. "I'll get my keys and drive myself." There was steel in her voice.

"Get your things and I'll drive you," I offered.

"Thank you." She reached out, almost touching my arm, before turning and gathering up her purse and phone from a hall table.

We drove in silence. I had a dozen questions that I wanted to ask and would eventually *need* to ask, but now was not the time or place. She deserved to have these few moments to come to terms with her personal tragedy.

I pulled over a hundred feet from the bridge.

"Listen to me. I will walk you to the bridge and let you look down at the scene, but you can't try to climb down. For right now, that will be as close as you can get to him. They will let you see him once the car is brought up out of the creek."

Sherry wasn't looking at me. Her eyes were fixed on the distant bridge and the crew working there.

"I need you to tell me that you understand what I'm saying," I pressed her. I wasn't sure that she had even heard me. "Please."

She turned and looked at me. "I understand. Can we go?"

I nodded and got out of the car.

I could tell by the look on Toomey's face as we

approached that he knew who she must be and didn't approve of her being there. I walked her to the edge of the bridge railing, then put my hand on her elbow stop her walking forward.

"He's down there?" Sherry's voice was almost a whisper.

"I'm sorry."

She leaned against the guardrail for support.

"How long ago?"

"A couple of hours. Wait here." I walked over to where Toomey was standing by the busted railing.

"What were you thinking?" He didn't look up.

"It was either bring her with me or she was going to come on her own."

"The wife?"

"Yes. Sherry Romano."

"Okay, I'll go talk to her."

"She's pretty shook up."

"Sometimes it can help to focus them." He looked up and frowned. "I'll be gentle."

He walked over to her and introduced himself. "I'd like to ask you a few questions about your husband's actions before the accident."

"I… thought… Is there any possibility that it isn't him?" Sherry asked.

Toomey shifted uncomfortably.

"It's possible, but we're sure that it's his car. Do you have any reason to believe that someone else could have been driving his car this afternoon?"

Now Sherry was the one looking uncomfortable. We both knew that she wanted to say yes. But "No" was the word that barely escaped her lips.

"When did he leave the house?"

"I don't know for sure. I was upstairs. I guess it was a little after noon when he said he was going into town. I didn't think much about it. He was always running into town for something."

"Do you know where he was going?"

An odd look came into her eyes before she answered. "I… It's Saturday and he wanted to pick up some things from the liquor store… and grab some groceries." She added the last bit as though to blunt her earlier statement.

"Had he had anything to drink before he left the house?" Toomey asked.

"I don't know." Her answer was blunt and most likely truthful.

"Would it have been unusual for him to be drinking that early on a Saturday?" Toomey watched her, his face passive and open.

There was another hesitation. "No. It's the weekend. He'd been working in the yard this morning, so a beer or two after… That's not unusual, is it?" Her posture and tone were defensive. It was like watching the quills on a porcupine bristle.

"You understand that we have to ask these questions?" he said, trying to get Sherry to let her guard down again.

"It's… I don't know. I haven't processed any of this yet." Tears formed in her eyes again.

"Do you have a current picture of your husband that you could text me?" Toomey asked, switching gears and handing her a business card. "Here's the number."

Numbly, she took her phone out of her pocket and started to thumb through her pictures. Without a word, she chose a couple, sent them and we all heard his text alert.

Toomey took a quick glance. "These will be fine. I've got your number. We'll do what we can to identify the driver without you having to make a visual ID."

"I think I want to see him," she said quietly.

"It will be better if you pay your respects after a mortician has cleaned him up." Toomey's voice was soft and kind. I had never seen him like this. Normally, he barked orders or grumbled about the idiots he encountered day in and day out.

"You probably shouldn't stay here," I told her. "Let me take you home. Sergeant Toomey's as good as his word.

He'll keep you up to date on what's happening."

"Maybe it's not Tommy down there." Sherry was staring down at the semi in the creek bed. "He could have been car-jacked. If they took his phone…" Even as the words of hope came from her lips, I could see in her eyes that she didn't believe what she was saying. "I better go back to the house in case he comes home."

"That's probably a good idea," I told her, not attacking the false hope she was indulging in. Better she hold onto something right now than have nothing. "Is there someone who can come and stay with you?"

"My mom lives in Tallahassee. I need to call her." She fumbled with her phone again. Her hands were shaking as I eased her back to my car.

By the time we got back to her house, Sherry's mother was on the way, so I left her with my card and instructions to give me a call if she needed anything.

I drove away thinking about the odd nature of life. Here was a woman I'd known briefly as a child, brought back into my life as a grieving widow of a man killed in an automobile accident that I'd assisted on. There was no understanding the twists and turns of fate.

I got back to the site of the wreck and Toomey told me to go home. He didn't see the point in all of us standing around waiting for the crane to arrive.

"Your dad isn't going to be happy with this bill. We finally got the owner of the crane to agree to come out after Major Parks negotiated the price down as far as he could. Last I heard, they're only going to charge us half of their usual overtime fees."

"We're probably lucky that they're coming out at all. What are we going to do? Say, 'No, we'll just let the body rot under the semi'?"

"Still going to be a hefty bill."

"Great," I said sarcastically. We'd been running a deficit ever since Hurricane Marcy had damaged our building and put the department behind the eight ball with our own overtime costs. Dad had been assured by the Feds that hurricane reimbursement money would be distributed any day, but he was still waiting.

I left Toomey waiting on the crane, glad that I wouldn't have to see the crushed and soggy remains of Tommy Romano.

When I got home, I found everyone in the household focused on the refrigerator. Cara, Alvin and Ivy were all crouched down on the kitchen floor. Cara's red head was crammed between the wall and the side of the refrigerator, while the other two watched from a short distance away.

"What's going on?"

"Your friend has hidden himself behind the refrigerator." Cara sounded a little exasperated.

"*My* friend?"

"You conjured him up at the haunted house. So he's yours." But from the way she said it, I could tell that she was only a little bit irritated.

"Do you want me to move the fridge?"

"I'm afraid you'll crush him if you try scooting it out."

She had a point. I'd have to rock the appliance back and forth to get it to move. Then a lightbulb went off in my head... a horrible, burning light. I knew exactly what would get Ghost out of his hiding place.

"He'll come out for Mauser," I said flatly.

"You *did* say that's how you caught him at the house."

"There's apparently some evil connection between those two." I shook my head, trying to think of an alternative.

"We can't leave him back there." Cara looked at me, quickly realizing how exhausted I was from the day's activities. "I'll go pick him up. If you don't think your dad will mind?"

I rolled my eyes. "Unless the mule dog has a personal appearance scheduled for tomorrow, I'm sure Dad won't mind letting him come here for a sleepover."

Cara gathered up her keys and phone, gave me a kiss and said she'd be right back. The moose wouldn't fit in Cara's small car, so she'd have to leave it at Dad's and drive his van back.

After Cara left, Ivy sauntered over and ate the small dish of wet food that Cara had been trying to use to bait Ghost out from behind the refrigerator. Alvin decided all the excitement was over and flopped on the couch for his after-dinner nap.

We had almost forty minutes of peace before Cara brought Mauser into the house. Mauser sniffed out the kitten immediately. As soon as his brick of a head was close to the bottom of the refrigerator, we heard a couple of cheerful meows. Mauser backed up and out pranced Ghost as though nothing had happened.

"You little scamp," I scolded Ghost.

"They're soooo cute together!" Cara fawned over them.

"There's a problem with this scenario. Mauser can't live here and Dad has a rule that excludes cats from his house. He's a barn-cats-only kind of guy." I went over and sat on the couch with Ivy, who was glaring at the kitten. "It's just you and me, girl," I said as we watched Alvin join the party in the kitchen.

After thirty minutes, everyone had settled down. Cara and I were on the couch with Alvin, Ivy was pouting on top of a bookshelf and Mauser was splayed out on the floor with Ghost tucked up in his armpit, watching us with his big blue eyes.

"I saw pictures of the accident online," Cara said. One of Tallahassee's local TV stations was pretty good about covering stories in Adams County on its website. "Looked awful."

I told her about meeting Sherry Romano.

"That's a horrible way to meet an old classmate," Cara said, dangling a feather on a stick in front of Ghost.

"It was unsettling. I felt more like a harbinger of doom than I normally do," I said, moving to the opposite end of the couch as the kitten launched itself at the feather… and Cara's legs.

"Is there any chance that it isn't her husband?"

"Slim to none, though stranger things have been known to happen."

"What caused the accident?"

"We're not sure yet. The good news is that the driver of the big rig should survive, so he'll be able to answer some questions. That, combined with Toomey's investigative skills, should give us some answers. Driving conditions didn't play a role. The road was dry and flat, and the only curves are a quarter mile away in both directions. Maybe a tire blew on the BMW and the driver lost control, or he got distracted by something and hit the bridge's guardrail."

"Scary what can happen in a car."

"Especially when people aren't paying attention to their driving," I said, thinking of all the people I saw looking at their phones or radios or God knew what else while driving down the road. "People should have to look at a couple dozen fatal accidents before getting their license."

"Didn't there used to be old driver education films that showed some pretty gruesome crashes?"

"You never saw those?"

"I never took driver's ed. Dad taught me how to drive when Mom wasn't around." I could imagine that Cara's hippie mom would not be the best help at driving instruction.

"I didn't either. The course had been dropped from high school a decade before I graduated, but Dad got copies of the films and made me watch them."

"You're kidding?" she said, then remembered who my dad was. "I guess not."

"Gruesome doesn't even begin to describe them. The wrecks in the films were all before safety glass and, at best, the victims were wearing lap-belts. The only saving grace was that they were in black and white. I'll admit they made an impression."

"Did it make you a safer driver?" The kitten jumped and flipped twice in the air, trying to catch the feather on the end of the stick.

"Maybe. I still did a few stupid things, like trying to see how fast Dad's truck would go. It broke a hundred one time before the side view mirror shook off."

"So the films didn't really help?" She smiled.

"I've never gotten behind the wheel after more than one beer," I said.

We played with the kitten the rest of the evening before heading to bed. As I fell asleep, I hoped I'd catch a break and not get called out on Sunday.

CHAPTER TEN

We spent the morning bonding with Ghost, trying to mitigate Ivy's jealousy and taking Alvin and Mauser for a walk in our woods. The cool, dry air was still a pleasant surprise after a long summer.

"Don't forget about next weekend," Cara reminded me as we sat on the porch. I tried to keep my face from showing that I didn't have a clue what she was talking about, but I obviously failed. "You *have* forgotten."

"Maybe," I said elusively.

"It's Pet-O-Ween on Saturday. Remember, you promised to help. And have you talked to your dad?"

"Dad?"

"How long have we been married? You can't be practicing selective memory already!"

"Married?" I said with raised eyebrows, letting my inner smartass shine through and earning myself a punch in the shoulder. "Ouch!"

"I asked you to find out if Mauser can be the grand marshal of the Pet-O-Ween parade." Cara actually said this with a straight face.

"I thought you were kidding." Even though I was being honest, I still got another punch in the shoulder. "You *weren't* kidding?"

"No. This has *got* to be a success. The Adams County Humane Society is damn near broke. They ran through a lot of resources during the hurricane, plus one of their storage sheds was damaged. Dr. Barnhill promised to sponsor the event and he asked me to head it up."

"I remember," I said, thinking about how so much of the county was still struggling to recover from the effects of a storm more than a year ago. "I just didn't think you were serious about having Mauser there. He's a wild card at the best of times."

"Which is why I want you to make sure that Jamie is there to handle him." Jamie was Mauser's dog-sitter. Dad had hired him almost two years ago and we'd all been amazed at how he'd been able to teach the big, four-legged lunk a few manners.

"But…"

"No buts. Thanks to your dad being sheriff and Mauser's larger-than-life personality, he's the best known canine in the county."

"Good Lord, don't ever let him hear you say that. He already has the biggest head I've ever seen on a dog."

"Just ask your dad." The firmness of her tone reminded me of my mother at her most unyielding.

"Texting him now," I said, pulling out my phone.

When I didn't get an answer after five minutes I looked at my watch. "That explains it. He must be at church."

Dad made it a habit to go to church most Sundays, both because he valued time in church to help remind him of his faith, especially after a long week of dealing with the darker side of society, but also because spending time with the different faith communities around the county helped him to stay in touch with the people he served. Every month, he'd pick different congregations to visit. I'd noticed that he had a tendency to use church bulletins to choose Sundays when the churches were hosting potluck dinners after services. Dad and Pete shared the church supper habit.

"You haven't gone with him in a while," Cara observed. Dad had frequently dragged me along with him to church, especially during election season.

"Part of my promise to the lieutenant not to use my special relationship with the sheriff to my advantage," I hedged.

"Going to church is taking advantage?"

"Dad and I don't seem able to *not* talk about cases."

"He *is* your dad."

"Maybe you're right."

"Johnson's not a total jerk. I'm sure he doesn't expect you to give up your personal relationship with your dad."

I changed the subject. "What do you want to do the rest of the day? Assuming I don't get called in."

"That's part of the reason I brought up Pet-O-Ween. I've got to pull some things together, like the entry forms and forms for the judges. And I need to talk to Bud Emery. He's been soliciting donations for the prizes. Do you want to help out?"

I'd walked into that. "Sure," I said, trying to sound enthusiastic.

"Great! You can stuff the giveaway bags," she said cheerily. I didn't let her see my grimace.

After an hour of putting coupons and cheap trinkets into little plastic bags with bones on them, I received a reprieve in the form of a request for help from one of our deputies. Andy Martel had been called to a scene where a man had been beaten badly enough that he wasn't able to answer many questions.

As I was driving to meet Martel, it occurred to me that there was a possibility this could be related to the murder of Gregory Wells. The attack had happened at the same Fast Mart where the miscreants had, according to Bart Crenshaw, beaten up Wells. I mentally shook myself, knowing I shouldn't jump to any conclusions until I'd at least had a chance to talk with the victim.

I found Martel standing with the victim, who was sitting

on a stretcher behind an ambulance. Hondo, Darlene's EMT boyfriend, was checking his vitals. We exchanged greetings as I walked up.

I took a close look at the man sitting on the stretcher. He was at least fifty, with unruly grey hair and blue eyes that wore a puzzled expression. His clothes were neat, though torn and marked with blood after the attack, and he was clean-shaven. The man didn't strike me as homeless.

"Mr. Reed, this is Deputy Macklin. He's going to ask you a few questions," Martel said.

"What can you tell me about the person who attacked you?" I asked.

"Not much. I… didn't see much." Something about his voice made me doubt that he was telling the truth.

"Okay. Just tell me what happened."

I could see the gears moving behind his eyes. This was not a person who was very experienced at lying, but he was certainly trying.

"I drove to the Fast Mart to get a six-pack. When I was going back to my truck, I heard a strange noise on the other side and went to see what it was. Next thing I knew, I was down on the ground with people standing around me."

"The woman who called 911 told us that he hadn't wanted the attack reported." Martel was letting me know that he also thought there was something hinky with the man's story.

"If we review the security camera footage from the Fast Mart, including the one in the rear of the building, will it tally up with what you're telling us?" The Fast Mart didn't have a security camera behind the building, but I was betting that Reed didn't know that.

There was a long pause. "I went to meet a guy," Reed finally said, looking at his feet.

"Why?" I asked, though I could make a good guess.

"I needed some… painkillers. You've got to understand, I fell down the steps a year ago and hurt my back. I need my pills." His voice was full of shame.

"How'd you contact this guy?" I asked.

"Messaging app on my phone."

"And you were going to meet him at the Fast Mart?"

"A public place. I thought it'd be safe."

"Let me see your phone." As soon as I said it, I knew that I'd made a mistake. Like magic, I saw Reed transform from a victim into a suspect. A suspect who didn't want to go to jail.

"You need a warrant for that, right?" The shame was gone from his voice, replaced by fear and suspicion.

"I don't want to take you to jail. What I *do* want is to find the asshole who beat you up before he hurts or kills someone else."

He seemed to think about this. "You promise me?"

"Give me your phone," I ordered like a parent talking to a naughty child. I wasn't going down the promises-and-guarantees road. I couldn't promise him anything, and I didn't feel like lying to him on a beautiful Sunday afternoon.

"I think I want to talk to a lawyer." Reed was playing full defense now.

"You don't need to. I can tell you exactly what he'd say. He'd advise you not to cooperate with us, but all that will do is force us to get a warrant based on the evidence from the security cameras. If I do that, I'll have to follow through and arrest you when I find evidence that you were attempting to purchase illegal substances." Okay, I told a couple of fibs, but I hadn't lied when I told him that I didn't want to arrest him. However, he wasn't making himself very likable.

"I..." Reed seemed very uncertain.

"I'm about done here. Cooperate, or we'll go with the other options." Since there wasn't a security camera in the rear of the store, I wouldn't be able to get a warrant for his phone. I didn't really *have* any other options if he stonewalled me, but Reed didn't know that.

With a heavy sigh, he took out his phone and pulled up an app called TawK. He showed me the messages he'd exchanged with a character whose username was Calhoun

Drug$$. After about thirty messages back and forth, they'd agreed on a price for two dozen Oxys. The time and place for the meet-up aligned with what we knew about the attack.

"So tell me what happened," I said again.

"I got here and saw a red Jeep parked at the back by the dumpster like he said, so I parked on the side of the building where I figured he could see me. I waited and nothing. So I got out and walked toward the Jeep. When I got close enough, I heard him tell me to come around to the dumpster." He paused. "It was stupid. I should have got out of there then, but…" He didn't have to explain that the addiction had been dictating his actions. That was how it worked. "At the dumpsters, a couple of guys jumped me."

"A couple? Two, three?"

"Three. I'm sure there were three. I was in the Army, so I'm not a pushover, but they slammed me into the dumpster and when I went down, they just started kicking the hell out of me."

"Did they steal your money?"

"Yeah. Took my wallet, but not until they were done kicking. I… think that's what they really wanted."

"What? To kick you?"

"They were laughing as they did it."

"How old were they?"

"Young. I'm not even sure they were in their twenties."

This was more than a little disturbing. "Could you see what they were wearing?" I asked.

"They were kicking the hell out of me and I had my head covered most of the time." He closed his eyes and I gave him time to think. "One of them was wearing sandals. I thought that was pretty stupid if you were trying to kick a person to death. One of the sandals came off as he was kicking me. The others had some kind of tennis shoes on. Rubber hurts. They had on jeans, I guess."

"Any tattoos or hair color? Skin color?"

"Yeah. I remember two were white and one was black. I remember thinking that at least they were equal-opportunity assholes. Funny what goes through your mind when you think you're going to die. Oh yeah, and one had long hair. I mean long for now. Kind of like that actor… the one that did that movie… *John Wick.*"

"Keanu Reeves?" Martel said.

"Yeah, that's the one."

"Black hair?" I asked.

"Yeah, 'cause I thought of that actor. It was that guy who called me over. I saw him for just a second before the others knocked me to the ground. I guess they were hiding on the other side of the Jeep. Look, I really am hurting here." I could see a darkening bruise on his chest. "My back's probably worse than it was."

"He's got a couple of cracked ribs and likely a concussion. We need to get him to the hospital," Hondo said.

"Fine," I agreed, but shook my head when Reed reached for his phone. "I'm going to keep this as evidence. I'll have our IT guy copy the information and then get it back to you."

"Hey…" Reed wasn't sure how mad he should be about it.

"On the bright side, I'm not going to arrest you for trying to buy Oxy."

"You don't have any evidence. I didn't even buy nothing."

"No, but this is probable cause for searching your truck. Any guesses what we might find if we did?" I asked.

"Okay," he grunted, resigned.

"There's one condition. You get help for your addiction. Trust me, I'll check with your doctor."

After the ambulance pulled way, I went into the Fast Mart to ask a few questions. The clerk was a newer guy who wasn't going to admit to knowing anything. But he called the owners, who were always willing to help us out since they relied on us to keep the store free of riff-raff and robbers. The man I spoke to promised to deliver two-weeks' worth of security footage to the sheriff's office on Monday morning. The only question was when was I going to find the time to watch all those hours of footage. Not to mention the video from the Khans' house behind the murder scene. I had an idea about who I could get to review the footage, but I'd need to run it past Lt. Johnson.

As I was getting ready to leave the Fast Mart, I finally got a reply to the text I'd sent to Dad. *I'll swing by and explain in person*, I replied. When I pulled up to his house, I found him in the front yard with Genie Anderson, his fiancée, and her son Jimmy, who was feeding apples to Dad's horses, Finn and Mac.

"We're going to be brothers!" Jimmy shouted when I got out of the car. He was about my age and had been born with Down Syndrome, but he was one of the happiest people I'd ever known.

"I couldn't be more thrilled. I hope you aren't too disappointed?" I kidded him.

"Oh, no, you aren't too bad," he said with a smile that covered every inch of his face.

"Have they set a date?" I asked him.

"Maybe around Christmas, they said."

"That would be nice."

I walked over to Genie and Dad, who were sitting in lawn chairs under a large oak tree. Dad had a beer and Genie something cool and green in a glass.

"Margarita?" she asked, giving me a big smile.

"I'm good."

"So what's this about Pet-O-Ween?" Dad asked, squinting at me.

"Cara would like the one and only Mauser the Magnificent to be the grand marshal of the Pet-O-Ween parade," I said, unable to hide my sarcasm.

"Yay!" Jimmy shouted. "Can I go?"

"It's next Saturday. Do you have to work?" Genie asked.

"I don't know. I got to check my schedule," Jimmy said, some of the joy gone from his voice. He worked as a bag boy at a Publix in Tallahassee and he usually loved his job, but not if it conflicted with a day spent with Mauser.

"Maybe they'll move you around if you ask. You never miss a day," Genie encouraged him.

"I'm never ever late either. Not like Jill, she's always late. I think they're going to fire her. I'll ask for sure," Jimmy said, smiling again.

"Then can I tell Cara that's a firm yes? You better make sure Jamie can come along too."

"We'll be there. I wouldn't want to stand between Mauser and his fans," Dad said with a grin.

I spent a pleasant hour visiting with them, then Dad walked me to my car.

"I ran into an old schoolmate in a rather uncomfortable situation yesterday." I went on to tell him about the wreck, but didn't bother to mention Sherry's name. While my mom probably would have known who she was, Dad wouldn't have had a clue. When I was in elementary school, he'd been working long hours on the road as a deputy and hadn't had much time for the details of my juvenile crushes.

"Toomey filled me in. The good news is that the trucker is going to be fine. Toomey's going to interview him tomorrow."

"I wouldn't mind being there." As soon as the words were out of my mouth, I put my hand up. "Not that I'm asking for your blessing. I'll ask Johnson if I can be in on it. The autopsy on Gregory Wells is scheduled for tomorrow too, so that could work out."

"I appreciate you falling in line with Johnson's point of view," Dad said.

"He has a point. Though it's tough sometimes not coming to you."

"It's not just for him. It's good for you and me too."

"So we're still friends?" My inner smartass was back.

"I don't know where you got so much jerk DNA."

"I'll give you a hint—it wasn't from Mom."

He took a faux swing at me and I dodged it, wearing a big

grin. Then I got back into my car and headed home to tell Cara that her grand marshal had been secured.

CHAPTER ELEVEN

At the office on Monday, my first stop was to talk with Sergeant Toomey, who had just finished roll call with the daytime patrol

"I'm ninety-nine percent sure that the victim is Tommy Romano," he told me. "I was able to pull a partial set of prints and sent them off to FDLE for comparison."

"His prints are on file?"

"Not what you're thinking." Toomey smiled. "He helped out with a Boy Scout troop for a few years. They fingerprint everyone these days."

"I'm glad it wasn't what I was thinking. His widow doesn't need any other surprises."

"I should hear back today."

"You going to talk to the driver today?" I asked.

"That's the plan. He was banged up pretty bad. Leg was mangled quite a bit. Still, the hospital said he should be able to answer questions."

"I'd like to come along."

Toomey gave me a look. "What are you thinking?"

"Nothing. Honest. I just want to be able to tell Mrs. Romano something about the accident."

"Do you also want to tell her when we confirm the ID?"

"I will. I appreciate you not making her do it in person."

"It would have been tough. His head was… damaged when the semi landed on the car."

"So what made you so sure?"

"Half his face was recognizable. I just had to imagine what the other half would have looked like. Plus, he was wearing a gold and emerald class ring that his wife verified as his."

"I've got to clear it with the lieutenant," I said. "I'll text you if he gives the okay to sit in on the interview."

"The more the merrier," Toomey responded. Not much phased him. I'd watched a guy spit on him while Toomey was reading his Miranda warning. Toomey had never missed a beat. As soon as he'd finished informing the man of his rights, he'd also told him that he was being charged with assaulting an officer as well. Cool as ice.

I now had two requests to run by Lt. Johnson. I decided that I needed to face the music before I had anything else to add to the list. I was on the way to his office when I saw him coming down the hall.

"Lieutenant, can I talk to you for a minute?" I asked with utmost politeness.

"I don't know, can you?" he said, stopping in the hallway and throwing me completely off my stride. I couldn't remember the man even attempting a joke before.

"Uhhh… I just had a couple of things I wanted to run by you."

"Great! I appreciate you bringing them to me. What's up?"

I took a good look at him. We were slipping into pod-person territory. "You're in a good mood." I just couldn't help commenting on it.

"I am." Johnson didn't elaborate, which just left me even more puzzled.

"I… uh… assisted with that tractor-trailer accident on Saturday and I'd like to be present when Sergeant Toomey questions the driver."

"Do you think there could be criminal charges brought?"

"I don't know," I said honestly.

"If it doesn't interfere with the other cases you've been assigned, then it's fine with me."

"Great! In fact, since I need to be in Tallahassee for the Wells autopsy, it won't even take me out of my way."

Johnson nodded. "Anything else?"

"On the Wells case, there's a couple of weeks' worth of security camera footage to review. I was wondering if you had a problem with me allowing a sort of unofficial intern to assist me?"

Johnson frowned and I immediately felt like we were back in familiar territory. "What do you mean by 'unofficial' intern?"

"The young lady who assisted me as a CI with a couple of investigations has been accepted at the law enforcement academy. I'd like to let her review the footage. That would save me a bunch of time and not cost the department any money."

Johnson worked his jaw back and forth and squinted as he thought about this. "She can review the footage, if you want. However, if she finds *anything*, then you'll need to review all of the footage yourself."

"I guess," I said, my puzzled expression causing him to roll his eyes up to the ceiling.

"I'll spell it out for you. If a suspect is discovered on the footage and that suspect is tried in court, then a defense attorney will want to question someone from our department about the tapes and what's on them. We can't hold up an unpaid intern. It will have to be an investigator who can honestly say that they reviewed all of the footage and can testify to what they found. That person will be you. Understand?"

I did and he was right. "Yes, sir."

"We done?"

"Yes," I said meekly.

"Have a great day," he said and headed for his office,

leaving me shaking my head.

"What's up with the lieutenant?" I asked Pete later when he came in and dumped a bag of pastries from the Donut Hole onto my desk.

"Wouldn't know."

"Aren't you on a diet?" I asked, picking a chocolate crème-filled donut out of the bag.

"I hiked three miles yesterday. I'm still in recovery." He looked at the bag and frowned. "You had to say the D-word. Now you've spoiled them for me."

I filled him in on the man who'd been beaten up the day before.

"We've got a lead!" Pete crowed.

"What do you mean 'we'?"" I poked him with a pencil. "I developed the lead while you were out playing wood nymph."

"I give. You're the king. So who's going through all the Fast Mart's security footage?"

I told him my plan and Johnson's response to it.

"So do you hope for a hit or not?"

"Surely the attackers go into the store on occasion. With the description we got from Reed, it shouldn't be hard to pick out the one guy. Even easier if they go in together."

"Did you question the clerk?"

"He wasn't saying much. But if the tapes show us our guys, that would make it easier to get the clerk to recognize them."

"Have you asked Jessie if she's interested?"

"Not yet. But is there any doubt?" Jessie was eager to do anything that involved chasing down bad guys. She'd irritated me at first, but now her eagerness seemed more energizing than off-putting.

"She's got more enthusiasm for being a cop than you ever had," Pete observed.

"Too true. Good thing I have such a talent for it." Pete rolled his eyes and I changed the subject. "I'm heading over to the Wells autopsy and then I'm gonna sit in while Toomey questions the trucker."

"I'd join you for the autopsy, but I've got a pile of my own cases to work." Pete looked thoughtful. "Let me know what the driver has to say. Toomey showed me some pictures of the semi. Took them five hours to clean it up."

"And that was *after* the crane got there."

"Toomey said they kept snagging the car when they tried to lift the trailer, and he didn't want to tear up the car before he had a chance to look it over."

"If I'm ever in a fatal accident, I want him to be the responding officer," I said.

"He's got dozens of notebooks filled with sketches of all the accidents he's been to."

"I know. I spent a month with him as one of my field training officers. Meticulous is the guy's middle name." While I was talking about him, I texted Toomey and confirmed that I'd meet him at two at the hospital.

I'd barely finished that text when I got another from Darlene wanting to know when I wanted my guided tour of the homeless camps. *Autopsy's today. Let's do it tomorrow, noon?*, I responded, and received a quick thumbs up in response.

Next I called Jessie. As I'd predicted, she was more than willing to go through all the video footage. The promised flash drive from Mr. Khan was already on my desk, so I stopped by the Fast Mart on my way to Tallahassee for the autopsy and picked up their footage as well.

"This was a determined attack," Dr. Darzi said two hours later, looking over the wounds on Gregory Wells's body. Andre was assisting him today, and the man looked even larger indoors. "Do you have a weapon?" Darzi asked me.

"We haven't found anything yet. I'm guessing it was done with an axe," I said.

"Good eye. Maybe something smaller, like a hatchet. I'm seeing…" He counted. "… evidence of eight blows. This one, an inch from the center of the forehead, is at an angle that suggests a right-handed assailant. The frontal blow would appear to be the lightest, though the hardness of the skull might have prevented the axe from penetrating as deep as some of the others." Darzi proceeded to measure and probe the various wounds.

"How big or strong would the attacker have had to be?" I asked.

Darzi paused and looked at the body. "I'd say that anyone of average strength could have done this. Clearly their right arm would need to be able to go through a full range of motion. Any average male or female would be capable. I think what will delineate your attacker more than physical ability is the psychological constitution that would be necessary to attack a human being like this. This was more than a single blow struck in the heat of a fight. This, my friend, indicates a dangerous person able to conjure up the will to strike and strike and strike again after his victim is on the ground."

"Passion," I suggested.

"But for what? If it was love, then they were clearly rejected."

"He was homeless, mentally ill and not… very clean. Not that I'm saying a homeless guy can't inspire love, but…" I shook my head.

"Anger then. What did this man do to instill so much anger in the murderer? If the killer is a psychopath, then Wells might have presented a roadblock to whatever plans the killer had."

"Projected anger? Maybe Wells just represented whoever the murderer really hated."

"Then let's hope your killer doesn't get ahold of the person that this corpse represented for him."

"We'll need a full toxicology report."

"It's highly doubtful that anything in toxicology will change my determination of the cause of death," Darzi said dryly.

"No, but assuming that we catch the person who did this,

we'll need to be prepared for their defense attorney. They'll be wanting to know if Wells was hyped up on something and highly aggressive, thereby contributing to his own death."

"I'm well aware of the machinations of defense attorneys. I can tell you one thing—the first blow was struck while the killer looked the victim in the eye."

"We also know that that first blow didn't knock him out. The crime scene shows that he stumbled to the edge of the porch," I pointed out.

"We'll know more about that first wound when I remove the skull cap and examine the brain. Though the time of death was only minutes after the first blow, so the question is almost moot. Just looking at the external injuries, I can state that the victim would have been left dazed and unable to defend himself. Proof of that can be seen in the total lack of defensives wounds, or even movement. You would expect that if someone was chopping at you with a hatchet, then you would squirm and twist in an effort to escape the blows. There is nothing here to indicate our victim did that. It appears that the assailant was able to strike repeatedly in roughly the same area of the back. If the victim was moving, then you'd expect to see wounds over a wider area of his body. Also, the blows seem to enter the body perpendicularly, no angled or glancing blows."

"Since most of the attack took place when he was face down and couldn't defend himself, then there's little chance of finding any evidence under his fingernails or in his mouth," I mused, disappointed. It was always helpful if a victim had a chance to scratch or bite their attacker.

"Wells was a long-time drug user. You can see old needle marks and signs of liver impairment. His teeth and gums also show evidence of long-term damage," Darzi pointed out as he continued the autopsy.

The autopsy was done an hour later without revealing anything new. Of course, it would be weeks at least before the lab reports came back with the results of the organ biopsies and the bloodwork.

"We have another one of your bodies waiting in the cooler," Darzi said, helping to lift Wells's body onto the stretcher to go back to the cooler, though Andre could have easily lifted the body by himself.

"You mean the car accident?"

"Yes. It's scheduled for tomorrow morning."

"I won't be back for that one. I was just an interested bystander."

"The evidence from the scene suggests that it was an accident."

"It looks like it. Sergeant Toomey is going to question the other driver this afternoon, then we'll have a better idea."

"Linda attended the scene and said that the body is in poor condition after having been crushed and submerged in the creek for several hours." Darzi almost sounded excited. He liked the unusual and the challenging.

"It certainly wasn't pretty," I agreed. "I didn't get down and look at the victim. Didn't need to. When you have tons of tractor trailer lying on top of you, you're not going to come out looking real good.

"Everything I saw at the scene seems consistent with an accident. The truck driver may be liable on some level since he did appear to rear end the car. Of course, it's possible that the driver of the car lost control and spun out, which would mitigate the trucker's responsibility."

Darzi listened attentively. A coroner was responsible for taking the events surrounding a death into consideration when deciding the cause of death.

I said my goodbyes, then headed down to the cafeteria. I had just enough time for lunch before I needed to meet Toomey. However, I found him in the lunch line in front of me.

"I thought all you patrol guys were fast food junkies?" I joked as he put a salad on his tray.

"Trust me. In twenty years, your doctor will be making unhappy sounds when he's reading your chart. I swore when I joined the force that I wasn't going to be one of the guys who has five ex-wives and a triple bypass by the time he's sixty. So…" He nodded toward the depressingly healthy items he'd selected.

I looked at the tasty Italian sub on my tray and almost put it back. Almost. Instead, I grabbed a bag of chips and a cup for soda and moved toward the cashier.

"We're in luck," Toomey said as we sat down in a sunny corner of the cafeteria. "The truck had a dash cam."

"Have you looked at the footage?"

"Not yet. I talked to the company this morning. They're being very cooperative. One of their tech guys is going to meet me at the yard later today. I had the truck cab pulled to our impound lot, along with the BMW," he said, referring to the small area behind the sheriff's office where we were able to store vehicles that needed to be scoured for evidence.

I didn't bother to ask Toomey what his current thoughts were about the wreck. Once he was enmeshed in an investigation, he was careful not to speculate ahead of the evidence.

Upstairs we found the trucker's room, and Toomey knocked gently before entering. A middle-aged woman greeted us at the door.

"I'm Lori Mansfield," the mocha-complexioned woman said, holding out her hand. Toomey shook it, then introduced both of us. "The doctor said Lennie shouldn't talk too much," Lori cautioned Toomey.

"I just want to ask a few basic questions about the accident, then we'll let him get some rest. In a week, providing he's doing well, we'll want to go over the events in more detail."

"Lori, let the man ask his questions," Lennie Mansfield said good-naturedly from the bed.

She shook her head before moving aside.

"Good news, Mr. Mansfield," Toomey said, walking over and standing by the bed. "Your bloodwork came back and there weren't any drugs or alcohol in your system."

"Tell me something I don't know," Lennie said.

"Can you tell me what happened?"

"Crazy. That's all it was. I don't know if the guy didn't know I was behind him or what. I'd been following him since the last intersection when he turned on the road in front of me. I'm used to that sh… crap." He glanced at his wife as though he expected a reprimand for almost cursing in front of law enforcement. "Just want to say I got a dash cam, so check that out."

"We will. I just want to hear your side of the events," Toomey assured him.

"Like I said, he pulled out in front of me, which caused me to brake. But he picked up speed fast enough, so I thought we were all good. That's until we came around the last curve before the bridge. He'd slowed down, which meant I was closer than I thought I was going to be when I got around the curve. No problem, there were still half a dozen car lengths between us and a straight, flat, dry road ahead. Just that bridge over the creek. I should have maybe left a bit more distance…"

"Lennie, don't be sayin' any of this was your fault," his wife scolded him.

He raised a hand. "I'm not. There wasn't anything I could have done, because once he got to that bridge, his brakes just locked up. There was nothing, I mean *nothing*, in front of him. I would have seen a rabbit or a dog. But there was nothing, he just locked up his brakes. By the time I slammed mine on, there was nothing I could do. The bridge is too narrow. I couldn't get around him. All I could do was watch as my grill plowed into the back of the car. 'Course, I'd put the brakes on so hard that the trailer was already jack-knifing as I pushed him into the creek. My tires snagged on the edge of the bridge, the guardrail or something, and I was pulled over the side with the car." Lenny stopped talking, obviously still baffled by the string of events at the bridge.

I thought of the scene when I'd arrived. The final pile of bent and twisted metal fit the scenario Lennie had described. I glanced at Toomey and knew he was wondering the same thing that I was. Could Romano have had a heart attack or stroke that caused him to slam on the brakes? Would Darzi be able to tell when he performed the autopsy?

Toomey asked a few more questions, then we left the Mansfields alone.

"Medical?" I asked once we were outside the room.

Toomey shrugged. "Or maybe Romano thought he'd forgotten something and slammed on the brakes. Or his foot slipped and he hit the brakes instead of the gas. Doesn't really matter. I'll take a look at the dash cam and if the footage backs up Mansfield's version, then we're done here."

"I guess." Something still felt... off about the whole situation. Maybe I just felt that way because I didn't know how to present the facts to Sherry Romano. Relatives always wanted to know the motivation of their loved ones in situations like this, or at least they wanted to know why everything had happened the way it did. Sadly, there was seldom an answer to that question.

"The only person who can be guilty of a crime is Mr. Mansfield, so if he's cleared by the video footage then I'm good."

"Could it be mechanical error?" I asked.

"Brakes fail, though I've never heard of them locking up without the operator pressing down on the brake pedal. Now it's possible that they were poorly adjusted and a small application of pressure caused them to lock up. Still..." He thought for a moment. "Ask Mrs. Romano when the car was last in for service. But the thing is, Romano appears to have driven it for miles at least on that day, so he would have had a chance to get used to the brakes, however they were adjusted. It doesn't take long for an experienced driver to figure out how much pressure to apply to the brake and gas pedals."

Toomey was right, but I couldn't help thinking that there was something we weren't considering.

CHAPTER TWELVE

I was headed back to Calhoun by three o'clock. My first stop was the library, where Jessie was manning the front desk.

"I've got all the footage. When can you start going through it?"

"I can come in early tomorrow and spend a couple of hours before the library opens." A thoughtful look came over her face. "Wait." She got up and disappeared into the back. When she came out, she was smiling. "I took tomorrow off. I'll spend the whole day going over the videos."

I wanted to tell her that she didn't need to miss work. On the other hand, I wanted to know as soon as possible if our attackers were on any of the footage. *What the hell, it's her life.*

"Great. We'll set you up in a room in the evidence lab."

I hadn't asked Shantel if I could use the room and I hoped she wouldn't be too miffed. The last time I'd turned it into a war room, she'd made me promise that it would be the *last* time. She'd had plans to give it to Marcus when he came back to work for us. *I hope he hasn't already taken it over,* I thought.

I got back to the office and decided to make a concerted effort to find Gregory Wells's next of kin. Using the fingerprints Linda had sent me, I ran a background check on him. His full name was Gregory Harlan Wells, and he'd been arrested a dozen times for possession of various narcotics and misdemeanors such as shoplifting, creating a public disturbance and public intoxication. All of the arrests and citations had occurred within fifty miles of Adams County, mostly in Tallahassee, and dated back to when he was twenty-nine. He was either a local boy or had come here for school.

I asked one of the interns in the records department to gather copies of all his arrest reports and court documents. The odds were very good that the paperwork would list some relatives. It was possible that Wells had been remanded into the custody of family members during or after the various hearings and trials.

I figured it would take a day or two for her to get all of that together for me, so I headed down to the evidence room to look over the items we'd collected from the shed behind the Lynch house. When I got to Shantel's empire, I found Marcus ensconced in his new office, dashing my hopes of setting Jessie up there to review the videos.

"Sorry," Marcus said, giving me a big grin.

"I never should have taken all of my stuff out of here."

"You didn't. There's still a box of things you left." He pointed to a cardboard box on the floor. "I also rolled the white board back to the interview room."

"What you lookin' at?" Shantel had snuck up behind me.

"Another man's office," I replied.

"It's not like you were paying me rent," Shantel chided me.

"I just need someplace for Jessie to review security footage."

"You're in luck. Lionel just moved into his new space back here. There should be plenty of room for her to set up in there and he can help her if she's got any questions." Shantel prodded me in the direction of Lionel West, our forensic tech guy.

Lionel was sitting at his desk with his dark face about six inches from a monitor. Two other monitors were set up on either side of the one he was staring at. Every few seconds, his hand would twitch on his mouse and the image on the screen would change.

"Lionel." I knocked on the open door. He raised a hand without looking at me and I waited patiently until he could give me his full attention.

"Hey, Larry," he said after a few minutes. "I can't do any rush jobs. Between this presentation that I'm doing for your dad and moving in here on top of all my regular work, I'm buried."

"Not what I'm here for. By the way, I like the new digs." The office still looked disorganized, but it had a lot more space than the glorified broom closet he'd been in before.

"It's nice to be able to spread my wings."

"All this new room is sort of what I came to talk to you about," I said and watched his eyes narrow. "Nothing permanent. I just want an… intern of mine to review some security footage. Could she set up in that corner over there?"

He pursed his lips and looked over his shoulder at the spot I'd indicated. "There's no work for me, right?"

"Absolutely not. Just provide some desk space… and maybe a monitor… and a computer, of course."

Lionel shook his head. "Whatever."

"Perfect. Thanks. She'll be here in the morning."

"I'll have something set up for her by then," he said grudgingly.

"I owe you."

"Many times over."

"One thing more." I pulled out the external hard drive from the Fast Mart that had been weighing down my pocket. "Could you keep this safe? Oh, and this too." I handed him the thumb drive that the Khans had dropped off.

"I'll hook it all up for her," Lionel said in the resigned voice of someone who was used to being taken advantage of. I left him feeling only mildly guilty.

I went to the large table in the center of the evidence room and began sorting through the items that we'd taken from the shed on Friday. At the bottom of a green canvas bag, I found a P38 can opener which I assumed was the one Wells had gotten from Bart Crenshaw.

"What's that?" Shantel asked, looking over my shoulder.

"It's a can opener."

"No way," she said, looking at it more closely. I unfolded the cutting edge and demonstrated how it worked.

"I'd show you with a real can, but this needs to be processed." I explained the can opener's role in the investigation. "It wouldn't do to damage it. I want to be sure that Bart didn't have anything to do with the death before I give this back to him."

"Always sad to see the folks wandering the streets," Shantel murmured. "I see the homeless and can't help thinking how lucky I am. Truly blessed."

"Want to help me sort through this? I'm hoping to find something that might point us toward a next of kin."

Finally I found a letter tucked into a well-worn paperback. The book was some esoteric tome on coding, which I thought was a very odd item for a homeless guy to be carting around. The letter itself was addressed to Gregory Wells, care off a men's shelter in Tallahassee. There was no return address.

I pulled a pink sheet of paper out of the envelope. It was the cheery kind of memo note that could be found in most people's kitchens. This one had a blue bird in one corner and ivy running around the edges. The note itself was plain and to the point.

Dear Gregory,

Your mother doesn't want to see you anymore. You broke her heart when you took Grammie's necklace and sold it. Please, Son, you know we want the best for you. Sober up and I'll get you all the help I can. Dr. French is a good man and could help you if you'd let him. Take your medicine! Get sober!! So we can help you. I can change your

mother's mind if you can meet us halfway. That's all I can tell you.
 Love,
 Dad

The postmark on the envelope showed that it had been mailed two years earlier from Tallahassee. Assuming that Wells was his given family name and that his parents still lived in Tallahassee, I decided then and there that I'd just start calling all of the Wellses in the phone book. With a little bit of luck, I should be able to find his parents.

The only other thing of consequence that we found with his personal items was a pair of notebooks filled to the brim with drawings and odd comments. Some of the doodles looked technical, while others looked like something out of a madman's nightmares, which they very well might have been. Flipping through the pages of the notebooks, I couldn't make any sense of them. But I'd still need to go through them, page by page, just in case there was a blatant clue written inside, such as: *This man threatened to kill me.* I would have done it right then, but I wanted to focus on finding his family, so I packed all the items back into the evidence box and headed down the hall to my desk.

There were twenty-seven households with the last name of Wells in Tallahassee. Of course, his family could have also lived in one of the surrounding communities like Havana or Crawfordville, but I'd leave those out unless I struck out with the ones in Tallahassee. I'd tallied up six no's and five no-answers when suddenly I had an incoming call from the front desk.

"You've got visitors," Sergeant Dill Kirby told me when I answered. I could tell by his voice that there was something odd about them. "They got a camera. A real one, not just their phones," he said in a whisper of warning before hanging up.

I headed toward the lobby, wondering what I'd done to attract the attention of reporters. But as soon as I saw the two of them, I was sure they weren't reporters. The woman was broad shouldered and carried an expensive-looking video camera. Her hair was tied back with a brightly colored bandana and she wore jeans and a T-shirt. The man wore cargo shorts and his hair looked like it hadn't seen the inside of a barbershop in a very long time. His T-shirt matched the woman's. In a blood-red, spooky-looking font, both shirts read: *Para-abnormal.*

"Hey man!" the guy said, sticking out his hand for a shake with way too much enthusiasm for anyone but a politician or an insurance salesman. "You've got to be Deputy Macklin."

"That's right. How can I help you?" I noticed that the woman was filming. "If you'd like to film our conversation, we should step outside," I said, moving forward in such a way as to push them toward the door.

"Sure, man. Not a problem. Great day for it. Vick, how's the light out there?" he asked the woman.

"We can make do." She pushed the door open and negotiated her way outside with the camera on her shoulder.

"Yeah, yeah, let's go."

"What is this about?" I asked once we were all outside, though I had a pretty good guess.

"Let's get set up first," the man said, studying the entryway. "Great, there's the sign. We can get that in the background. Wish you were in uniform," he tossed over his shoulder at me.

"I can hold my jacket back so you can see my badge," I offered sarcastically.

"That would be fantastic!"

"Not happening. Come on, what's this all about?" I let a sharp edge creep into my voice. I was starting to dislike the guy.

"Don't get your panties in a wad. We just want it all on record," he said with a smile and raised eyebrows. He had to be less than thirty.

I wanted to respond in a suitably rude and vulgar manner, but the woman was already filming, so I let my better nature prevail. "You've got ten minutes."

"All we'll need. Damn it. I haven't even introduced myself. I'm Sly Harris and this is Vicky Bradford. We're the Para-abnormal Group. Like the shirts say. We do a regular web series that's been picked up by the All Ghost Channel. But this!" He waved his hands theatrically. "*This* could be the pilot for a bigger show. I'm still working on a name for it, but the show would focus on cases where the paranormal and true crime intersect. What luck to have a murder at the Lynch house while we're here filming."

"I don't think the victim would think it's very lucky," I said with a frown. I looked them up and down, trying to come up with an excuse to arrest them.

Sly didn't look embarrassed. "Nah, you know what I mean. Look, we just want to ask you a few questions." He was all smiles.

"That's my line."

"What?"

"You can ask me questions if I get to ask you a few," I said, remembering that Howard Tippets had mentioned seeing a pair of filmmakers at the Lynch house.

"Okay, sure."

I let them decide where we would stand and gave Harris the first shot at asking questions.

"Does this new murder fit the pattern of the Lynch murders?"

"No," I said, and Harris made cutting motions at the woman.

"I thought that he was chopped up like the Lynches?" Sly asked with a hint of frustration in his voice.

"Where did you hear that?" I shot back, causing him to look a bit confused.

"Ah, well, it's the word on the street."

"I can't give out that information."

"Come on! That's not fair. You know he was killed with an axe. I'm not asking for all the super-secret details. Just make it sound like it could be related to the Lynch murders."

"I'm not part of your show. Whatever you've heard is just a rumor. We haven't even had a chance to notify the next of kin. In fact, you interrupted me as I was trying to find the victim's relatives."

"Fine. We'll just go with another murder at the Lynch house," he muttered to Vicky. "Let's start over." With the camera rolling again, he said, "There's been another murder at the Lynch house?"

"Yes," I said without any animation.

More cut gestures toward Vicky. "Come on, now. Give me something I can work with," Sly moaned.

"Tell you what I'll do. Let me ask my questions and I'll give you a couple minutes of real footage."

"Perfecto! Then let's get on with it. Shoot!"

"You were in town before the murder?" I asked.

"Yep!" he said, giving the one-word-answer treatment right back to me.

"How long have you been watching the Lynch house?"

"We went by there a few times," he said, looking suddenly uncomfortable. I found some satisfaction in that.

"Did you ever see anyone around the house?"

"A couple of times. The old man across the street asked us questions once." He threw a quick glance at Vicky.

"Anyone else?" I pressed.

"The woman neighbor on the other side of the house spent a lot of time staring down at us." He paused for a moment as though considering his next statement. "Also, we met a homeless guy."

I was instantly alert, wondering if they'd encountered Gregory Wells.

"Actually, he scared the hell out of us," Sly continued. "We were just looking around. It was the middle of the day and I noticed that shed in the backyard. So we went over to it and when I opened the door, this awful sound came from inside. I damn near pissed my pants. The loon… guy just howled for a minute and then started to throw stuff at the door. I thought it was great footage and waited until he calmed down so I could talk him out of the shed and get him on camera." Sly paused to look at me, no doubt trying to assess how I was taking his story.

"Did he come out?"

"Yeah, yeah. We've actually got footage. Yeah. You can see it was all friendly-like after he quit that freaky howling."

"Did he tell you his name?"

Sly nodded. "Yeah, said his name was Gregory Wells."

This was moving from an annoyance into a possible lead. I worked hard to keep a poker face and said, "I want a copy of the footage."

"Sure! Vicky will get it for you."

"I've got it in the van," she said without taking her eye from the viewfinder of the camera on her shoulder.

"Was that the only time you interacted with him?"

"We just asked him about the murders and the ghosts." Sly shrugged.

"It's all on tape?"

"Start to finish."

"I'd like to have the copy now."

"Will you answer a few more questions? Like, *really* answer them?"

"There are things about the case that I can't discuss right now."

"Yeah, yeah." He waved away my excuses. "Understood. Just a few basics."

"The copy?"

"Give me the camera," he said to Vicky. She took it off her shoulder and handed it to him, then ran to their van. Sly turned the camera on me. "Now, what can you tell us about the murder?"

"The victim was a homeless man," I began, and saw Sly's eyes widen.

"Was it—" he started, but I shook my head.

"I can't confirm his identity until we've notified the next of kin, but he was thirty-seven years old. He'd been living in the shed behind the house for a few weeks."

"Did he have any connection to the haunted Lynch house?"

"Not that we know of. And let me say that the sheriff's office doesn't believe in haunted houses." I figured they'd cut that part, but at least I had tried.

"Do you have a line on who killed him?"

"Not at this time."

"Do you think it was the ghost of Daniel Lynch who killed him?"

"No. As I said, the Adams County Sheriff's Office doesn't believe in ghosts."

"We talked to several of the neighbors who reported strange goings-on at the murder house. Have you investigated any of the weird activity?"

"If by 'weird activity' you mean homeless people and neighborhood kids, then, yes, we've responded any time we got a call."

Behind Sly Harris, I saw one of our unmarked cars pull into the parking lot. I muttered a small curse under my breath when I realized that Lt. Johnson was behind the wheel. He'd have something to say about me talking to anyone on camera without clearing it with him first.

"One more question. Do you think Daniel Lynch killed his family?"

I almost threw up my hands. *How the hell am I supposed to comment on a case that's eighty years old?* I thought.

"We have no plans to reopen the case," I responded diplomatically. Out of the corner of my eye, I saw Johnson get out of his car and start toward the front door, which would lead him right past us. I was shocked to see him smiling, even after he took in Harris, the camera and me. I came close to fainting when he gave me a little wave and a nod, then continued on through the front door. *What kind of drugs is he on?* I wondered. *And why hasn't he been taking them before this?*

Vicky popped out of their van and came back over to us while I was still trying to understand what had just happened with Johnson. She held out a thumb drive. I took it and traded it for a pair of my cards.

"Thank you. Call me if you think of anything else you might have seen or heard around the Lynch house." I waited and, when Sly didn't say anything, I added, "I'd like a number where you can be reached."

He dug a card out of a pocket of his cargo shorts and passed it to me. "You'll let us know when you have a break in the case?"

"Sure. Are you staying in town?"

"At the Roads Best, unfortunately."

Back inside the building, I tried to decide if I should talk to Lt. Johnson about Sly and Vicky. Part of me argued that since he hadn't said anything, then I should just leave things well enough alone. Another part promised that he was just setting me up and if I didn't go to him now and confess, I'd pay a heavy price later. I opted for the path of least resistance and went back to my desk to finish my survey of all persons with the last name of Wells in Tallahassee.

CHAPTER THIRTEEN

Half an hour later, I dialed one of the last numbers on my list and Eugene Wells answered the phone. I could tell that he was an older man from the timbre of his voice.

"What?" was his greeting.

"I'm Deputy Larry Macklin from the Adams County Sheriff's Office."

"Oh, for Pete's sake, I'm not giving any money to whatever benevolent society to help blah, blah law enforcement that you're soliciting for. And take my name off your list."

"No. I don't want any money," I managed to say before he could hang up. As soon as the words were out of my mouth, I felt something change in the man on the other end of the line.

"Oh. You said you're in Adams County?"

"Yes, sir. I'm looking for any relative of Gregory Wells."

"Of course you are." His voice was somber.

"I'm…"

"Whatever he's done, we aren't responsible," he interrupted calmly.

"You're Eugene Wells?"

"I am."

"And you are related to Gregory Wells?"

"I was his father," he answered oddly.

"I don't understand."

"Yes, Deputy Macklin. I am Gregory Wells's father. Now what is it you want?"

"Sir, I'm sorry to tell you, but your son is dead."

There was a long pause. Then he said, "We expected as much."

"How's that?" I asked, though I thought I knew. Resignation was not an uncommon response from the families of addicts or the mentally ill, especially if the person was over twenty-five.

"He's been… ill a long time. The last time we saw him, we knew that we'd get this phone call one day."

"When was that?"

"Three years ago. We'd sent him to rehab out in Arizona six months earlier. It was one that specializes in addicts with mental health issues. He did great for a few months and then he started skipping his pills and… he hit his mother. We couldn't do it anymore. My wife couldn't even look at him. We knew he was sick, but that didn't change what he did. If he would have let us take care of him, we would have. Greg just couldn't give up control. Couldn't let us give him his medicine and watch over him. In the end, we knew it was just a matter of time before his… problems destroyed him." I could tell that the man was holding back tears.

"I'd like to meet with you both."

"I guess there are arrangements that have to be made."

"Yes. And there's a bit more to your son's death that you should know."

"How's that?"

"Someone murdered him… in a particularly gruesome manner. I wouldn't be giving you these details, except that you're going to hear about them in the media."

"What are you talking about? Murdered?"

"If we can meet face to face, then I can tell you everything we know."

"Of course… I don't know how my wife is going to take the news. I told you that we expected something bad would happen to him eventually. However… murder. In spite of everything, she dearly loved that boy." His voice cracked.

"I can be there in an hour," I told him, feeling an obligation to do everything I could to give them as much information and comfort as I could without them having to wait for it.

"That'll be fine. I'll have time to break the news to Miriam."

I verified the address and headed for my car. On my way, I bumped into Pete and filled him in on the parents.

"Rips your heart out. Do you want me to go with you?" Pete asked.

It was big of him to offer, since I knew how much he hated to notify parents of a child's death. He'd told me once that he got strange flashes where he felt like he was the parent and not the deputy, which left him feeling broken.

"I'll be all right," I assured him.

"At least they'll know," he said.

I found the Wells home in the northwest section of Tallahassee. The neighborhood had sprung up in the post-World War II housing boom. The house was an all-brick ranch that probably didn't look much different today from when the builder had stuck the original "For Sale" sign in the front yard. I saw a man staring out the bay window as I pulled into the driveway.

"I'm Eugene Wells," the stout man said, meeting me at the door and giving my hand a firm shake.

"I'm sorry that I have to bring you such awful news," I said, following him into the house.

"Miriam isn't taking it well at all. I've called our minister." He led me into the living room, which was furnished directly from a 1975 Sears home catalog. Miriam Wells was sitting on the couch, and even in her grief I could tell that she must have been very attractive in her day. She had high cheekbones and the posture of a model. The only thing that marred her looks were her red eyes and the tears running down her cheeks.

"Don't get up," I told her as she started to rise from the couch.

"Please have a seat," she said, pointing to an overstuffed chair across from the couch. I let myself settle on the edge of the chair.

"I can't tell you how sorry I am." I looked at Miriam as her husband sat down beside her.

"I thought that I'd already grieved for him." More tears formed in her eyes.

"You said that he was… killed?" Eugene asked.

"Yes. I'm afraid it was a rather savage attack."

"Who would do such a thing… I guess it must have been one of the… the addicts he hung out with," Miriam said.

"We don't know yet. When was the last time you saw him?"

"That's a rather painful memory," she said. "Gene and I had tried to help him, but nothing we could do made a difference. It was three years ago last month. He'd gone off his medication and… well, I'm sure he was high on something. I caught him trying to steal some of my jewelry. When I tried to stop him, he hit me."

"Did you report it?"

"No. I kicked him out of the house," Eugene said.

"You were there when it happened?"

"I'd been outside. I heard the fight and ran into the bedroom. He had her jewelry box in his hand and she was lying on the floor." He took her hand and squeezed it. "I knocked the box out of his hand and ordered him to get out."

"I thought he was going to hit you too," Miriam said, leaning into her husband.

"He just pushed me back and ran out. You need to understand that nothing about that boy is evil. I guess I mean *was*. Lord help us." Tears fell from Eugene's eyes too.

"That's the worst part. He was brilliant as a child. No parents could have wanted more from their boy."

"She's right. He never had a problem in the world until he was twenty-nine."

"What happened?"

"He'd been working at U.S. Auto, at their office up in Tennessee. He was the head of the security section in their R and D division. All of it was a mile over my head. Computer stuff."

"He had a beautiful house, a girlfriend, Miranda. We hoped they'd marry." Miriam was squeezing her hands together nervously.

"Then in October, Miranda called us," Eugene said. "She was all upset 'cause Greg was acting odd and had written all over the walls of the house. We couldn't calm her down and I asked to speak to Greg. He wouldn't come to the phone, but I could hear him in the background, ranting. Something about the phone sucking his brains out. Crazy talk."

"We didn't even pack, we just took off in the car."

"Got up there in the middle of the night to find Greg locked in his room. Took us hours to talk him out." Eugene paused, lost in his memories. "There were dozens of doctors and endless tests over the next couple of months. Even after they diagnosed it as paranoid schizophrenia, we took him to more neurologists, hoping that something... I don't know... physical could be done for him. I think I'd known from the beginning what we were facing. He was hearing voices and his paranoia was making him fear everyone and everything. Finally I had to admit that my son was facing a lifetime of confusion and pain. We took him to some of the top psychiatrists in the nation."

"We spent every penny we had," Miriam added.

"And a lot we didn't. We still have a mortgage on this house."

"We make it sound like we just took him here and there and had doctors exam him. In truth, it was horrible. He fought us every step of the way. We'd be in a doctor's waiting room when he'd suddenly stand up and yell at us before storming out," Miriam said.

"There were some good times too. We eventually got him on some good meds that evened him out. I wouldn't say it made him better, just not so crazy."

"He hated them. I can understand that. There was a period of time during all of it that I took valium. The washed-out feeling was helpful on the one hand, but… it wasn't living. That's what he complained about all the time he was on medication. No matter how the doctors adjusted his meds, he would still be so unhappy. Eventually he started medicating himself."

"It was pot first, which I thought, okay, maybe that can help. You know, mellow him out," Eugene explained. "But it didn't do much. If he couldn't get anything else, he would drown himself in cheap booze. He was into heroin at one point, which scared us to death, and I don't know what all else. I don't think he cared."

"I can't imagine how difficult that all must have been for you," I said, wondering how anyone could deal with that type of pain and loss. "Can you think of anyone who might have wanted to hurt your son? I realize that you haven't been in touch with him in a long time, but anything you can tell me could help."

"When he got… sick, Greg would get into fights with people all the time. Usually about nothing," Eugene said.

"Anyone in particular that he got into it with? Maybe something serious enough that the person might hold a grudge?"

"Burton," Miriam said.

"Yeah," Eugene agreed.

"Who?"

"Trip Burton. Gregory hit the man's car about four years ago. It happened when Gregory was on medication and was sober, miracle of miracles. Unfortunately, he was at fault in the accident."

"So was Burton," Miriam added.

"Which was the problem."

"Problem?" I asked.

"The police ruled it a no fault or, more accurately, a double fault," Eugene explained. "Gregory turned in front of Burton, but it was a thirty-mile-an-hour zone and Burton was doing almost sixty. Burton and his wife were late for a dinner date and rushing. Luckily, Gregory was driving our old van and Burton hit him at the sliding door. If Burton had hit the driver's door, he'd have killed Gregory."

"But he blamed Gregory?"

"Burton's wife was half out of her seatbelt, fooling with her makeup when the accident happened. She slammed into the dash hard enough to cause significant brain damage. Since she wasn't properly belted in and Burton shared the guilt for the accident, our insurance company refused to pay. In fact, it went after Burton and *his* insurance for Gregory's damages. Of course they refused to pay as well, but our insurance company was able to bluff them well enough that they refused to pursue the case and even refused to pay Burton for his damages. So he was left holding the bag with a woman who needed almost constant medical care."

I could hardly imagine a more horrible situation. "Did Trip Burton ever threaten Gregory?"

Eugene nodded. "And us. He didn't seem to understand that we didn't have anything to say when it came to how our insurance company handled the claims."

"What happened? Did he write you letters or emails? Confront Gregory in person?"

"We've got emails he sent telling us that Gregory ruined his life. In the emails, he outlined all the things that he had to do for his wife now that she wasn't... wasn't herself. They were awful to read. I felt sorry for him, but what could we do? We'd already spent all of our money trying to help Gregory."

"I'd like to see the emails. Do you know where Burton lives now?"

"I think he's still in town, though I'm not sure. He hasn't contacted us in more than a year. I'll get you copies of the emails." Eugene stood up.

"You can just email them to me later." I took out one of my cards and handed it to him and he sat back down.

"What about his body?" he asked.

"The coroner has already conducted an autopsy. His body can be released to you at any time. I'll be glad to help you navigate the red tape. Nothing too complicated."

"It sounds awful, but we've already thought about his burial. Even before I kicked him out, we knew this day would come."

"But to be murdered." Miriam shook her head in confusion.

"I'll do everything I can to find his killer." I paused, not quite knowing how to bring up the other issue concerning his death. *Just plow ahead*, my inner voice told me. "There's something else that you will have to deal with. Your son was murdered on the front porch of the Lynch house."

"What house?" Eugene looked confused.

"Lynch. A family was murdered there back in the 1930s."

"I don't understand."

"The murders are a well-known true crime case. Also, a lot of people in Adams County believe that the house is haunted."

"What does any of that have to do with Greg's murder?"

"Probably nothing. The thing is, your son's murder will garner more attention simply because it took place at the Lynch house. I've already run into a couple of people filming a paranormal show about the house and the original murders. I think it's a sure thing that your son's murder will be included in any story they do about the house."

"I see," Eugene said, working his jaw. "I guess there's nothing we can do about it?"

"It's a free country. Unless they tell falsehoods about your son, I don't see how you can stop them. Even then, it is very difficult to do anything when the subject is deceased."

"I understand," Eugene said, patting his wife on the arm. She was staring off into space now and I could understand why the events had left her dazed. To expect that your son would come to a bad end because of his lifestyle was one thing, but to be confronted with his murder and the possible exploitation of it was another situation altogether.

The drive home was dreary. A cool front had rolled in and a damp wind brought stinging rain. I listened to the thumping of the windshield wipers and wondered how I could find justice for Gregory Wells. The poor man had been given everything—brains, health and a loving family—only to have it all ripped away from him by an insidious disease. For a final indignity, he'd been butchered in a way that would bring unwanted attention to his life and death.

When I opened my front door, I was welcomed home by a thundering loose cannon.

"What are you still doing here?" I said, trying to fend off Mauser's affectionate and painful greetings. I winced as I saw Ghost weaving in and out between the Dane's manic paws. Miraculously, the white ball of fur managed not to be stomped or kicked across the room.

"The kitten loves him," Cara told me from the kitchen. I could smell something delicious. "I fixed a chicken casserole. I've already eaten. Do you want me to warm some up for you?"

"I'm going to grab a shower first. Give me fifteen minutes."

Forty-five minutes later, clean and full, I settled on the sofa with Cara as she told me about her day.

"Mauser was a hit at the clinic, as usual. At least with most of the patients. Mrs. Woolley's Australian Shepherd tried to herd him and Ed Neel's Boxer wasn't very fond of him, but overall he had a good day."

"Where was Ghost when you got home?"

"Haven't a clue until he came bounding out to play with

Mauser."

"You know, the big idiot will need to go home tomorrow. Ghost needs to learn to live on his own."

Cara leaned in to kiss me and we stopped thinking about the animals for a while.

CHAPTER FOURTEEN

Tuesday dawned clear and cool. I got up early enough to take Mauser for a walk through the woods. The ground was damp from the night's rain, but that didn't spoil the mood. It was nice to know that fall was really on the way. With a little imagination, I could hear the sound of high school bands and shouts of "Happy Halloween!"

By the time I got to the office, Jessie was already waiting in the lobby with a visitor badge pinned to her shirt. Dill Kirby was bending her ear about the good ol' days when a patrolman could do some detective work for themselves.

"Nowadays all they do all day is drive from one call for service to another. If there's a real case, you have to turn it over to one of these suits," he told her, winking at me.

"You're going to convince her to go into another career," I warned him.

"Nah, she'll be just like you—on the street for a couple of years and then she'll be climbing up the ladder."

"What ladder? I'm on a stepstool."

"Yeah, right. Fifteen years from now, he'll be sheriff like his old man," Dill joked. "Me, on the other hand, I've been here longer than his dad and you can see where I am." His wide grinned belied his words.

I don't think there was another deputy in the South who enjoyed wearing the uniform more than Dill Kirby. He'd retired and been miserable, so Dad had brought him back to work the front desk. It had been one of Dad's best decisions. When Dill was there, calls were logged, sign-in sheets were signed and all visitors were properly screened. On the days that one of the younger deputies filled in, it was inevitable that something would slip through the cracks.

I finally pulled Jessie away from Dill and we headed for the evidence room.

"Did you eat?"

"I had some cereal," she said, all serious about being in the office with a job to do.

"If you get hungry, you can go down to records. Beth Miller always brings in some great cookies or pastries of some sort."

Lionel had everything ready to go for her. I hung around while he made sure she was familiar with the equipment.

"You can start with the flash drive. That's security footage from the house next to the Lynch house. That should be easy. Just capture stills of anyone in the video. The camera they use is motion-activated, so there shouldn't be that much to cover."

"Then I'll go over everything from the Fast Mart," Jessie said, obviously anxious to get started.

"I'll be right over there if you need anything. You might have to yell if I've got my headphones on," Lionel told her.

"Is that the footage from the trucker's dash cam?" I asked, pointing to one of his monitors which was showing an image of a country road above the hood of a truck.

Lionel nodded. "It's got good resolution too. You were at the scene, right?"

"I got there about fifteen minutes after the accident."

"I'm not there yet. They gave us the whole day's footage."

"Mind if I watch?"

"Sure." He shrugged.

I looked over to make sure that Jessie had settled in before I turned my attention back to Lionel's monitor. He explained what the different numbers at the bottom of the footage represented as he began to jump forward.

"I'm not going straight to the crash footage. There's a good chance that the time and date stamps aren't right. People don't set them properly, or they're set for a different time zone. This way, I can see if there are any jumps in the footage where someone edited it or disconnected the camera."

Lionel pushed the toggle and sped through fifteen-minute segments with his eyes glued on the meter in the corner. It actually wasn't a bad idea to review the whole day's footage. There was always the chance that an event earlier in the day could shed light on the cause of the accident. Of course, I didn't expect to see anything obvious like the truck weaving or other near-accidents. But sometimes you never knew what you were looking for until you saw it.

"We should be getting close to the time of the accident," I said after almost half an hour of this.

"Sergeant Toomey said that it happened just after two," Lionel said as he let the footage play out across the screen. It was surprisingly hard for me to figure out exactly where the truck was until I saw an intersection with a sign that jogged my memory.

"We're close," I said, remembering that I'd passed that sign only a few minutes before coming up on the accident. "That's him," I said, pointing to the BMW on the screen. "Back it up. I was so busy trying to see landmarks that I think I missed when Romano pulled onto the road."

Sure enough, when we backed it up I could see the BMW at the intersection as the truck approached it. The car pulled out and accelerated at a good pace, but the truck still caught up with it.

"Do you want me to slow it down?" Lionel asked.

"Let's watch it at normal speed first."

In the time that it took me to answer, the bridge

appeared in the distance. The truck driver had slowed down after running up to within a couple of car lengths of the BMW. He wasn't as far back as he should have been, but his driving was well within the norm.

As both vehicles approached the bridge, the BMW was moving farther out in front, but not by much.

"I can't tell if the truck is accelerating as the BMW does, or if the BMW is maintaining speed and the truck is slowing down," I said.

"As Einstein would tell you, it's all relative."

Since the bridge lacked shoulders, the road appeared to narrow and the driver of the BMW slowed down a little in response, which caused the truck to close some of the distance between the vehicles. Then, just as the BMW got about twenty feet onto the bridge, its brake lights came on and it stopped so suddenly that it was possible to see the smoke issuing up from the locked brakes. The BMW skidded sideways as the truck bore down on top of it. Everything had happened so fast that Lennie Mansfield hadn't had time to react.

In the video, the truck was braking now, but it was way too late. The camera's view swung left as the cab was twisted around by the jack-knifed trailer pushing it sideways. The rest of the footage was chaotic as the cab went through the guardrail and down into the creek.

"Wow!" Lionel stopped the video and leaned back in his chair.

"Let's see it again in slow motion. I want to see if we can determine any reason for the BMW's driver to have put on the brakes so fast."

Lionel rewound the footage and we both leaned in toward the monitor.

"I'm going to go at one-third speed. If I slow it down any more than that, it will become jerky and hard to make out objects."

"I don't see anything," I said as we watched the video again.

"The camera is only picking up about fifty yards ahead of the car."

"Yeah, but that's well past the end of the bridge. You wouldn't think anything much farther ahead would cause Romano to slam on the brakes like that."

"He obviously wasn't paying any attention to what was behind him," Lionel observed.

We watched the footage three more times at various speeds, but still nothing stood out.

I called Toomey and told him that we had the footage queued up if he had time to check it out. He showed up half an hour later bearing muffins and coffee.

"Don't think you're special," he said as our eyes lit up. "Dill brought a whole tray into the briefing this morning. We've been sharing them around."

"Thanks!" Jessie said, picking out a muffin and a cup of coffee from the tray.

"You can watch, if you want," I told her after introducing her to Toomey.

The footage rolled across the monitor four more times without showing us anything we hadn't seen the first couple of times.

"That fool just slammed on his brakes." Toomey's eyebrows were raised. "Can't blame the truck driver, though technically he should have left more room between him and the BMW. But that's ideal-world stuff. I don't know any driver who would have done anything different."

"Who expects someone to slam on their brakes in the middle of a bridge?" I said.

"I'm calling this an accident. I'll run it by a few folks, but there wasn't anything in Mansfield's bloodwork and I checked his phone. He wasn't texting or talking to anyone. I'm inclined to let it go," Toomey said. "Before this, he had an absolutely spotless driving record."

"Have you heard from Darzi about the autopsy yet?" I asked.

"Yeah. Darzi didn't see anything obviously medical, but

he rattled off half a dozen things that could have happened. He said that Romano died so quickly that there just wasn't time for most medical issues to leave evidence that they had happened."

We watched the footage a couple more times, trying to focus on Romano.

"You can't see him well enough," I grumbled.

"I can't enhance it any more than this," Lionel apologized.

"Don't you think he moves around a little just as the brakes come on?" Jessie said.

"I agree; it looks like there's some movement. But there's just not enough detail to tell what he's doing. I don't think he's falling over, but he could be reaching for something. Did you check his phone?" I asked Toomey.

"Yes. No calls at that time. No texts and no evidence on the phone that he had been using it. Of course, with a car like that, he would have been hooked into it through the phone's Bluetooth."

"I'll confirm that with his wife when I go over there." I'd already decided to visit Sherry Romano as soon as we were done. She deserved to know that the accident appeared to be just that… an accident.

"Good. Let me know if she has any concerns." Toomey stood up. "I need to get back out on the road." He radioed himself back into service and almost immediately had a couple of calls for advice from deputies under his command.

By the time I left, Jessie had finished with the footage from the Khans, printing out half a dozen obscure figures that had walked past the back of their house. Several of the figures could have been Wells, but none of them would do us much good. She moved on to the Fast Mart footage, hoping for a better result. I made sure that she had the very vague descriptions Mr. Reed had given us of the kids that had roughed him up, then wished her luck.

I just had time to run over to Sherry Romano's before meeting Darlene to go through the homeless camps. I called as I left the office, so I wasn't surprised when Sherry met me at the front door, which was decorated with a black wreath.

"I put the wreath on the door without thinking about the fact that it's October. At least Tommy loved Halloween. I think he would have seen the humor in the situation." She was dressed in a black turtleneck and jeans.

"I know this is awful for you."

"Why don't we talk out back on the patio? The weather is so nice and I need to get some fresh air. I've been on the phone for hours with his relatives and mine. Most of Tommy's extended family is coming in for the funeral."

"Did you have any problems making the arrangements to get the body from the hospital?"

"The funeral home took care of everything. I appreciate you asking." She touched my arm lightly. I had to admit that I found Mrs. Romano to be a very charismatic woman.

As we walked through the house, I noticed framed architectural drawings on the wall. "Was your husband an architect?"

She turned and gave me a sad smile. "No, those are mine."

"I'm sorry?"

"Believe me, it's a problem. That's just one reason that I decided to go into real estate. The sexism in the profession and the fact that Tommy liked to travel, so I needed a job with flex time."

"I saw the real estate signs against the garage."

She nodded. "I'm an agent with Adams Real Estate, though I don't know when I'll feel like going back to work. Luckily, Angie, a friend of mine, is more than happy to fill in for me. She's been having a tough time getting listings lately." Sherry sighed. "It feels so strange to think about my ordinary concerns when, in truth, my whole world has been turned upside down."

"What did your husband do?" I asked as we sat on the patio.

"He imported furniture."

"I would think you'd need to live in a major city for that type of job."

"Flying out of Tallahassee could be a little problematic sometimes. A lot of times, he'd just drive to Jacksonville or Tampa. Of course, these days he was able to do most of his work from home. A lot of it involved emails and having good contacts in Europe and the Middle East."

I took a deep breath, then delivered the bad news. "I wanted to let you know that the dash cam images from the semi showed that your husband applied his brakes when he was on the bridge. The trucker could have been maintaining more distance than he was, but having said that, there were no indications before your husband slammed on the brakes that he was going to attempt to stop."

She shook her head. "But why would Tommy just stop in the middle of the bridge?"

"We don't know. There was nothing on the video to indicate a reason. Nor did we find anything at the scene that might have explained it." I decided I would go back to the scene when I had a chance and take another look around. No one had done a thorough search of the area. Maybe I could find the body of an animal, something too small to show up on the dash cam.

"Tommy was a good driver," Sherry said quietly.

"No one's saying otherwise. Did you ever know him to use his phone while he was driving?"

"He had it hooked up so he could use it hands-free through the car's... what do you call it?" She put her hand to her forehead as though she had a headache. "I'm sorry. I just can't imagine what could have happened."

"I've seen a number of accidents. Some fatal, some not. Even in the ones where people live, you can't always figure out what happened. A slick patch on the road. A moment's inattention. I'm just sorry that it happened to your family."

"I'm glad that the truck driver won't be charged. If, as you say, it's something that could have happened to anyone, then he shouldn't have to suffer for it."

"Is there anything else that I can help you with?" I asked.

"You can talk to me for a few minutes." Sherry looked at me with a small, sad smile. "About anything else."

"I…"

"Tell me about your life since we saw each other in… what was it… sixth grade?"

"Not a very extraordinary life. My mother passed away when I was in college. That's what prompted Dad to run for sheriff."

"He'd been a deputy, right?"

"That's right. All my life."

"I think I remember him coming to school once for show-and-tell, or bring-your-parent-to-school day or something." She smiled at the memory.

"You're right. I'd forgotten that. I think I was so embarrassed that I just scrubbed it from my brain."

"He was very manly. Told us to be good and we might be lucky enough to become cops one day. There was also something about, if we were bad, we'd end up wearing handcuffs. He was going to put his handcuffs on a couple of us until Mrs. Swinton told him that she didn't think it would be a good idea."

I cringed. "Ugh! It's all coming back. No wonder I'd forgotten."

"Really, he seemed like a great father. I wanted a dad like that. One who could protect me from all the evil in the world." She had an odd look in her eyes. I wondered what darkness lurked in her childhood.

"What about you? Ah… what happened when you moved?" I'd almost asked how she met her husband until I remembered the reason I was there.

"It's all very boring. We moved to Tallahassee where Dad went to work as the manager of a supermarket and Mom was a teacher. I went to the FSU and got my architectural degree… went through a few bad relationships before I met Tommy six years ago." She shook her head. "I… I guess it's going to be a while before I can talk about him." She wiped at the tears that were rolling down her cheeks.

"I shouldn't have asked," I said, wanting to comfort her. I could only do so much as a deputy, and our childhood acquaintance wasn't enough to qualify me as a friend now.

"It's okay. Tommy and I had such great times." Sherry waved the memories away. "I can't break down now. I have to get things ready for the funeral."

I stood up. "I'd better go."

"If you can make it to the funeral, it will be on Friday morning."

Suddenly feeling very awkward, I made my excuses and told her I'd try to be there.

CHAPTER FIFTEEN

I drove to the city police station. It still felt very odd to walk into the station and see Darlene's name on the glass door. The building had originally been built as a bank in 1920, but the bank had folded during the Great Depression and the city had taken it over for back taxes. When the city formed the police department in 1946, they had converted the building into a state-of-the-art police station. The joke was that they had never spent another dime on the place, leaving it like a grand dame of the theatre who still had great bones, but everything else was sagging a bit.

Darlene's assistant waved me into her office, where I found the chief talking on the phone while she looked something up on her computer. She nodded at me and pointed to a chair near her desk. It had been several years since I'd been in the office—I hadn't exactly been welcome by her predecessor, Charles Maxwell. I remembered the room as cluttered and dusty, but Darlene had always kept her desk and car very tidy, and this office was no different. The wood of her large oak desk gleamed, and her diplomas and law enforcement certifications were hung neatly on the wall.

After assuring the person on the other end of the phone

that their burglary was the most important case in the history of the city, and promising to keep them up to date on the police department's findings, she hung up.

"Everyone is my boss now. Piss someone off and they run screaming to their city commissioner, who complains to the city manager, who gives me a call and asks why I'm ruining their day."

"You're important now," I said with a grin.

"So important that I don't have time to devote to a murder four blocks from here."

"I told you I'd handle it."

"Why don't I feel better?" she joked.

I filled her in on the results of the Wells autopsy, my interview with Bart Crenshaw and my meeting with Eugene and Miriam Wells.

"Good job finding his folks. At least they were close enough that you could notify them in person. I never feel more helpless than when I have to notify a loved one of their loss over the phone."

"They've had a hard time of it. Wells was very gifted before he became schizophrenic."

Darlene nodded. "There's a man I went to high school with who suffers from schizophrenia. It's not paranoid schizophrenia; his is another type. Happened during his senior year. The school and his parents were sure that it was drugs, which just resulted in a draconian lockdown and search of the school, followed by a grilling of any students who knew him. No one seemed willing to accept that his brain chemistry had just gone wrong. Sad. His parents did get him somewhat straightened out, but..." She shrugged. "Let's go look at those homeless camps."

"I'll follow you," I told her once we were outside and heading for our cars.

The first camp was all but abandoned. A local business had recently changed the drainage for their parking lot and the area was muddy from rain. There was only one young guy and his girlfriend still hanging out there. The couple were muddle-headed from drugs, drinking or both. They claimed to be traveling down to the coast and Darlene strongly suggested that they should be on their way.

The next place we visited had three campers who were regular panhandlers downtown. The camp was neat, and they claimed to be selective about who they let join them. They had all heard about Wells's murder and each of them admitted to seeing him around town. As a group, they agreed that he was just the type that they didn't want camping near them. When I pressed them as to why, they just said he was crazy.

The third camp was a five-acre vacant wooded lot near the railroad tracks. It was conveniently located near a couple of major intersections and two churches that served meals to the homeless. A few beaten paths crisscrossed the lot. They led to several small clearings where men had thrown up tents and makeshift shelters. The campsites were a collection of their possessions and usually a shopping cart or a wagon.

"Howdy Miss Chief!" shouted a man with poor teeth and even worse hygiene as we approached the first tent. He was sitting on a lawn chair with a broken back that had been repaired with duct tape. "You goin' to kick us out today?"

"I told you that I'd let you know before we cleared the area," Darlene answered. "Vetter, this is Deputy Macklin. He'd like to ask you a few questions."

The man, who was probably in his thirties but looked twice as old, stuck out his hand. Trying not to show my reluctance, I reached out and gave his hand a brief shake.

"I'm looking for people who knew Gregory Wells." I didn't see any recognition in his face, then I remembered Crenshaw's nickname for Gregory. "Some folks called him Gory."

"Oh, yeah, that wack job. I saw him around a few times. Not here. He and Bart hung out a bunch. I think they normally dug in over at the Sawmill camp."

"You didn't like him?"

"What, 'cause I called him wack job? Hell, I'm a lush.

See, that's what I like about living loose. I can call someone a wack job without a judgmental prick like you giving me a hard time." His eyes had become hard and flinty.

"You'll excuse me for not recognizing wack job as a term of endearment." I gave him my best no-bullshit stare.

Vetter shrugged. "He was a bit crazier than the average. Some of the other guys warned me that he'd stolen stuff. That's not good."

"Can you give me the names of the guys who told you about the stealing?"

"Can't and won't. Next question."

"You know that Wells was killed?"

"People die. Lesson one out here in the real world."

"You aren't afraid that one of your fellow travelers could have hacked him up with an axe?" Knowing how fast information traveled among the street people, I didn't think I was giving anything away mentioning the cause of death.

"I treat everyone I meet like they're an axe-murderer. That's the smart way to be."

"Can you think of anyone who had a grudge against Wells?"

"You're determined, I'll give you that. But you aren't getting any names out of me."

"*Were* there people who had a grudge against him?"

He gave me a slant-eyed look. "You tryin' to trick me?"

"What I'm trying to do is find out who murdered Mr. Wells."

"Vetter, do you remember two weeks ago when one of my officers found you drunker than a skunk over by the elementary school?" Darlene asked with ice in her voice.

Vetter looked down at the ground. "Guess so," he mumbled.

"I knew you didn't mean any harm. School was out for the day and there weren't any kids for you to scare. But the law says that drunk people have to stay more than a thousand feet from school grounds. It doesn't mention anything about school being out. Remember that when the deputy asked me what to do with you, I told him to take you over to Reverend Tolliver's to dry out?"

"Got a damn lecture from him too," Vetter mumbled so low that I barely heard what he said. Unfortunately for Vetter, Darlene's hearing was better than mine. She yanked the handcuffs off of her belt and tossed them into his lap.

"You want to be wearing those the next time I have options?"

"No."

"Then give the deputy some names. And don't be an ungrateful bastard. You've already earned yourself a workday at the church. When I ask Reverend Tolliver if you've been over to volunteer for a day, his answer had better be yes. If it isn't, I'll have you in the county lockup for as long as I can."

Vetter looked like he wanted to say something, but a strong sense of self-preservation kept his mouth glued shut. Darlene held out her hand and he meekly returned the cuffs.

"Do you have any names for me now?" I asked.

"Tex and the skank he hangs out with."

"Does she have a name?"

"Dot, something like that." He was muttering again.

"What exactly did they say about Wells?"

"Exactly? You think I've got a recorder—" Vetter stopped when Darlene took a step forward. "All I remember is them saying he was a thief. That's all I got to say."

"Where can I find Tex and maybe-Dot?"

I thought Vetter was going to try stalling again, but instead he pointed down the path. "You know I'm goin' to get a right good ass-beating if word gets around that I gave you their names?"

"It's a risk. Seems to me that you better want me to care."

"I get you. I honestly don't remember nothin' but that they said he stole some stuff. I'm not even sure it was their stuff." It was pretty obvious that Vetter was telling the truth.

"Your name won't come up," I assured him.

We left the man and headed farther down the path. But

before we could conduct another interview, the next tent we came to turned into a situation. The young man lying in a makeshift cardboard lean-to had a cut on his leg that was so infected I could smell it from ten feet away.

"He's sweating like a pig," Darlene said as she leaned in to get a good look at him. When she poked him with her baton, he started thrashing around in the dirty bedding.

"This needs to be looked at." She pointed to the filthy rag wrapped around his calf. Flies buzzed near him as he shifted back and forth in his delirium.

"I'll call for an ambulance," I said and radioed dispatch with the details.

"I'll wait here," Darlene told me. "You go on and find the couple. Once they hear the ambulance, everyone in the woods will make themselves scarce."

"Will you be okay here?" I asked. She just gave me a look that I remembered from our days as partners—half "You're an idiot" and half "You're wasting time."

"I'm just going to stand here and wait for the EMTs. Give them directions if I have to. What I'm *not* going to do is go anywhere near that leg."

I found half of the couple at the second campsite I came to. Dee, not Dot, was cleaning a few shirts with a pan and a couple of jugs of water.

"I didn't steal the jugs, if that's what you're thinking," she said when she saw me looking at her.

I shook my head. "I'm looking for Tex," I said, going with the name that Vetter had seemed surest about.

It wasn't necessary to tell her that I was a deputy. She'd already figured that much out on her own. Suspicion and fear fought for control of her face. "Why?"

"I'm not here to give anyone a hard time. I'm just looking for some information."

Some of the fear left her eyes, but every bit of the suspicion remained. "So what do you want?"

"I just want to—" I was interrupted by the sound of approaching sirens.

"What's that?" Dee gave me a piercing look.

"The fellow back up the path has an infected leg. The police chief called for an ambulance."

"He can't pay for no hospital visit."

"Does he have enough to pay for a coffin?"

"It didn't look that bad."

I tried to get the conversation back on track. "I have some questions about… Gory."

"He's dead."

"Someone *killed* him."

"I heard something about that." Dee was getting curious in spite of herself.

"You and Tex told someone that Gory was a thief."

"That no-good Vetter. Bastard!"

"I don't know who you're talking about," I tried to bluff, but she wasn't buying any of it. "Look, I'm not here to cause you any problems. I just want to find the person who killed Gory Wells."

"Wasn't me or Tex," she said emphatically.

"Who do you think it was?"

"Don't have a flippin' clue. Probably someone he stole shit from."

"Did he steal something from you?"

Dee's eyes narrowed as she tried to work out her answer. "Maybe."

I didn't say anything and an uncomfortable silence grew between us. I looked her in the eye, letting her know that I expected more.

"All right, all right. An old phone, a flashlight and a little fan I carried with me." From the look on her face, I could tell that Dee was still upset about the losses.

"When was this?"

"I guess a few weeks ago. Before he moved to that old house."

"Was Tex mad about it?"

"Hell, yeah, what do you—" Dee caught herself. "I mean, he wasn't happy."

"Where is Tex?"

There was another pause, but Dee knew she'd already lost the battle. "He's at the Supersave trying to get a few bucks."

"Did he confront Gory about the stolen items?"

"The guy was crazy."

"What do you mean?"

"Not mean crazy, exactly. Just kinda like… explosive. One minute he was fine, not botherin' no one. Then he'd just go off spouting loony stuff and pointing fingers. He liked to point fingers." She made jabbing motions with her index finger.

"You haven't answered my question. Did Tex confront Gory about the items that were stolen?"

"You can't let someone steal from you."

"Is that a yes?"

Dee sighed. "When we figured out it was him, Tex went over to their camp and told Gory that he needed everything back. Gory wouldn't give it back, so Tex hunted through his stuff until he found everything."

"And Wells let him do that?"

Dee looked down at the ground. "Nah, he tried to stop Tex. You ain't seen Tex."

"What do you mean?"

"He's a big fella. First time I saw him at a Flying J truck stop, I said, 'That's the man that can keep me safe.'"

"So he didn't have any trouble from Wells?"

"Oh, Gory tried. I followed Tex over there, so I seen most of it. Tex is a big fella. He just pushed that little shrimp away every time he'd try to stop him from looking for our stuff."

"No one got hurt?"

"Gory got thrown on the ground a dozen times, but he kept getting up, so I don't think he was hurt none."

"What did Wells say?"

"Just kept yabbering about his work or something. He was always telling everyone he was working on some secret project or other. Crazy as a bedbug in June. Over the years, I seen a lot of crazy folk. I don't guess he was any crazier than most."

"So you got your stuff back, but you still told others that Wells was a thief?"

"That's part of the code, like. You let others know when there's trouble around. Gory was trouble."

"You think that's why he moved camps?"

Her expression changed like she'd just remembered something. "No. That's right. He got beat up, but it weren't Tex. Gory got rolled pretty bad."

"Who did it?"

"I don't know. Thumpers."

"Who?"

"Thumpers. There's some in every town. Young creeps that like to roll homeless guys. That's how they get their jollies."

"Do you know if anyone saw these… thumpers?"

"Nope. Just heard about it. We didn't even see Gory. Bart was mad at us for tearing up their camp, so Tex and me didn't go back over there."

I'd just decided that she'd told me all she knew when Tex strolled into camp. Dee had not overstated his size. The man was several inches taller than my six feet and couldn't have weighed less than two-fifty. There were enough tattoos on his skin for three normal-size men. I recognized a few as standard, home-grown prison tats. He was putting on a tough-guy act, but I could tell that he was nervous to see me there.

"You a cop?" he asked. His eyes darted between me and Dee.

"I'm an investigator with the sheriff's office," I said, showing him the star hanging on my belt.

"What happened?" He nodded in the direction of the man with the infected leg. We could hear a little as the EMTs worked on him.

"Guy's got a serious infection. They're taking him to the

hospital. But I'm here because of the murder of Gregory Wells. Gory."

"I don't know nothin' about that," Tex said with fire in his voice. I'd met his kind before. Throughout their lives, they'd used their size to intimidate others in order to get their way. Looking at him, I was sure that it had worked ninety-nine percent of the time. Since he was physically capable of killing me with a single blow from one of his grizzly bear paws, I hung back and let my right hand rest on my holstered Glock.

"I know about the stolen items and the altercation you had with Wells."

"The what that I had with who?" he said, pushing his head out at me and taking a step toward me, flexing his hands.

"The fight you had with Gory," I said in a flat tone that I hoped was a reasonable facsimile of Clint Eastwood's voice.

"I didn't have no fight with Gory. All I done was get our stuff back. The man was a damned thief!"

"I heard what happened. I just want to ask you some questions. Have a seat." I nodded toward a plastic chair.

Tex looked at me with all the experience of a man who'd seen a good bit of trouble in his life. "Damn questions is how you end up in jail," he growled.

"No one is going to jail today," I said honestly. The only way I would have been prepared to make an arrest was if I'd seen a bloody axe in their campsite. As it was, I didn't even see anything that looked like it could chop wood.

He relaxed a bit and walked over to the chair, lowering his bulk down like a bear in a circus. Dee came to stand behind him, her arms crossed over her chest. Tex stretched his huge booted feet out in front of him. "My feet are killing me anyways."

"So Gory stole some items from you?" I asked.

"Damn straight. Not for long."

"What happened when you went to retrieve them?"

"That pipsqueak? Not much. I just went to his campsite

and got 'em."

"Was he mad?"

"Who cares?"

"You weren't worried about confronting him?"

"Like I said, nothin' to be worried about. He couldn't do nothin'."

"Did you tell everyone that he was a thief?"

"People got a right to know."

"Did you see him again after you retrieved the stolen items?"

"Nope. Bart came over a couple of times and told us to quit telling people that Gory was a thief. I told him to take a hike."

I stood up and asked to see their IDs so that I could take a picture of them. "I don't want you leaving the county without telling me."

"We ain't done nothin' wrong," Tex said belligerently.

"I didn't say you had. But I might need you as material witnesses."

"Witnesses? We don't grass on nobody," Dee chimed in.

"Just do as I ask." I was weary of arguing with them. "You know we have vagrancy laws in this county. I could take you both in right now."

"Reverend Tolliver said we could tell people that we live there if anyone harassed us." Tex watched with a smile as Dee made her case.

"Do what you want. I'm just telling you that I won't be happy if you run off."

"Yeah, so?"

I let her have the last word. I walked back up the path to find Darlene wrapping up the young man's tent. She'd put his stuff inside and rolled it all up into a bundle.

"I don't want his stuff to get stolen." She frowned as she tried to lift the tent. I grabbed an end. "I got ahold of his father. He's going to come by the station and pick up his stuff. Stinks. I'll cram it in the back seat, so at least I can spray it out. The weather is nice enough I can drive with the windows down." Darlene was talking to herself as much as to me.

We had gotten back to the cars when my phone rang. It was Alistair Hinson.

"I wanted to make sure that there aren't any restrictions to me using the house," he said as Darlene got in her car and drove off.

"I still want to do a full walk-through of the house, on the off chance the killer had access to it at some point."

"Yes, of course. It's just that I've gotten an offer to rent the house for a week. A generous offer. I'd like to accept it."

"Like I said, once I've walked through the house, you can do what you want with it." I didn't have any legal or practical reason to keep the crime scene locked down much longer. "Who wants to rent it?"

There was a huge sigh from the other end of the line. "If I didn't need the money… They're some ghostbuster wannabes with deep enough pockets. Like I told you, I might have to sell the place to pay off the debts that my daughters are accruing and, from what people tell me, these days a national reputation as a haunted house is actually a real estate plus."

"I can't tell you not to do it, but…" Knowing who he was talking about didn't make me feel better about it.

"This could mean I won't have to sell the house, at least not right away. Maybe I can find some more people who want to film in it, or the guy said that I might be able to rent it out to paranormal researchers and people who just like to sleep in haunted houses."

"You have to do what you have to do. I'll pick up the key from Samantha Rutledge and let you know as soon as we're done with the walk-through."

"If you don't mind, go ahead and give the key to Sly Harris when you're done."

That suited my plans, since I wanted to have another talk with Sly anyway. A talk *without* the camera.

"Sure thing. I'll—" My phone buzzed with another call

and I apologized to Hinson so I could take it. It was Lionel.

"She's freaking the hell out!" he said and I could hear crying in the background.

"Jessie? What happened?" I was baffled.

"I don't know," Lionel said, pronouncing each word emphatically. "She was watching the Fast Mart footage, then next thing I know, she's hysterical."

Jessie was wired a little tight, but this was out of character for her. "I'm ten minutes away," I said, hopping into the car.

CHAPTER SIXTEEN

I hustled down the hall to Lionel's office to find Jessie still crying, but calmer.

"What's wrong?" I pulled a chair next to her and sat down so I'd be on eye-level.

"It's her. I know it's her," she said, wiping at her tears.

"Who?"

"Terri, on the camera." She pointed her finger at the monitor where a hoodie-wearing individual was frozen in time. Terri Miller, an acquaintance of Jessie's, had disappeared five years earlier. Despite Pete's intense investigative efforts and Jessie helping Terri's mom to paste the county with missing posters, there'd been no sign of her since.

"You think that's her?" I pointed at the screen, not sure I could believe it.

"Yes! Here, watch." She rewound the tape to show the hooded figure entering the store, waiting patiently behind a large man, then having a brief exchange with the clerk and handing over what appeared to be several bills. The clerk took the money and rang it up before turning to a machine hidden from the screen by the cash register. I knew it was the terminal used to activate the gas pumps. The woman, if it was a woman, was already out the door by the time the cashier was done.

"You can't see her face," I said gently.

"No, but look." Jessie rewound the tape again. When she found the right spot she let it go forward at half speed. "Right there." She pointed to the figure as it swiped back a strand of hair that had slipped out from under the hood. "She always did that."

"Jessie, lots of women do that. Heck, lots of guys sweep their hair back like that."

"No, not just like that. The way she walks, it's just like Terri too." I could tell that Jessie was utterly convinced the person in the hoodie was the missing woman.

"Okay, look, I'll give Pete a call. See what he thinks." After a brief back and forth with Pete, I hung up. "He's over at the jail and will be here in a couple of minutes."

While we waited, Jessie played the images of the woman a dozen more times. I made note of the time and day. It had been less than a week earlier.

Pete arrived looking tired. "Interviewing suspects in a knifing free-for-all. Everyone is innocent and nobody did nothin'." He rolled his eyes.

"Show him." I turned it over to Jessie to make her case, since I was unconvinced that anyone could make an ID from the three minutes of screen time.

Jessie explained her reasons for believing the figure was Terri, while Pete concentrated on the moving images on the monitor.

"I'm not doubting you," he said slowly. "I just want to go over what we know. If I remember correctly, you weren't a close friend."

Irritation flashed in Jessie eyes. "I saw her a lot. I... She kinda inspired me. I got to recognize some of her quirks. You know?"

Pete held up his hands defensively. "I'm just asking the questions that anyone would. The walk and the way she sweeps back that lock of hair... Is there anything else in the video that suggests it's Terri Miller?"

Jessie stared hard at the image on the screen.

"Clothes, hair color, maybe the hands?" Pete encouraged.

"The hands. I think that's part of it. See how long her fingers are?" She touched the screen.

The image was high resolution, but it was still difficult for me to make out that sort of detail.

"I'll talk to the clerk. I don't want to show her mother until we have a little bit more to go on." Pete looked at Jessie the way a mentor would look at a protégé.

I could tell that Jessie wanted to argue, but finally she nodded. "I'm so sure."

"If you're wrong, it would be very hard on her mother," I said, backing up Pete.

"I know. And if I'm right and we still can't find her…" Jessie pursed her lips and slowly shook her head. Terri's disappearance was a large part of why Jessie wanted to be in law enforcement.

"Terri had a couple of close friends. I'll look them up and get their opinions on the video," Pete said, nodding to himself. I could tell that the idea that Terri could still be alive was as appealing to him as it was to Jessie. One of Terri's missing person flyers was tacked up on the wall next to his desk and his file on the case was never buried too deep in the stacks of his ongoing cases.

"How much of the footage have you looked at?" I asked Jessie after Pete had left, trying to get her to focus back on the main assignment.

"Maybe a quarter of it."

"Why don't you knock off for the day?" I suggested.

"No."

I sighed and left her to it, knowing that she would be looking as hard for more images of the woman in the hoodie than she would be for our male suspects.

I headed to Samantha Rutledge's house to pick up the keys

to the Lynch house.

"Alistair said you'd be contacting me. I got the keys right here." Sammy stepped over to a safe built into the wall of her garage. "Can't believe someone was murdered there. Oh, okay, maybe I can. I gotta admit, the place has been a challenge over the years. I've always half worried that someone was going to burn it down. I usually hire an off-duty cop for the week of Halloween to keep an eye on all my vacant properties. Number one on the list is always the Lynch house. Honestly, I'll be glad if he sells it. The only reason I keep it on is 'cause I liked his father so much. It's a creepy old place."

"Do you believe it's haunted?" I smiled.

The older woman gave me a level gaze. "I spent a night there back in the '80s. There've only been a handful of folks who can say that they've stayed in the murder house overnight. There'd been some arson cases and Mr. Hinson was out of town. He asked me to have someone keep an eye on the place. I figured I'd pocket the twenty bucks and watch over the place myself. My husband thought I was nuts, but I was into all that ghosts-and-ghouls stuff back then. I thought it'd be a thrill."

"What happened?"

"Nothing. Well, almost nothing. I slept fine. Got up the next morning and was like, that was a big nothing. Then as I came down the stairs, that's when things got weird. I could swear I heard someone in the kitchen. I'll be honest, it spooked me. The sun was up, which didn't seem typical for a ghost, or at least not what I thought of as a ghost. Anyway, I called out to whoever it was and continued down the steps. Then I thought I heard someone drag something across the floor. Now, I wouldn't want to say it was an axe, but... it sounded like an axe. Damn near wet myself. I sat down on the steps and just waited. Maybe five minutes, maybe twenty, I eventually crept all the way down and into the kitchen." Sammy stopped for dramatic effect and I realized that she must have told this story a hundred times. "There was nothing. Absolutely nothing. No one was in the kitchen. But I looked around for that axe. Never stayed there again." With that, she dropped the keys into my hand.

I called Pete as I left Sammy's. "I'm heading over to do a walk-through of the Lynch house. Wanna come?" In my head, I was making chicken clucking sounds for asking someone to go into the house with me.

"Afraid to go in by yourself?" Pete asked, calling my bluff.

"You too afraid to come with me?" I shot back in my best nine-year-old voice.

"I'll meet you there," he said bravely.

I arrived first and pulled into the driveway. The crime-scene tape around the porch fluttered in the breeze as I got out of the car. I didn't see anyone at any of the neighboring homes. I thought of the Khans, the elderly Mr. Tippets and the Holders. How would they feel if the Lynch house suddenly gained a higher profile and became a destination for every spook hunter in the country?

Pete pulled in behind me and clambered out of his car.

"Did you know that Samantha Rutledge stayed in the house overnight back in the '80s?"

"She's got bigger cojones than I do." Pete hiked up his pants, girding himself to confront whatever lurked inside.

"You really look worried," I said with a grin.

"Don't you have any childhood fears?" Pete asked, glaring at me.

"Sure. I hate heights. Anything much over thirty feet. I remember being on the twenty-second floor of the state capitol building once when I was a kid. When I walked over to one of those tall observation windows, I got hit with vertigo and almost threw up. Scared the hell out of me. I've never been back there again."

Pete nodded. "This house does that for me. Around Halloween one year when I was in elementary school, some older kids told me all about the murders in vivid and, looking back, ridiculous detail. For weeks afterward, every night when I'd go to bed, those images would come back to haunt me."

"Sounds a bit like the guy in *'Salem's Lot*," I said, thinking of one of my favorite Stephen King novels.

"I think that's part of why I became a deputy. Part of me wanted to be able to defend myself and my family, and the other half wanted to be able to hunt down creeps who would chop up a family."

"Let's go face your fears," I said, pushing him toward the porch.

"Fine. But only if I can take you out on that glass bridge they have at the Grand Canyon."

"That ain't gonna happen."

We looked closely at the porch, on the off chance we'd missed something.

"Shantel came out with some interns and scoured the area looking for the murder weapon. She even got permission to look around the outside of the neighbors' houses. Nothing," I said, putting the key in the lock.

"There are a lot of woods and open fields nearby. We should probably organize a search party to cover a few hundred yards in every direction," Pete suggested.

"I imagine our killer either kept it or tossed it in a body of water somewhere." Lakes, rivers and streams were favored dumping grounds for criminals. Why more of them didn't just go off into the woods and bury their weapons a few feet down, I didn't know.

The inside of the house was eerie, not helped by the fact that all the furniture was covered in ghostly white dust sheets. *This house is certainly haunted by its past*, I thought.

"At least it's not nighttime," Pete said.

"Sammy said she heard the ghost in the morning."

"Thanks a lot."

The rooms in the house were spacious, with the high ceilings typical of homes built before air conditioning. Everything was clean. I figured Sammy must have arranged for the house to be cleaned from time to time, otherwise there would have been a foot of dust on everything.

I remembered the stories of the bolts on the doors and windows, and turned around once we were inside. The heavy iron bolts were still on the front door. A padlock hung open through a hole in the bolt.

"No one is going to get through these." I tapped on the lock. Then I fumbled along the wall until I found the old-fashioned light switch by the door. I was a little surprised when the lights came on.

"They're on the windows too. I can't see how anyone other than Daniel Lynch had the opportunity to kill the family." Pete walked toward the stairs and pointed at the bottom step. "Here's where Mrs. Lynch was found."

"Before we go looking around, let's check all the windows down here and the back door, just to be sure."

Everything was secured. The only door without a closed bolt was the front door, and it boasted a quality deadbolt with a good two-inch throw on it.

"No one's gotten into this house who didn't have a key," Pete said.

"Let's look over the rooms down here first, then head upstairs." There was always the outside possibility that our killer *did* have a key. Sammy had obviously hired a cleaning crew, and we didn't know how many Hinson relatives might have had keys.

We finished our tour of the downstairs in the kitchen, staring at the spot by the back door where the original murderer had picked up the axe.

"Nothing there now," Pete said.

"So the primary theory was that Daniel Lynch was stealing his father's money, got caught and then killed everyone, right?" I asked.

"Yeah, so?"

"Then what did he do with the money?"

Pete looked thoughtful. "Good question. I don't remember any of the stories talking about him spending money he shouldn't have, and they didn't find the money in his room or anywhere else in the house."

"Of course, Mr. Griffin *did* say that many folks thought Thaddeus Lynch was going crazy and that no one was stealing his money."

"In that case, the motive for the boy could have been that he was driven to do it by a crazy father and a madwoman for a mother. Children have killed abusive parents in the past."

I'd wandered back into the room that had served as Thaddeus's office. There was an enormous desk at one end of the room with over a dozen drawers in it.

"That's pretty imposing. Do you think it originally belonged to Thaddeus?" I asked.

"I bet it did. By the size of it, I'm not sure you could get it out of the room. I bet they built it in here."

I looked at the door into the room. "You're probably right."

We went upstairs where we found six bedrooms. Besides the furniture, there wasn't much else in the house, which made the rooms easy to search. The right front room was obviously the master bedroom, with an en suite bathroom that would have been a unique luxury when the house was built.

"This place is big enough that I believe Daniel Lynch *could* have slept through the murders," I said. "It's a pretty amazing house."

"Creepy," said Pete emphatically.

I wanted to make light of his fears, but there really was something spooky about the place. *Any house that has sat empty for as long as this place has would feel strange*, I told myself.

I took one last look around the landing, then looked at Pete. "I'm good. There's nothing here that has anything to do with the Wells murder."

Pete shuddered. "I thought it'd make me feel better about the house, seeing the inside of it. It doesn't. Let's get out of here."

I locked the front door, then we took down the crime-scene tape. I didn't want to provide Sly Harris with any props for his little horror show. As Pete drove away, I called Sly and told him that I was ready to drop off the key.

"Cool, man. I'm in that dump of a hotel by the interstate. Room 104."

I was standing at his door fifteen minutes later.

"What exactly are you going to film in the house?" I asked, once Sly had opened the door.

"Oh, come on, surely you've watched some of those ghost hunter shows. It's that kind of thing, only with the added thrill of a recent crime. Not that I'd even thought of that angle until after that poor guy was killed." Sly didn't sound like he cared at all about Wells or his murder. "The original plan was just to mix the unsolved crime genre and the ghost hunter shtick, with our own brand of crazy." He sounded like he was pitching the show in Hollywood.

"Glad you can benefit from all the murders," I said sullenly, wishing there was a way to put a stop to his grisly made-for-TV gawking. But the truth was, I had no leverage to stop him. Then I remembered that I hadn't yet reviewed the footage where Sly had interviewed Wells. Maybe something useful would come out of their presence, after all. "When are you going to film?"

"We're putting a script together now. I've gotten some funding, so I've been able to order some new equipment. It's just come in. Our plan is to film on Friday night. Would you like to come out and be interviewed again? This time inside the Lynch house?"

"No."

"Very well," Sly said, dismissing me and holding out his hand. "The key, please."

It was late afternoon, so I swung by the office to pick up the flash drive containing the interview with Gregory Wells so that I could review it at home that evening.

"Where's the monster?" I asked, stepping into the house

already braced for Mauser's greeting and being surprised not to receive it.

"We took him home to his daddy. I think it's clear that Ghost is over the trauma." Cara was trying to work on some orders for Dr. Horvath, but the little white devil was scurrying across the top of the table, scattering her paperwork.

"I look back on our life with only two critters in the house with great fondness," I said, pulling leftovers out of the refrigerator.

"Oh no!" I heard Cara yell.

I turned just in time to see Ghost slide off of the table and land hard on the floor. In a split second, he regained his composure and went tearing off to find Alvin.

"We visited the haunted house today," I told Cara, sitting down across from her with my dinner.

"Spooky."

I told her about Sammy's story and what the inside of the house had looked like.

"I looked it up when I was on my lunch break and read about the murders. Very strange. I really thought that, in the case of most family murders, there were indications of problems beforehand."

"There were *lots* of indications from Thaddeus and his wife. Maybe the boy just seemed normal by comparison."

"If the murders had been done with a gun, or even a knife, you could think that maybe the mother or father killed the others before committing suicide. But with an axe..." Cara said thoughtfully.

"Yeah. But the locations of the wounds on both of them made it physically impossible for either to have inflicted the wounds on themselves. People have killed themselves in some odd ways, but whacking themselves half a dozen times in back with an axe isn't on the list."

"Is there any other way into the house?"

"Even the upstairs windows have bolts on them. The sheriff at the time testified, rather regretfully, that he found all the bolts and latches in place. The only window that was open was the one that the neighbor busted to get into the house."

"The pictures of the son at the trial are heartbreaking. There's something… haunting about his eyes."

"I'd be surprised if he didn't look lost. Either he killed his family with an axe, or he slept through the slaughter of his parents and siblings. And if he was innocent, he had the additional pain of being accused of the killings."

"Figure out who really killed that family," Cara told me.

I guffawed. "Sure. Are there any other miracles you'd like me to perform while I'm at it? Maybe find Amelia Earhart's plane or figure out if there was a second shooter in Dallas?"

"I don't want him to be guilty. The obvious answers can be very unsatisfying," Cara pouted as she tapped at keys on her laptop.

"I've had to arrest the guy who *was* guilty instead of the one I *wanted* to be guilty more than once in my career," I agreed.

After dinner, I took my laptop over to the couch to watch Sly and Vicky's interview with Gregory Wells. There were no bombshells in the footage. But even without any major revelations, being able to see and hear the victim only days before his murder helped me to understand what the witnesses had been trying to tell me. Wells seemed to go from calm to agitated in the blink of an eye. One moment he was talking about electronics and experimental physics, and the next he was ranting about the underground people who talked to him through his feet. It was disorienting to listen to him. They had filmed him in several different locations, so the images occasionally cut from one location to another. Even when they were in the same location, there were often breaks in the narrative. It had to have been difficult to film a subject who was as unpredictable as Wells was.

I couldn't see where they had gotten anything useful out of him, since he'd never said more than a word or two about the ghosts that supposedly haunted the house. Every time they had asked him a question about the paranormal, Wells had given a one- or two-word answer before going off on another rant about whatever had popped into his head.

For the most part, I spent the next two days concentrating on all the other cases that had been dropped on my desk. A few could be handled with phone calls and an interview or two, but a couple would require a full investigation that could take weeks.

Gregory Wells's parents had arranged for his funeral to be held Wednesday afternoon. I drove over to Tallahassee to attend the graveside service. Other than his parents, I saw only one other person who wasn't obviously part of the funeral home's staff. I updated Eugene and Miriam on the investigation, assuring them that their son's case would not be lost.

By the time I got back to the office, Eugene had emailed me all of the information on the man that had threatened them after being involved in an accident with Gregory Wells. It didn't take me long to eliminate him as a suspect. He had moved to Arizona with his wife for her health and he had a solid alibi for the day of the murder.

Jessie had identified three possible candidates for Wells's tormentors after reviewing the convenience store footage, so Thursday afternoon I made the rounds of the Fast Marts. I included a picture of Jessie's mystery woman when I asked the clerks if they could give me names or any other information. None of the clerks could give me a lead on the woman, but they all thought they knew the guys. Unfortunately, they only knew street names and hadn't seen them in weeks. I spent most of Friday running around town, trying to turn Dirk, Speck and Rod into real names so I could run background checks, but had no luck.

"Did you remind your dad?" Cara asked me that night.

"Yes. That's the third time I've told you," I said with only mild exasperation.

"I want Pet-O-Ween to come off tomorrow without any

major flubs," she said as we carried gift bags out to her car.

"You've certainly lucked out on the weather. It's going to be perfect."

As if on cue, a cool breeze rustled the leaves in the old live oaks. The sun was on the horizon and I thought about Sly and Vicky filming at the Lynch house. I briefly thought about going by to check up on them, but as much as Sly irritated me, I decided to pass.

"How is your friend doing?" Cara asked out of the blue as we walked back to the house.

"Sherry Romano? She's not really my friend. Just an old acquaintance," I demurred.

"Those middle school romances never go away," Cara teased.

"Quit," I said, bumping her hip and leaning in for a kiss. "She seemed okay at the funeral today. There were tons of family. I wasn't sure which were hers and which were his. Everybody was crying."

"Are they bringing any charges against the trucker?"

"No. Toomey got the telematics report from the trucking company and it all matched up with the dash cam and the trucker's account. He was also able to get the infotainment data from the BMW, but the chips with the telematics were mostly damaged from being waterlogged. We could hire a recovery company to try to get what's available out of them, but all the quotes Toomey got were in the mid-four figures and that isn't reasonable for information that wouldn't make a difference anyway. It's obvious that Romano braked right in front of the truck. Now, I guess there's a possibility that the brakes or something else on the car malfunctioned, but that would only matter if Sherry were interested in suing BMW. If she wants to do that, then *she* can pay to have the information retrieved."

Later that night I was flipping through channels and caught the tail end of a ghost hunter show. I wondered again about how Sly and Vicky were doing, but then Cara distracted me and I didn't give them another thought once we locked Ghost out of the bedroom.

It was midnight when my phone rang. I reached for it before realizing I'd forgotten to put it on the nightstand. Hopping out of bed, I stumbled toward the kitchen where I tripped over Ghost and banged my knee on the table. I said a few choice words as I tried to get the phone to respond to my fingertips.

"What?" I answered gruffly, having seen that it was dispatch.

"A man named Sly Harris just called and reported a possible homicide at the Lynch house."

CHAPTER SEVENTEEN

I rolled the windows down as I drove, trying to wake up and digest the news that another murder had happened at the Lynch house. My mother had always talked about ghost chills that caused you to shiver from fright rather than the cold. I felt them now.

The street in front of the house was filled with emergency vehicles and unmarked cars. Most of the cars still had their headlights and flashers going, casting the house in a bright mix of blue and red. With all the lights behind them, everyone walking around the yard was throwing huge shadows that reached across the lawn. There among the shadows I found Pete and Darlene.

"Who, what, when and why?" I asked.

"You forgot how," Pete reminded me as Darlene finished up with a phone call.

"Always did. That's probably why I didn't become a reporter. Now knock it off and tell me what happened."

"You aren't going to believe this one. That woman from the paranormal show, Vicky something. She was hacked to death. She was inside while her partner, Sly what's-his-name, was outside. Get this: he claims the door was locked and no one could have gotten inside."

"What?"

"And the murder weapon is missing."

Darlene put her phone back in its holder on her belt and looked at me. "This is quite the wingding." She shook her head. "I hope you've got your electrodes tuned to very, *very* smart, Poindexter."

"Who says this is my case?" I raised my eyebrows.

"It's a wild guess, but I'd say this might be related to the Wells murder," Darlene said.

"I'm thinking it was done by the same bad guy as the original murders." Pete didn't look like he was kidding.

"Have either of you seen the body?"

"I was the first officer on the scene and went in to check her for life signs," Darlene said. "Not that I had to touch the body to see that she wasn't going to be put back together by anyone at the hospital outside of the morgue. She's in the hallway just past the stairs. Her head... Let's just say that someone really worked her over with that hatchet."

"No murder weapon?"

"I cleared the house, but it could still be hidden on the premises. All I can say is it isn't lying out where you can easily find it. And since I can't imagine why anyone would hide it at the scene if they were able to escape, I'm guessing that the killer took it with them."

"You searched the van they came in?"

"They brought separate vehicles, but nothing was found in either one. No weapon, no noticeable blood stains or anything else suspicious." Darlene shook her head. "One possible explanation is that Harris is lying about the timeline and the events surrounding the murder."

"What's his story?"

"They arrived here around nine o'clock and spent a couple of hours scouting for the best backgrounds and doing sound checks with him reading from the script. Anyway, around eleven he got a text from someone who wanted to talk with him. It said to meet them out by his van." Darlene pointed to the van, which was parked behind a Mustang convertible about halfway down the driveway.

"This was a stranger?"

"Not exactly. He didn't recognize the number, but they identified themselves as someone he'd talked to earlier in the week. They said they had some information about a person the filmmakers should interview."

"That all sounds rather fishy," I said.

"Harris says that it's not unusual for him to get this kind of contact after he's been handing out his cards all over town. Anyway, he went outside and waited around. No one showed up, so after twenty minutes he went back up to the house, unlocked the door and found Vicky on the floor in the hallway."

"He locked the door when he left?"

"According to him, Vicky insisted."

I thought about that. "I guess I can understand that. There were still blood spots on the front porch from Wells's murder. Of course she was a little nervous. Do you think it's safe to assume that the phone call was from the murderer?"

"Seems too convenient otherwise," Darlene agreed.

"Or the murderer is Daniel Lynch."

"The boy who hung himself eighty-odd years ago?" Darlene looked at Pete like he was nuts.

"I'm kidding, but…" Pete looked at me. "Would *you* spend the night in there?"

"Right now, no. Not that I think the ghost of a long-dead murderer is hanging around, but this is the second murder here in a week."

Shantel and Marcus arrived and Darlene and I took them up to the house. I wanted to go in and look at the scene, but we couldn't take the chance of contaminating the site any more than had already been done.

"Where's Harris?" I asked Darlene once Shantel and Marcus were inside.

"He was hysterical." She pointed to the ambulance.

"Was it real?"

"I don't know. He *does* make movies. I'd say it was a little over the top."

"But he *makes* movies, he doesn't act in them."

"Exactly."

We decided to perform an informal interview with Sly Harris. We found him sitting on a stretcher at the back of the ambulance. Hondo was with him, taking his blood pressure.

"Ladies and gentlemen in blue and green," Hondo greeted us. "Our patient is calmer now. He'll be fine."

"I'll never be fine again." Sly was looking down at the ground, all of his earlier bravado completely gone.

"What happened?" I asked.

"I already told her," he said in a voice that was barely a whisper.

"I'd like to hear it from you."

He looked up and shook his head.

"Listen to me. Someone did this to Vicky. I'm giving you the benefit of the doubt by believing that you want the bastard brought to justice as much as I do. Every second counts and everything you can remember is important. So get your head out of your ass and tell me what you remember."

For a moment I thought he might tell me to go screw myself, but instead he shook himself like a bear, took a deep breath and closed his eyes.

"I'm trying to envision what happened," he said. He kept his eyes closed as he began to tell his side of the events. "We got here around nine. The sun had already gone down, so it was dark as we unpacked our cameras and lights. We carried everything to the porch where I got the key out to unlock the door."

"What kind of mood were you both in?" I asked.

"Good. Though now that you ask, I thought that Vicky was quieter than normal. Not that she's ever very talkative. Just that something was off. I felt great. We had some money for the first time in a while."

"Was the door locked or unlocked when you got here?"

"Locked. I know it was locked because I tried to open it before getting the key out. I remember feeling really stupid."

"Go on," I encouraged.

"We went inside. It was dark, very dark. I felt for the switch, but it was a weird, old-fashioned kind so I had to fool with it for a minute before I figured out that you turn the knob. Vicky wanted to do a walk-through to pick out the best spots to set up, so we started with the downstairs. I had printed some pages with the story of the original murders so we could understand how the scene would have looked on the morning when they found the bodies."

"Where are those papers?" Darlene asked.

"I don't know. I guess with the rest of our stuff. We left everything in the library." I figured that he meant Thaddeus Lynch's office

"Did you see anything unusual as you walked through the house?" I asked.

There was a long pause. "No. In fact, we were disappointed that everything looked normal. Old-fashioned, sure, but not, you know, spooky. We weren't worried, though, since we had the blood on the front porch. That was going to be our punchline."

I wanted to punch *him* for thinking of Wells's lifeblood as a hook for their paranormal documentary. Gritting my teeth a little, I asked, "What did you do next?"

"We had chosen five spots to do set-ups. So Vicky started doing sound checks and capturing background noise. You know, you have to be sure that there isn't a leaky faucet or a buzz in a light that you're going to pick up with the audio. And the background is for any voiceovers we might need to do so it still sounds like we filmed them in the house."

"What did you do while she was doing all that?"

"I sat at the dining room table and finished the script. I had a solid narrative. I just needed to add specific comments based on our different set-ups."

"Did you do any filming?"

"Yes, when Vicky was done we shot two scenes. Mostly trying to get the lighting and my marks right. That's when I got a text."

"Where's your phone?"

"I already bagged it," Darlene said. "I checked the number, but nothing came back on it. I haven't tried calling it."

"No better time." I pulled out my phone and Darlene handed me a piece of paper where she'd written down the number from the text. I dialed and, after several rings, was informed that the owner of the phone had not set up their voicemail.

"We should try from his phone after it's been dusted," Darlene suggested.

"Can't hurt," I agreed. "What did the text say?"

"Just that they had a person who would be great to interview for our documentary," Sly said.

"They also mentioned that the person had seen a ghost at the house," Darlene added, since she'd read the text before bagging the phone.

"Yeah, that's right. Said they would meet me out in front of the house."

"Did other people know you would be filming here?" I asked.

"Sure! I told the guy at the motel, my sister, our editor. I mentioned it to a couple of people we talked to about the ghosts. And my angel too."

"Angel?" Darlene asked.

"And investor."

"Who is?" I asked.

Sly went quiet again, grinding his jaw back and forth. "I'd rather not say. He's put up a bunch of cash and I think he wants to stay anonymous. He told me that he absolutely doesn't want his name in the credits or in any of the publicity."

"How much is he giving you?"

"I can't say."

I stared at him. "How much?"

"Really, I can't say."

I kept staring. Finally, he said, "It's a good chunk of change."

"Has this person already given you the money?"

"What does this have to do with the murders?" Sly protested.

"If he hadn't given you the money, would you and Vicky have been here tonight?" Darlene's question caused him to look up at the dark sky. A cool breeze rustled the leaves in the trees above.

"I guess I see your point. I'll tell you that the person promised low six figures and gave me access to a quarter of it to buy equipment."

"Did you know this person before he contacted you?" I asked.

"I knew the name. He's a money guy. I'm not the first person he's backed. He likes all the paranormal, alien stuff. I'd sent him a dozen emails in the last year. Last week, I sent another telling him about my idea for a true crime/paranormal crossover show. Wham bam, he got back to me right away. No one was more surprised than me."

"And you didn't look a gift horse in the mouth," Darlene said sagely.

"Oh, hell no! It's not about making movies; it's about begging for money. And when you get a chunk of change, you grab onto it and guard it with your life," Sly said with undeniable honesty.

"Where does this guy live?" I said.

"Connecticut. Okay, now that's all I'm going to tell you about him. He's my angel and I'm going to protect him."

"How do you think he's going to feel about Vicky being killed?" As soon as I mentioned Vicky, I saw Sly's face change from defiant to defeated.

"I don't know. I don't even know how I feel."

I narrowed my eyes.

"No, no, don't get me wrong. I hate what happened to

Vicky. I mean about the project. My angel makes it tough. If it were up to me I'd change the project now. The trouble is, if I do that then I might lose the money." He saw us looking at him with more than a little disdain. "Don't give me that holier-than-thou crap. You fight for years to get a project off the ground, living in shitholes and kissing ass, then have the money drop into your lap. You think that's easy to just throw away?"

I decided we'd hassled him enough about this financial backer. "Go back to the text you got tonight. What did you do?"

"Vicky was fooling around with the camera, getting ready to move to one of the other locations, so I figured, sure. I'd get a little fresh air and I could find out what this guy had to offer."

"Think. Did anything strike you as odd or suspicious about the text?"

Sly closed his eyes again and let a few seconds pass before answering. "No, but I'll tell you what struck me as odd was Vicky's reaction. You'd have to know her. She's pretty unflappable. Before she started helping me out, she did hardcore BDSM shoots. Some of them were for personal use by the clients and others were for commercial use. She told me about some of the stuff she'd seen. It would have freaked me out. Her? Nothin'. Two years ago, we had an accident in our van. Pretty bad. Rolled over a couple of times in the median of I-95. She gets out like it was no big deal and starts picking up the equipment that flew out all over the interstate."

"How'd she react to the text?" Darlene asked.

"Kind of freaked out. She didn't want me to leave." For a moment, Sly looked like he was going to break down, but he got control of himself. "This is where I blame myself. She asked if she could come out with me. I told her she should stay and get ready for the next set-up. She tried to convince me that we had plenty of time, but we didn't. I didn't want to be there until four in the morning, so I told her I'd lock her in and she'd be fine."

"And she was okay with that?"

"Not really, but we'd gone around and filmed the deadbolts and the locks on the windows, so she knew that the place was practically a fortress."

"Did she say what she was scared of?" I asked.

"All she said was that someone could come in there and do to her what they did to that homeless guy."

"That's all?"

"She followed me to the front door to make sure I locked it."

"And that was the last time you saw her?"

"Except…" He looked visibly upset. "…you know, when I found her."

"There's one more thing you can help us with," I said. "Do you have numbers for any of Vicky's next of kin?"

"Wow, I didn't think about that. I guess it would be her mother… or her husband, but they're getting a divorce. They were only married a couple of years."

My ears perked up at the mention of an ex. "Where does he live?"

"Maryland. That's where Vicky's from."

"Do you have his number?"

"Yeah." Sly sounded a little surprised that I wanted to call the ex.

"Good. I want you to call him and inform him of Vicky's death."

"I guess." Sly sounded reluctant.

"And we want you to ask him a couple of questions." Darlene took out her notepad and started to write. She'd picked up on what I had in mind. "We want you to ask him where he is and who's with him."

"Oh…" I saw understanding dawn in his eyes. "I guess the ex is always a suspect."

Sly placed the call while we listened as best we could to both sides of the conversation. According to the ex, he was in Maryland with his quote, new family, unquote. I was inclined to believe him, but I made a note to contact someone with law enforcement up in Gaithersburg to check out his alibi.

Darlene made the difficult call to Vicky's mother. We'd decided that it might go down better coming from a woman, though no good news ever comes when the phone rings after one in the morning. We were fortunate that her brother's family was visiting at the time, so she had a strong support network with her. After the woman began crying uncontrollably, her brother came on the line and Darlene gave him our contact information.

Finished with the calls, we asked Sly a few more questions, but he couldn't tell us anything new.

CHAPTER EIGHTEEN

"So?" Darlene asked as we walked back toward Pete, who was coming from the direction of the Khans' house.

"He seems sincere. Trouble is, if we rule him out then we have a lot of figuring to do."

"My thoughts exactly."

Shantel came out into the yard and joined us as we caught up with Pete.

"While you were talking to Sly, I went over to the neighbors on both sides. They're freaked out, to say the least. The Khans didn't notice anything over here until the police cars started showing up. On the other side, the Holders wanted your dad's number. 'I want to speak to the sheriff!'" Pete completed his report in a fair imitation of Lucy Holder's tone, if not her voice.

"Terrific," I muttered. "Did they see anything?"

"Mrs. Holder saw the cars pull into the driveway tonight and she talked her husband into coming over and asking Sly what was going on. They were up in arms about that too. In fact, I think they had a mixed reaction to the news of Vicky's murder. On the one hand, they weren't thrilled that another murder had taken place next door, but on the other hand, they're hoping that the murder will put a stop to the production."

"They'd feel a lot worse if they saw that girl in there." Shantel shook her head sadly. "Dead is dead. If this job's taught me anything, it's taught me that. But to be chopped up like that. I feel horrible for her family."

"Have y'all documented everything?" I asked her.

"We've filmed the scene. Marcus is putting down markers now for the various pieces of evidence and blood. It's gonna take a while."

"The hallway and staircase were something out of a nightmare," Darlene said.

"I'm going to give you my opinion, whether you want it or not. The same evil soul who killed that homeless man killed this woman," Shantel told us.

"What makes you say that?" I wasn't challenging her. Shantel was an expert at finding and interpreting evidence, but she seldom speculated on a case, so I was curious what she might have observed.

"It looks like the same weapon, same methods of attack. And just as vicious."

"From what I saw, I'd agree," Darlene said, nodding. "With both bodies, the wounds were to the head and back. None of the wounds that I observed were more than a few inches below the shoulder blades."

"Overhead blows," Pete stated.

"The first blow to the front of Wells's head was not a decisive strike," I reminded them.

"That might have been the killer's first time attacking a person with an axe. Also, the victim was facing the killer," Pete said.

"And even so, it wasn't a tentative blow. It almost took him to his knees. Wells just managed to stagger toward the edge of the porch before the killer delivered the second blow," Darlene pointed out.

"Whoever did this is evil," Shantel declared again, in case we'd missed it the first time.

"Certainly a psychopath," Darlene said, "which means

we're looking for someone who's able to appear normal most of the time only to go batshit crazy when the urge hits them. I'd bet you a dollar that five minutes after a murder like this, they're back to looking and sounding like everyone else."

"That's what I said, evil." Shantel looked toward the house. "I better get back and help Marcus."

"When you're done, I want us to go around and check every door and window," I told her. She raised a hand in acknowledgement. I turned back to Pete and Darlene. "We need to do more than just eyeball the bolts. We need to lock them and then try to get the locks to fail. Someone got into that house."

"Or they were hiding inside before Sly and the Family Stone showed up," Pete suggested.

"There's a thought. Could they have escaped after the attack without being seen or leaving evidence of their departure?" I said.

"Evidence like an unlocked window," Pete added.

"I cleared the house after I established that the woman was dead. Sly was standing at the door the whole time, so nobody could have slipped out while I was going through the house," Darlene insisted.

"But he came in and found the body first," I pointed out. "We need to ask him if someone could have slipped out while he was in the house alone."

We all looked over to the ambulance where Sly was walking around under the observation of Hondo and the other EMT.

"I'll go talk to him." Darlene started off in that direction while Pete and I watched closely to see how she would interact with Hondo.

"Are they completely on the outs?" Pete asked me.

"They aren't seeing much of each other, whatever that means."

Darlene and Hondo exchanged nods.

"Did he smile?" I couldn't tell.

Pete nodded. "Yeah, though for Hondo it wasn't much of a smile. But it was a definite upturn of the lips."

Darlene talked to Sly for a few minutes before walking back over to us. "What are you two looking at?"

"Nothing," Pete and I said in unison.

She gave us a squint-eyed glare, then reported, "Sly claims that he never left the doorway, and I will testify that the woman's body is clearly visible from the door. Also, with the amount of blood around, it wouldn't take a doctor to know that she was in need of professional medical attention. So it's not unreasonable that he opened the door, stepped into the hallway, saw the body and backed out to call 911."

"Did he go back to the van or leave the porch?" I asked.

"No. Again, I'll vouch for the fact that he was on the porch when I arrived. Which—" She held up her hand and called dispatch. After a brief exchange, she hung up. "I got here less than four minutes after dispatch received his call. The dispatcher said that she asked him several times if he could see the victim and he answered affirmative each time. She tried to talk him into going in and checking the body for a pulse. He refused."

"The big question is, is there another way in and out of the house?" I said.

"There's another question. Is he lying?" Pete reminded us.

"Agreed. That remains a possibility," Darlene said.

"A thought just occurred to me. Do you think Vicky could have been filming when she was attacked?" The other two looked at me with wide eyes, the impact of my statement sinking in.

"I'll see if Shantel can go ahead and process the camera. I think it was lying about three feet from the body." Darlene was already moving toward the house.

"We couldn't get that lucky," Pete said.

"I'd be happy with one big fat clue. I don't have to see the person's face. A shot of their shoes or hands would be enough. At least we might be able to rule out half the population of the county."

"The camera was on," Darlene said, unable to keep the excitement out of her voice as she rejoined us. "Shantel said they'd already filmed and photographed it. We can walk through the crime scene before they start bagging, tagging and dusting evidence."

We all donned protective clothing on the front porch before entering the house. Behind us, I heard another vehicle and turned to see the coroner's van park on the edge of the yard.

As we approached the front door, I tried to see it from Sly's viewpoint before he knew that Vicky had been killed. As I stepped across the threshold, I looked around. Marcus hadn't moved the camera yet and it was the first thing that drew my eye. *What the hell is the camera doing on the floor?* might have been Sly's first question.

As I looked up from the camera and down the hall, I could see the body of Vicky Bradford sprawled on the floor. Because her head had been so savaged in the attack, the body looked odd. It might have taken a second for Sly to realize what he was looking at. However, a step or two into the hallway and there would have been no doubt that he was looking at a dead body. Unless he'd felt compelled to check the body for signs of life, there would have been no need for him to leave the door.

I think we all had a hard time looking directly at the damage done to Vicky. Repressing my gag reflex, I noticed that a professional mini-lamp was lying on its side near the body. At some point, the tripod had been knocked over. I wondered how much noise that would have made. Could Sly have heard it out by the van? At that hour on a Friday night, there would have still been some traffic moving around. That, combined with being outside and possibly on the far side of the van, could certainly give him wiggle room to claim that he hadn't heard anything.

The blood spatter was almost artistic in its looping spirals running up the walls. The twelve-foot ceilings were clear, but the wood floor had a heavy coating of blood.

"There!" I said, pointing to a spot near the body's shoulder. There was a fresh, three-inch gouge in the floor.

"Our killer missed." Pete smiled.

"I've already photographed it," Marcus said. "I'm pretty sure I can get some idea of the shape of the head of the axe."

"Or hatchet," I said, looking closely at the gouge. "If the murderer is using a hatchet, which is what Dr. Darzi thinks, then they would have had to be kneeling when that happened."

"That's up close and personal with your victim," Darlene said, frowning. "Assuming the body was already there, then the killer would have had to be kneeling on or straddling the body. That is one crazy son of a bitch."

We looked around the rest of the house without finding much different from when Pete and I had been there. Mostly, we noted the items that Sly and Vicky had brought with them. As we went through each room, we tested all the windows. Two of us checked each window so there was no possibility of missing signs of tampering, or a bolt failure that would have allowed someone to get into the house. All of the windows were still secure, as well as the back door.

"If the windows and doors were closed and bolted, there is no way anyone got through them," Pete declared.

"I looked at all the windows and the back door when I cleared the house. I'd swear under oath that they were all locked and bolted," Darlene said.

All of us knew what this meant. We had an impossible situation. If Sly didn't kill Vicky, then who had? Or, more accurately, who *could* have?

"We need to know if any of their video equipment is missing, or if anything lying around wasn't something they brought with them," I said.

"One of us will need to lead Sly around so he can point anything out," Pete said.

"We can wait until the body has been removed." I didn't

see the point in traumatizing the guy anymore.

As we were leaving the house, Marcus told us he would dust the camera, bag it and join us outside.

Waiting for us on the front porch were Linda and Andre from the coroner's office. "Sorry it took us so long. We've been running to all the best parties tonight," Linda said.

"Parties?" I asked with raised eyebrows.

"We had a coronary, which we wouldn't necessarily have picked up, but the man was found dead in the bathroom of a club down by the university. He was young and everyone's thinking drugs, though I sure didn't see any indications. According to witnesses, he wasn't acting intoxicated, only sweaty. After that, we went to an anniversary party where the husband decided to stab one of the guests."

With that lovely image, we left them to their examination. Fifteen minutes later, Shantel and Marcus joined us in the front yard. Marcus was carrying the camera in an oversized evidence bag.

"I can rewind the tape and we can see what's on it. I'll keep it in the bag to preserve any DNA evidence until we get it back to the office and can vacuum and swab it," he said.

"Works for us. We just want to see if there's any glaring evidence that might tell us who the killer is," I said.

We went over to Pete's car where we could stabilize the camera on the hood. Huddled around the device, we let Marcus search back through the footage. The last half hour was the same shot of the bottom step of the staircase.

After that, figures appeared on the camera's small screen. Marcus stopped it and let the video play forward. The footage was of Sly doing a monologue. The sound was muffled from the bag, but his TV-presenter excitement still came through clearly. Then we heard the sound of applause and we all looked at each other, puzzled, until Sly took his phone out of his pocket and looked at it.

The footage cut off after that, then picked up again with a shot looking up the staircase. Slowly, the camera backed down the stairs and continued to film as it swept the front entryway. Then, like a flash of lightning, the picture went wild. We heard a grunt as the camera fell to the floor with a hard, cracking sound, facing the edge of the front door. After that were the spine-tingling sounds of something weighty hitting flesh. None of us had a hard time figuring out what we were listening to. We waited in hopes that the murderer would walk in front of the camera, but there was nothing.

Eventually, all the sounds stopped. Marcus made a move to stop the tape, but I put my hand out. "Let it play," Pete said at the same time.

After five minutes, we heard the front door open and Sly call Vicky's name. A split-second later there was a high-pitched scream that could have been made by a nine-year-old girl. Then the door slammed and all was silent. Five minutes later the door opened again, and we could just make out Darlene's feet as she entered and exited the house, then there was silence again. This time I let Marcus turn off the camera.

"We'll have to let Lionel analyze the part of the tape when the attack takes place to know if there are any usable clues," I said.

"I thought I saw an arm at one point. Whether it's the victim or the perp, I couldn't tell." Darlene was frowning. "That backs up Harris's story. Though, with him being a filmmaker, he could have set this all up with the intent to reinforce his alibi."

"That's what I was thinking," Pete chimed in.

"This isn't going to be a magic bullet, that's for sure. One thing that would help is if we could find the murder weapon," I said.

"Any chance the killer left it somewhere on the property?" Pete asked.

"We can't be sure that the killer isn't still here." I nodded toward Sly.

"Searching the area would help to eliminate him as a suspect," Darlene admitted.

"If we don't find anything. The camera *does* establish the amount of time that he would have had to get rid of the weapon," I said.

"Five minutes, tops. He could maybe get five hundred yards and back without being out of breath when you arrived," Pete said, looking at Darlene.

"And he's not in the running for a spot on anyone's Olympic team," I quipped.

"I've got two officers working tonight. They can come and search," Darlene offered.

"I'll call and see who we have available." I pulled out my phone and called the watch commander. When I got off, I said, "We've got six deputies working tonight and can have them when they're available. Bad news is that it's Friday night, so they've been running pretty hot and heavy."

"Assuming we have a dozen people, we can cover the grounds pretty thoroughly in a few hours," Pete said.

"Let's each take one of the neighbors and go tell them what we're doing. They can walk around the outside of their homes with us." I had already decided I didn't want to visit the Holders.

"Of course *they* can't be ruled out as suspects," Darlene said.

"Exactly. So not only will this provide an opportunity to look for the weapon in their garages, outbuildings and yards, but it will give us a chance to observe them."

"They weren't happy, but none of them appeared suspicious to me," Pete said.

"Did you talk with Mr. Tippets?"

"The lights weren't on," Pete said and we all looked across the street.

"I'll go check on him." *Is it possible that he slept through all this commotion?* I wondered, worried that something might have happened to him.

Pete volunteered to take on the Holders while Darlene headed for the Khans. I quickstepped across the street to check on Mr. Tippets.

After the fourth ring of the doorbell, I went around to peek in the window of the garage to see if a car was parked there. I saw a '90s vintage beige Cadillac. Worried now, I went back to the front and rang the doorbell a few more times before I decided to try the back door. Just as I was walking away, lights came on in the house and I relaxed.

"What in Sam Hill is going on?" Tippets said as he opened the door. He was wearing a robe over his pajamas. "I was asleep." That was obvious from the tousled grey strands sticking out from his head and the unfocused eyes blinking at me.

"I'm sorry to wake you. There's been another murder across the street."

At this, he opened his eyes wide and gave his head a little shake. "No kidding! You're that deputy I talked to the other day. Guess you ought to come in. Another killing? Who was it?" He backed away from the door, giving me room to slip by.

After I explained the situation, he rubbed his hand over his head. "I took some pills the doctor gave me. She said they might make me sleepy. Guess she was right. Can't believe I slept through all that excitement."

"I'd like to look around the outside of your house. We're looking for the murder weapon."

"Now?"

"It's important."

"Heck, yeah, I guess. Let me get a flashlight and put on some real shoes." He held up a foot to show me the slippers he was wearing.

Ten minutes later, we were walking around his yard. I was sure that he was the one neighbor we could rule out as a suspect. Ten years ago, he might have been capable of clouting someone over the head with a hatchet, but today, not so much.

"You say it was an axe or a hatchet?" he asked. "I've got one of each in the toolshed."

"Point the way when we get close." We were still working

our way down the south side of the house. There were half a dozen camellias and several large gardenias on this side of the house, and searching under them took time in the dark.

When we got to the backyard, I shined my flashlight on an old one-car garage. Even though it was well maintained, it was showing its age.

"The shed was here before the house. It was in better shape than the old cracker shack that had been home for the caretaker of the Lynch house. When we bought the property, I had the house torn down and left the shed."

Tippets pulled open one of the big wooden doors of the old garage. Inside I saw a collection of old bikes, a motorcycle, a fairly new riding lawnmower and an assortment of power and yard tools. Tippets stepped inside and pulled a string that hung down from a bare bulb in the ceiling. The light from the bulb was so bright that I had to squint for a couple of seconds.

"There's the axe," he said, pointing toward a wooden-handled axe with a double-sided head. He started toward it.

"Don't touch it!"

"That's right, fingerprints and all that DNA stuff. I watch those shows." He pointed his own flashlight at the tool as I walked over to take a look. "I don't see no blood. Looks like it hasn't moved. Not that I've used it in years."

I had to agree with him. Dust and cobwebs were generously spread around that area of the shed, including one cobweb stretching from the handle of the axe all the way to the wall.

"I think you're right. It hasn't been moved recently," I said. "Where's your hatchet?"

Tippets turned left and then right. "It should be right there," he said, pointing to an empty spot on a peg board screwed into the wall. There were lots of other tools there, including screwdrivers, wrenches, a hacksaw, a square and a long level. He looked under the bench that was against that wall. "Don't know what to tell you."

"When was the last time you saw the hatchet?"

Tippets stood up and scratched his head. "Now that's a good question." He looked up as if he were adding up a string of numbers. "Guess it's been a couple of years. I've got a yard man now who cuts my grass and takes care of the lawn."

"Can you describe it for me?"

"Sure. Come to think about it, I've had that hatchet most of my life. Bought it when I wanted to go camping before I was drafted. The wooden handle, though, that I replaced twenty years ago. Had some rust on it last time I saw it, even though it still had a good edge to it. My initials are carved in the handle. You think someone stole it and used it to kill those people?"

"I don't know anything right now." I thought it was just as likely that Tippets's hatchet had been misplaced. Maybe the yard man had used it and it'd gotten mixed in with his tools. There was also the chance that Wells had stolen it at some point. He was known to have sticky fingers. I looked around to see if there was anything else that looked valuable. "Is anything else missing?"

"No," Tippets said, though he looked uncertain. "Like I said, it's been a couple of years since I've even been out here."

We closed the shed and looked around the rest of the yard. We found nothing and I sent a very tired old man back to bed.

Over at the Lynch house, Darlene and Pete were already organizing our small band of searchers. I told them about the missing hatchet while explaining that Mr. Tippets hadn't seen the hatchet in years.

We spent several hours walking the grounds, flashlights in hand, looking under bushes, cars and houses for the murder weapon.

"We've covered a lot of ground," I finally said, completely worn out. "I think we should stop and look around again tomorrow when we have some light." As dark as it was, it would have been possible for one of us to walk right by a tree where someone had stuck the hatchet, or to not see the handle sticking out of a pile of leaves.

"Agreed," Pete said. "Sarah wants us all to go to Pet-O-Ween tomorrow…" He rambled on for another minute or two, but inwardly I was groaning and trying to think how I was going to make it through the event which, as a glance at my watch informed me, started in only four hours.

"I don't have a choice. Cara is helping to put it on," I said as much to myself as to Pete.

"Take a chair with you," was his solemn advice.

CHAPTER NINETEEN

"Just two hours. Then I'll be fine," I told Cara as I crawled into bed. "You leave when you have to, and I'll try to get there by ten."

"No, really, you don't have to go," Cara said. But what I heard was: *I'll be horribly disappointed if you don't come to the event.*

"Just let me get a nap. Set my phone for nine-thirty. Already had a shower." I was half asleep before Cara slipped into the bathroom for her morning routine.

When the phone started buzzing at nine-thirty, all I could think of was how sweet it would be to ignore it. I was talking myself into ten more minutes when I woke with a start and realized it was now almost ten. I dressed hurriedly, nearly tripped over Ghost as he threw himself at me when I came out of the bedroom, grabbed a couple of slices of bread and cheese, and ran out of the door, apologizing to Ivy that she was going to have to babysit.

I remembered Pete's words of wisdom and snatched up one of the lawn chairs off of the porch on my way to the car.

Feeling tired and numb, I drove with extra caution like a drunk leaving the bar on Saturday night. There weren't any parking places within a hundred yards of the city park, so I found what I could and accepted the walk as a way to wake up.

The park was full of dogs in Halloween costumes, and a few less conventional pets, including a goat dressed in lederhosen and a llama wearing a drape with the masks of comedy and tragedy on one side and the name "Drama Llama" on the other, for those who didn't get it.

I found Cara working the registration desk, signing people and their animals up for the costume contests. I waved and got a quick smile in return as she collected forms. She spoke to a ten-year-old girl who was standing beside her. The little girl walked over to me, trailing Alvin, who was prancing and panting in his pumpkin costume.

"Mrs. Macklin says for you to take Alvin." She held the leash out to me.

"Thank you," I said, then led Alvin over to a shady spot where I could set up my chair and we could stay out of everyone's way.

I'd just gotten comfortable when I saw the world's ugliest pirate trotting through the crowd, dragging three more pirates behind him. Alvin gave a quick, sharp bark that must have gone straight to Mauser's oversized ears. He perked up and pulled hard in our direction.

"Thanks, now you've done it," I grumbled at Alvin.

Dad and Genie followed Mauser, while Jimmy kept getting distracted by all the funny animal costumes. They were ten yards away when Mauser lunged and broke free of Dad's grip. I didn't stand a chance. He slammed into me, sending me and the chair over backwards. He then proceeded to dance on top of me while attempting to lick my face. Alvin joined in with the latter endeavor. The many spectators to my pummeling expressed various levels of concern, from uncontrollable laughter to asking if I needed an ambulance.

"Get him off me and I'll be okay," I told Genie, who was one of the few expressing concern for my welfare.

"He'll live," Dad assured her. He, of course, was in the uncontrollable laughter camp.

"Yeah, I'm peachy," I growled, rescuing myself from the onslaught only to find that my lawn chair was bent out of shape. "Thanks, Jughead," I told Mauser, who was still trying to wipe my nose off my face with his tongue. "I thought Jamie was coming to keep the beast in check," I said to Dad.

"He couldn't make it," Dad said, still smiling.

"He knocked you on your butt!" Jimmy informed me, loud enough that everyone in the park who hadn't seen it now knew.

"I'm fine," I said, trying to put my chair back together.

"Long night?" Dad said with some sympathy.

"They're selling cupcakes to help the shelter animals," Jimmy informed Dad and his mother, not so subtly.

"Why don't y'all go get some. I'd really like chocolate," Dad said, taking a twenty out of his wallet and giving it to Jimmy.

"Yes, sir!" Jimmy and Genie headed for the Adams County Animal Shelter tent as Dad tried to convince Mauser to sit down.

"Is this murder connected to the first one?" Dad asked me when they were out of earshot.

"I don't see how it can be. And I also don't see how it *can't* be connected."

"I don't have to tell you that we need to be able to show some progress on this case sooner rather than later. I've already been contacted by some regional news outlets. The nationals can't be far behind."

"I'm sure they will eat up the ghost angle."

"Two phone calls from media in Atlanta and Miami and that's all they could talk about."

"I don't know what to tell you. This is a genuine locked-room mystery," I said, trying to make myself comfortable in my damaged chair.

"Are you sure that there wasn't a way the killer could have gotten in?"

"Dad, I *am* still committed to keeping Lt. Johnson in the loop," I reminded him.

"You don't need to feel obligated to that agreement anymore."

My eyes widened. "What's going on? I've noticed that he's been in an unusually good mood lately."

Dad nodded. "He's taken a job as a major with the Panama City Police Department."

"That explains a lot. Doesn't he have a house at the beach?"

"Yeah. He and Angela go down there all the time. He told me how much he loved being near the beach when he took the job with us." Dad adjusted his tricorn hat with its skull and crossbones.

"Nice costume, by the way."

"Jimmy's having the time of his life," Dad said, with just the hint of a smile.

"When's Johnson leaving?"

"Two weeks."

"So who's going to be in charge of CID?" We were already short a sergeant. Dad hadn't filled a position a couple of years ago after he'd promoted Darren Goodmen to lieutenant and given him one of the watch commander positions.

"I probably shouldn't be telling you. Insider information." Dad touched his nose, teasing me.

"Like you said, that agreement is off the table now."

Dad chuckled at my quick reversal. "I'm leaning toward promoting someone to sergeant and letting them oversee CID. The other option is to consolidate auto thefts, accident investigations and the vice squad under CID, and place one of the existing lieutenants in charge."

"Who?" I asked.

"For sergeant? Don't know. Until I make a decision, Major Parks will fill in as head of CID."

"My money would be on Pete." With one daughter already in college and the other following soon, the man was going to need some extra income. Plus, he was about as fair a person as I'd ever met.

Dad just shook his head, putting his finger over his mouth. "I'm willing to give you a little insider information, but I'm not discussing promotions with you."

"Back to the Lynch house murders—"

"Great. You've already given them a media tag." Dad was only half joking.

"I was going to tell you that Darlene, Pete and I checked every window and door in the place. All of them were locked."

"Who was first on the scene last night?"

"Darlene was the first LEO; Pete was the first of our people. Darlene cleared the house and was willing to swear that the windows and back door were locked when she did it, same as how we found them later."

Dad looked grim. "Did this filmmaker do it? That would seem like the obvious solution."

"Slim chance. There's evidence in the form of a video camera that was running during the course of the murder that backs up his account. If you eliminate the camera evidence, then it *might* be possible."

"He *is* a filmmaker."

"We're going to have Lionel give us his opinion on the tape. Hopefully the date and time stamp can be verified."

"Pardon me if I hope that the man's alibi falls apart. Could he have committed the first murder?"

"It's possible, but we'd need a motive. I've already decided to check his alibi for that murder. Without a motive, we hadn't yet followed up on any alibi for him and his camera woman."

"Prioritize both murder cases," he said. I figured that, with Johnson leaving, Dad was going to be giving a few more direct orders to investigators. Major Parks was a great administrator, but he was not a guy to get down in the trenches, at least not at his age.

Jimmy came back bearing a sugary treat. "We got you the chocolate with chocolate sprinkles," he said in his most serious tone.

Mauser stood up to greet Jimmy. Dad took the cupcake while Jimmy dug in his pockets and gave Mauser some treats. Mauser took the opportunity to also clean the icing from Jimmy's fingers.

"Where's your mom?" I asked.

"Helping Cara," he said, pointing to a cleared area where I could see that Genie had been roped into setting up the ring for the contests.

"Are you just going to sit on your butt all day?" Dad asked me and Jimmy laughed.

"Two-and-a-half hours' sleep," I reminded him.

"Back in my day…" Dad gave me a look that told me he was kidding.

"Besides, I'm keeping a handle on the pumpkin." I nodded toward Alvin, who was lying with his feet stretched out and panting.

The day was practically perfect. I did get up and help a couple of times, but I mostly sat staring at the crowd and wondering how someone had gotten into the Lynch house through locked doors and windows.

Pete, Sarah and their daughters showed up with their part-Bassett, part-something-fuzzy. The dog was wearing a deer stalker and had a pipe tied to his side.

"Sherlock Hound. Get it?" Kim, Pete's youngest, said with a wide smile.

"Why aren't you dressed up as Moriarty?" I asked Pete.

"Please," he said dismissively. "They had to drag me out of the house as it was. Remember, I was with you all night."

"Yeah, you don't look your usual, well-groomed self." I noted his shirt half tucked in and a stain on his pants, all of which was normal weekend wear for him. He gave me a subtle but clear finger.

"You'll want to step up your game. You're my chosen candidate for sergeant," I told him, once Sarah and the girls had headed for the contest ring.

"What are you talking about?"

I repeated what Dad had told me which, of course, was

part of the reason he'd told me in the first place. I'd learned a few years ago that when he wanted to disseminate information to the department without making it formal, he'd tell me knowing that I'd spread it around.

"Too much paperwork and meetings," Pete said, dismissing the suggestion.

"You'll need the money for college," I said, nodding toward the ring.

"Time or money. I'd rather have these last few years with them before they get careers, husbands and houses on the other side of the country."

"They won't move that far away."

"You don't know that. Kids, they break your heart." I was surprised by the sincere melancholy in his voice, but then again, like me, he was working on only a few hours of sleep.

"Speaking of eating up your free time, what are you doing tomorrow? I'd like you, me and Darlene to get together to really think these murders through."

"Tomorrow afternoon, maybe. Those murders are bugging the hell out of me too."

"Something is missing. The first murder doesn't line up with the second," I said, trying to formulate my thoughts into words. Being muddle-headed from lack of sleep didn't help.

"I'm just focused on opportunity for last night's murder. Is there a chance that Lionel can break Harris's alibi?"

"If the footage has been tampered with, then he's our man. But… I don't know. We have to come up with a motive for the first murder."

"Let's leave it for tomorrow when we'll have Darlene's brain to pick too," Pete said.

He was getting ready to walk away when I spotted Jessie coming our way. She had a determined expression on her face as she eyeballed both of us.

"Have you gotten anyone else to look at the security camera footage?" she asked when she was close enough to be heard.

Pete sighed. "I've talked with two of Terri Miller's friends, and they've both agreed to come in after they get off work on Monday. I'll let each of them see it separately first, and then together." He shrugged. "That's all I can do for now."

Jessie looked thoughtful. "I *do* understand why you don't want to tell her mother yet. I just… I really know that's her."

"I know you do," I said, glancing at Pete. "But it would be difficult to identify anyone from the little bit that can be seen in that footage. There are people who have the same quirks. I've seen someone from behind and thought they were someone I knew because of the way they walked, and it turned out to be a stranger. Stuff like that happens."

"You all think she's dead."

"I'm sorry, but that's what the odds would tell you. Again, it's not a guarantee. People go missing, don't tell anyone and show up later. Having said that, I'll add that it's seldom *years* later," I said.

"She had a steady job, was reliable, and she and her mother were close," Pete said with a sad shake of his head. "She had no reason to just disappear. But no one would be happier than me to have her show up alive."

"I know," Jessie said sadly.

"As soon as her friends have had a chance to look at the footage and make up their minds, I'll let you know," Pete assured her. "If both of them think it's her, we'll call in her mother and give her a chance to see it."

After a little more small talk, Pete went to join his family and Jessie headed back to the table she'd been working for the library. Alone again, I looked across the crowd of dogs and people to see Dad, Genie, Jimmy and Mauser, all dressed alike and laughing at something I couldn't see. Maybe it was the fatigue, but for a moment I felt like I was looking at a family that I wasn't a part of.

I tried to remember a time like that when Mom, Dad and I had been that relaxed and happy. Nothing quite fit. Dad had always been serious and focused on his job as a deputy. We had done things together and had fun, but a part of him had always seemed to be elsewhere. And, to be honest, I had never felt like I lived up to his expectations. Maybe there was a beauty in the fact that Dad now had Jimmy in his life. The only expectation that Jimmy or Dad had for any moment was that it would be fun. I couldn't be jealous of that. How low would I have to be to want anything but joy for the three of them? At that moment, Cara walked across my field of vision and my eyes followed her. *And how can I be jealous of another man when I have her in my life?* I thought.

My eyes closed, and I let the warm fall sun lull me to sleep. But after what seemed like only a few minutes, I heard someone yelling at me.

"Wake up! It's time to go home." Cara nudged the lawn chair. I jumped and the damaged chair fell over, dumping me onto the ground again. Cara had to cover her mouth to suppress her laughter.

"Ha, ha! That's the second time I've rolled around on the ground today," I huffed, trying to clear my head.

"Hey, I let you sleep through Mauser winning the giant dog costume category," she said, holding out her hand to help me up.

"You made up that category just for him, didn't you?"

"I've got video. You should have seen Jimmy's face when they won."

Cara's smile was wide and bright. I hugged her, then picked up my broken chair in one hand and a sleeping Alvin in the other and we headed for the cars.

CHAPTER TWENTY

Cara and I spent Sunday morning enjoying the cooler weather and just lazing around, not doing much of anything after a long, tough week. Predictably, I couldn't get the murders out of my mind, but I was able to keep from talking about them as we took a long walk in the woods with Alvin.

Around one o'clock I started to get restless. I called Marcus and talked him into meeting me at the Roads Best Motel. When I'd finally left the Lynch house on Saturday morning, I'd made a quick stop by the motel to seal off Vicky Bradford's room. Normally I would have looked at it right then, but I'd been too tired and hadn't wanted to risk missing something or screwing up evidence.

When I got to the motel, I checked the seals I'd put on the door and was satisfied that they hadn't been broken. Inside, we found a room in considerable disarray, but it didn't take us too long to determine that Vicky had just been a messy person. She kept her room the way you'd expect a sixteen-year-old boy to keep his. There were clothes thrown about, food wrappers on the nightstand and towels on the floor of the bathroom. I'd made note of the "Do Not Disturb" sign that had been hanging on the door when I'd sealed it Saturday morning, and now I realized Vicky had probably never let the maid in to clean the room.

I let Marcus photograph and videotape the room before I started to actively search it. We didn't find anything useful. There seemed to be little more than personal clothes and hygiene products. I wondered if she kept all of her work items in the van, which Shantel had taken and secured in the fenced area behind the sheriff's office.

"Have you all tackled the van yet?" I asked Marcus.

"Nope. I have it on my schedule for tomorrow afternoon. I did film it and take pictures at the crime scene."

"Do you remember if there was a laptop or other items that might have belonged to our victim?"

Marcus shook his head. "It was a mess. Cables, lights, tripods, monitors, other cameras. It's going to take me all day to sort through and catalog everything."

"Keep an eye out for any personal electronic items of our victim. We didn't find her cell phone at the scene."

The thought that we didn't have any of her electronics bugged me enough that I walked a few rooms down and knocked on the door of Sly Harris's room.

"Did Vicky have her phone with her Friday night?" I asked when he answered, looking like he'd just woken up.

"Is that a joke? Vicky would have gone mad if she didn't have her phone in contact with her body."

"Did she have a laptop?"

"Is this officially Ask a Stupid Question Day?"

"Just tell me," I said with enough fire that he backed down.

"Sorry. I'm just going a little mad here." He ran his fingers through his tangled hair. "This motel is so depressing, and I still can't believe what happened... Yes, yes, she had a laptop. That's how she did all of the editing. We looked at dailies on it every day we after we filmed. It's a top-of-the-line MacBook."

"Would it be in your van?"

"I don't think so. Let me think... No, she didn't bring it with her Friday night. She only brings it along if we're going to look at some footage or if she needs to download video from the camera when it's getting short of storage."

"We can't find it in her room."

"Really?" Sly looked surprised.

"Do you have any idea where she would have kept it in the room?"

"It's a big silver thing. You can't miss it. I think it was on the table whenever I was in there." He paused and seemed to realize what he'd said. "Which wasn't often. I only went to her room when we were working."

I thanked him and headed back to Vicky's room.

"Have you all cataloged everything we took from the crime scene?" I asked Marcus.

"Come on, man. Hell no. We were out as late as you that night." Marcus frowned at me.

"Okay, you're right, that wasn't a reasonable question. When you *do* go through it, let me know if you find a motel keycard." I had a bad feeling that our killer had been in the room already. If they'd stolen Vicky's keycard, then they could have easily gotten there before we did and taken whatever they wanted, which didn't make any sense unless there was something on Vicky's phone or laptop that would incriminate them.

The motel was old-fashioned and the rooms opened onto the parking lot. The only security camera on the property that I knew of was in the office. I'd been after the owners for years to put up cameras that would cover the parking lot around the motel. However, they avoided it like the plague, knowing that a percentage of their clientele used the motel for the very reason that it offered a level of anonymity.

I would have to wait until Monday to get a warrant for Vicky's phone records. It was possible to get one on the weekend, but it was best to only make that request when it could be argued that time was of the essence.

Nothing else in the room provided us with any answers. We locked up and I stopped by the office to make sure that the locks would not accept Vicky's original key to the room.

I was assured that when they had issued me a key on Saturday morning, the lock had been effectively changed.

Darlene and Pete had agreed to meet me at the sheriff's office at three. When I got to the conference room, I found Pete in shorts and a garish Hawaiian shirt with his feet up on the table.

"Don't judge me; it's Sunday," Pete said when I gave him the eye.

I told him about the missing phone and laptop.

"You think that's why she was killed?"

"Maybe. I don't think these murders are the work of a thief. There had to be something on those items that the killer didn't want anyone else to see."

"They darn sure didn't kill Wells for his valuables. They even left his ten-dollar Walmart watch on him."

"The murders might have had different motives. I guess I figured that anyway," I said.

"I'm still trying to figure out the locked-up house."

Darlene showed up a few minutes late, wearing her uniform.

"Don't you ever take a day off?" I asked her.

"I'm making twenty percent more money to work fifty percent more hours. How's that for a good business decision?"

"We were discussing the locked house," I said.

"I've been thinking about that. Is it possible that someone snuck inside while Sly and Vicky were filming in some other part of the house? Then Sly leaves, they come out of hiding, kill Vicky, and then sneak out of the house. The only part that has me baffled is the video camera. It's pointing toward the front door as soon as Vicky falls to the ground. So how could the bad guy get out without any part of him being caught on film?"

"Unless they were still in the house and you missed them when you cleared it," I said.

Darlene glared at me, but said, "I don't blame you for suggesting that. However, let me be clear. *No one* got out of that house after I arrived. Even if I missed them, which I wouldn't have, then Sly would have seen them since he was standing on the front porch. I'll be glad to show you how I cleared the house, and you and your buddy can see if either one of you can sneak out."

"That's not a bad idea," I said thoughtfully. "We could set up a camera at the same angle and see if it's possible to sneak out without being picked up."

"Or if we can get past the super cop." Pete gave Darlene a wave.

"You're on, pork chop," she told him.

"We can tackle that later. My problem is with the two murders. I'm sure they're connected, but what do they have in common other than the choice of weapon?"

"And location," Pete added.

"Though one was outdoors where they could have been seen and the other was indoors," Darlene pointed out.

"It doesn't sound like a serial killer," Pete said.

"Can we come up with a motive for both murders?" I asked.

"Wells was struck in the forehead. Does that mean that he knew the killer or not?" Darlene asked.

I rubbed my jaw. "I think it *does* indicate that he was relaxed with the person who attacked him, since there were no defensive wounds to his hands or arms. If you were facing someone who you knew might attack you, then you'd probably be able to mount some sort of defense."

"Why would you allow someone to stand in front of you with a hatchet?" Darlene wondered.

"Because you thought they were completely harmless even with a hatchet in their hands?" I shrugged.

"That would eliminate the guys who attacked him at the Fast Mart," Pete said.

"I think there could be other explanations for why he wouldn't put up a defense. Like there were three people there and the other two were distracting him, or even holding him," Darlene suggested.

"There weren't any bruises on his arms or hands like someone had a tight hold on him, but maybe they weren't holding him that tightly," I said.

"Until there is some other evidence, I still think the Fast Mart guys have to be prime suspects," Darlene said.

"I don't disagree. But here's the rub: it makes sense that they might have killed Wells, but how do you see them being involved in Vicky's murder?" I asked.

Pete and Darlene pondered that question for a minute.

"Maybe she saw something?" Pete suggested.

"But why would she withhold that information?" Darlene challenged.

We pondered some more.

"Doesn't make sense," Pete said after a while. "So the question is, could we be looking at two different murderers? The guys killed Wells and… maybe Sly killed Vicky, hoping that we'll be stuck like we are trying to make one killer fit both murders."

"Makes as much sense as anything. Of course, that all hinges on us proving that Sly fudged the camera footage," Darlene said.

"It's not a stretch to believe he could alter the footage. With deepfakes, you can't believe anything you see on video anymore. We just have to prove it. As it is, I'd be uncomfortable accusing him without proof that the camera is lying," I stated.

"Then that falls into Lionel's lap," Darlene said.

"I've already told Shantel to make sure Lionel has a chance to study the camera as soon as he comes in tomorrow. Dad's given these cases priority."

"Dad? You're back to using your familial connections?" Darlene asked with a grin.

"For all practical purposes, he's our direct supervisor now," Pete told her. "Lt. Johnson is moving on to sandier pastures. At least that's what *Dad* said." Pete gave me a smirk and I repaid him with the finger.

"I should have stayed on here. Big Daddy could have made me y'all's supervisor."

"Okay, guys, enough with the dad stuff. Let's get back on track. We're agreed that the camera footage is crucial to the second murder, right?"

"With all of us keeping our fingers crossed that it's been fudged. otherwise we're up the proverbial creek without a paddle," Darlene said, nodding.

"There's one other possibility. We figure a way out of that house other than the front door," I said.

"Or in. If Sly can convince us that no one could have snuck in while they were filming," Pete muttered.

"Yeah. Okay, then for right now we're looking at two separate murders. Bad boys for the first and Sly for the second." Darlene leaned forward and looked at me. "Though I'm with you. I think we're missing a connection. I just don't like the 'two murderers' solution."

"We don't even know if Sly had a motive for Vicky's murder," I sighed.

"Boy and girl. There are always motives." Pete was right. The love connection was ripe for motives. "You add all the possibilities with a business partner and I don't think motive will be our sticking point."

"We still have to find the men who attacked Wells. Jessie found some possibilities on the security footage. I've asked around at the Fast Marts, but so far all I've got are street names that I can't connect to real human beings."

"Maybe Sly killed both of them. We know that he'd met and interviewed Wells. Maybe some bad blood developed between them," Pete suggested.

"Wells took drugs. Maybe Sly does too. That would solve all of our problems if Sly is our mastermind," I said.

"Hate to base an investigation on feelings, especially me being a woman and all that, but Sly just doesn't strike me as the axe-murdering type." Darlene flipped her hands up in the air. "Just a feeling."

"I know what you mean. I'd also give him an Academy Award for his performance on Friday night. He was very convincing as the scared and baffled witness to a hideous crime," I said.

"Let me hope that he turns out to be our villain. That would just make life so much simpler." Pete, sitting there in his leisure wear, looked the part of a man trying for a simpler life.

I filled them in on a few more case details.

"I sent the blood photos off to my contact at FDLE. He said to give him a couple of weeks for a full analysis. I don't think it's going to help us find the killer, but it might help to convict them," I said.

"And we've eliminated Vicky's ex," Darlene said.

"Still have to follow up on that, but yeah, most likely. I've also established an alibi for the person who wrote those threatening emails to Wells's family," I told them.

"All I see are a lot of dead ends," Pete grumbled, though we all knew that was part of the job. All leads were dead ends except for the ones that weren't.

We kicked around a few more ideas, then headed off in our own directions. As I was walking across the parking lot toward my car, I saw Sergeant Toomey getting out of his car. He raised a hand and I stopped to wait for him.

"I wanted to talk to you about a phone call I got yesterday," he said.

"Sure."

"It's about the accident. The victim's sister called me."

"Romano's sister? What did she want?"

"That's the funny thing. She told me that Romano had enemies and that she thought the accident might not be an accident."

I hadn't seen that coming. "Did you tell her what was on the dash cam?"

"Yep. I couldn't be sure over the phone whether she believed me or not. She just kept saying that he had enemies and that we should take a closer look at it."

"Did she name any of these enemies?" I asked.

"She mentioned his business. Apparently his family made money running the Romano Couch Company. I've heard of it. They were a big thing back in the '70s and '80s."

"Oh, yeah. I think we had one. Their convertibles were all the rage. Are they still in business?"

"They don't build couches anymore. They import furniture and sell it wholesale."

"Is this sister in the business?"

"No. Apparently Romano pushed the rest of the family out."

"Then could this be an interfamily thing?" I asked as we walked toward my car.

"I don't know. She didn't sound like she was angry about being bought out. Just that there were rumors that Tommy had wanted full control. And that he might have been involved in drug smuggling. I pressed her on specifics, but she couldn't give me anything. I thought it all sounded like whispers and guesswork."

"I guess we could look into his business dealings a little. And I can talk to his wife again."

"Would you mind checking it out for me? Unless something glaring comes out, I don't know how much further we can go."

"What about the car's telematics?"

"I can check with BMW and see if they'd be interested in attempting to recover the data."

"Maybe the family would be willing to foot the bill."

"Here's the sister's number. Her name is Gloria, if you want to give her a call as well." Toomey handed me one of his cards with her number written on the back.

I waved as he left, then I looked down at the number. It was not uncommon to get odd phone calls from the family members of victims. Grief and fear often caused people to do and think things that were not always one hundred percent rational. *Is that the case here?* I wondered. The only way to know was to follow up on it. That was my punishment for sticking my nose into a case that wasn't my concern. No good deed goes unpunished.

I texted Sherry Romano to make sure she was available. After an immediate affirmative response, I called Cara and asked if she minded me making a stop before I headed home.

"I guess you earned a few brownie points by dragging your tired self to the event yesterday."

"I'll be home as soon as I can."

Sherry Romano answered the door and invited me in.

"I just have a few questions," I said, trying hard to find a safe place to put my eyes. She was wearing one of the most revealing tennis outfits I'd ever seen outside of a men's magazine.

Sherry either misunderstood my expression or deliberately ignored it. "I just got back from playing tennis at a friend's house. I hope you don't think too poorly of me for getting some exercise. My doctor told me that the best way to combat my depression is to be as active as I can."

"That makes sense."

"We can sit in here or out back if you'd like?"

"Outside would be great." For some reason, I felt uncomfortable being inside with her dressed like she was.

"When I got your text, I wondered what questions you had for me." I could have sworn that there was a suggestive hint in her words.

"Actually, I need to ask you a few more questions about your husband."

"Sure. Can I get you something to drink?"

"I'm good," I said and she slowly sank down into the patio chair across from me. "Can you tell me if your husband had any enemies?"

I was sure I saw her eyes narrow a little. "That seems like a very odd question under the circumstances." There were no seductive nuances now.

"We're just being thorough in our investigation."

Sherry relaxed again. "I appreciate that. If this wasn't an accident, then I'd like to know it."

"We're still waiting on the toxicology reports to come back. We do know that your husband's blood alcohol level was only mildly elevated and there wasn't any THC in his system."

"He might have had a drink or a beer before he headed into town, but nothing more, and I don't think he even tried pot in college."

"What about his business? Did he have any competitors that might have been enemies?"

"I don't think any more than most businessmen. Some of the people overseas could get pretty crazy with their threats. But you turned around, and the same people who'd been calling him a son of a cur dog would be selling him everything they could get their hands on. I think it's just the way some of them negotiate."

"And what exactly did he import?"

"Furniture. His family made a name in couches, so he marketed that."

"Are any other members of his family involved in the business?" I thought I saw her tense a little at this question.

"No."

"They didn't have an interest in the business anymore?"

She frowned and looked thoughtful for a moment before answering. "You've obviously heard something. Okay, there was a knock-down, drag-out fight over the rights to the name fifteen years ago when Tommy's parents died. Tommy won. He was always better at the business than any of his siblings."

"And there were hard feelings?"

"At first, but Tommy was generous and bought his brother and two sisters out. Over time, as they watched him struggle through the recession in 2009, I think they learned that he'd done them a favor. He managed to turn everything around, but not without working his ass off. You saw his family at the funeral. Did it look like there were any hard feelings?"

"I'll admit that everyone behaved. Were all the siblings there?"

"Yes. As far as the business goes, I don't know what I'm going to do with it. The import furniture business isn't my thing. I'll probably sell it. I bet you none of the family will be interested in making me an offer."

"Do you have any examples of the threats he received?"

"I'm sure there are any number of them in his emails. I'll be honest, I haven't even logged into his accounts since he died."

"Would you mind if we went through them?"

Sherry hesitated as she considered my request. "After I let his lawyer go through them. He's running the business until I decide what I'm going to do with it."

"The sooner the better."

"I still don't understand. I thought you all had decided that the wreck was an accident?"

"Someone could have poisoned your husband, or done something to his car to cause it to stop in the road."

"I suppose so. I… don't know where you heard that he had enemies?" she said, her voice going a little high to make it a question.

"Just some rumors. Did he have anyone working for him or with him?"

"It was pretty much a one-man operation. That's what he liked about it. He contracted with a number of people. You know, to ship and pack and do whatever you have to do to get furniture from one country to another. He also had a few people who were trusted to act as his agents when buying furniture from local manufactures."

"If we could get some of their names, that would be helpful."

"Again, the best person to ask would be our lawyer." She bent her head and rubbed her neck. "I'm sorry. I… just was never involved in Tommy's business. Now you're saying that someone might have killed him. It's a lot to take in. Maybe this is all my fault. If I'd been more interested, I might have seen something that could have saved him." She wiped at her eyes.

"We don't know anything. We're just checking out all the possibilities. It very well might have just been an accident."

She bit her lower lip. "Thank you for that. I hope you're right. I would hate to think that someone was responsible for his death. That would just make it worse. An accident is just an accident, but… I guess you'd call it murder. That would be horrible."

"If you'll give me your lawyer's number, I'll follow up with him."

"He's in Jacksonville. His name is Kassim French. I'll text you his number," she said, standing up and clearly done with the conversation.

At the door, I apologized for coming by on a Sunday.

"We still need to make a date to catch up," she said, letting some weight fall on the word date.

I left feeling a little dirty and with an odd notion about Sherry Romano. I wasn't sure how upset she really was about her husband's death. A lack of grief wasn't as uncommon as some people might think. I'd met one woman who'd laughed when I told her that her husband had died in jail, and a husband who'd told me it was the best news he'd received in years when I informed him that his wife had been hit by a car.

I'd been suspicious of a few other spouses who'd put on very good acts, even though I had been sure that there'd been a hint of a smile as they mourned the loss of a husband or wife. Nothing in the law required grieving the death of anyone, family or not. Still, something about Sherry nagged at me.

CHAPTER TWENTY-ONE

I got home just as Cara was taking a pan of lasagna out of the oven.

"Don't get used to this," she said, putting the pan on the counter. "The cooler weather just has me in a cooking mood."

Ghost started meowing as he hopped around the living room, chasing invisible enemies to the amusement of Alvin and the distain of Ivy, who was letting her nose lead her toward the smell of meat and pasta.

"It looks amazing." I meant every word. Drool was actually escaping my mouth as I watched her slip the garlic bread into the oven.

"Did you learn anything?"

"At our meeting or when I went by Sherry Romano's house?"

"Both. Either."

"The takeaway from our brainstorming session was that we're screwed if we can't break the evidence presented by the camera. And what I got from Romano was that she isn't that upset that her husband is dead."

As we waited on the garlic bread, we talked about the locked house, which meant going over many of the same ideas that Darlene, Pete and I had explored.

"Seems like you've got the same problem that the owner, what's-his-name, had." Cara sliced the lasagna with a spatula and pulled out a piece for my plate.

"Huh? What problem?"

"The guy whose money was stolen." She filled her own plate and sat down at the table across from me.

"Thaddeus! I thought you were talking about the current owner, who's actually trying to use the murders to sell the house. I wouldn't be surprised if he encourages Sly to keep filming there." I ate several bits of lasagna, not taking in what Cara had said. Then it hit me. "Wait. What did you mean about the money?"

"I said that you have the same problem as Thaddeus. He had money disappear from his office and you have a murder that's taken place inside the house. Both of you are sure that no one could get into that house, but obviously someone did. Seems to me that there must be some way to get in that he didn't know about back then, and that you don't know about now." She put a hefty bit of lasagna into her mouth.

I stared at her for a full minute.

"What? Do I have sauce on my face?"

"No. You're absolutely right. And you're brilliant. If someone was getting into that house when it was bolted and locked eighty years ago, then maybe our killer is using the same way to get in now."

"You just have to figure out how," Cara said with a smile.

Now I was dying to look over the whole house again. Was there a trick to the locks? A hidden door? I finished my dinner with all of the possibilities swirling in my head.

Later, I debated calling Tommy Romano's sister, Gloria. The yes side of the argument won. Once she answered the phone, I introduced myself and heard hesitation from the other end of the line.

"Let me go into the other room," she whispered. I waited and in a minute she was back. "Sorry, my husband doesn't think I should get involved."

"You told Sergeant Toomey that you thought one of your brother's business associates might have had something to do with his death. Why do you think that?"

"I… I've got my reasons. I just think you need to look more closely at the accident."

"Had he received threats?"

"Yes… that's part of it." Gloria was very hesitant.

"You can tell me what's bothering you," I encouraged. "This isn't a formal interview."

"I don't want to say something that might get me into trouble," she said, and I was sure I heard fear in her half-whispered words.

"You think that someone might come after you?"

"Yes," Gloria said bluntly.

"Who?"

"No. I'm not going that far. Just look into the accident. I could be wrong. I pray that I'm wrong."

"If you have suspicions about someone, just tell me and I'll look into them discreetly. You have my word."

She gave a short laugh. "I shouldn't have called."

"Please don't hang up. I need your help. We were going to close the investigation before you called."

"Shit! Look, just check everything. I don't know what to say." I could hear the fear and frustration in her voice.

"Okay. You said his business associates. You mean the ones overseas?"

There was a lengthy pause. "Everyone that he's done… business with."

"I spoke to Sherry. She said that he'd received threats from some of the people he bought and contracted with. Is that who you mean?" I was trying to get her to narrow down her suspicions.

"Everyone!" Gloria said in a desperate whisper before abruptly ending the call.

I looked at my phone and thought about calling her back, but I doubted she'd answer. I wouldn't try to call again until I'd looked into Tommy Romano's business dealings a little more closely. Contacting his lawyer would be my priority on Monday morning. It would mean ignoring Dad's directive to prioritize the Lynch murders, but talking to Romano's sister had caused the hackles on the back of my neck to rise. Something funny was going on, but I wouldn't know if it had contributed to his death until I dug a little deeper.

I kept my promise to myself and called Romano's lawyer first thing after I got to the office on Monday. His assistant told me that he would get back to me in the afternoon. I pressed him and explained the situation, with the hopes that the lawyer would be prepared to talk when he called, rather than tell me that he'd have to "look into it." I'd had more than a few go-arounds with lawyers and their stall tactics. The assistant assured me that he'd pass the information on to Mr. French.

I pushed Romano's accident to the back of my mind and headed down to Lionel's office to make sure that he was on top of the video camera footage. The sooner we could find out if there was any evidence of tampering, the quicker we could move on.

"You're lucky I'm not a superstitious person," Shantel told me when I walked into the evidence room. "Calling me out in the middle of the night to your haunted house for another murder."

"Not *my* haunted house," I said.

"They're *your* murders." She paused, then dropped, "Sergeant."

I gave her a hard look. "That's not gonna happen. Besides, I'm not a supervisor kind of guy."

"I thought that when I got promoted to crime scene supervisor."

"Dad is not going to promote me." I was convinced of that.

"Won't be entirely up to him. It will be the advancement committee that makes the recommendations. Our ranks are thin. I say you got a chance."

"Dad can veto anyone the committee sends to him."

"We'll see."

Gossip was the grease that made the gears turn around the sheriff's office. Everyone would be speculating on the promotion. CID shouldn't be considered any more important than any of the other divisions, but it seemed to get the most attention when it came to promotions and personnel decisions.

"And with you stepping out and working cases that aren't even yours." I knew she was talking about Tommy Romano.

"I'm just helping Toomey a little."

"One sergeant to another," Marcus said. He'd been quietly cataloging evidence at a counter. He and Shantel worked as a team when it came to gossip.

"Enough!" I gave the word an extra dose of dramatic anger and waved them away. I knocked on Lionel's door and went inside his office.

Lionel was sitting in front of his three monitors, zipping footage back and forth so quickly that I couldn't tell what he was working on.

"I've got to finish this file and get it to Julio. It's due to the State Attorney this afternoon."

"Did you get the word about the video camera?"

"Yep. I'll get the footage off of it as soon as I finish Julio's home invasion case."

Julio had joined CID from patrol just a few months earlier and was working burglaries, both home and auto. He'd been given this home invasion case as a bonus.

"He got lucky with that footage," I said.

Julio had told me all about it. The creep had beat the hell out of the cameras and the onsite recorder. Unfortunately for him, technology had done one better and the footage had been auto uploaded to an online storage site. As a result, there were almost crystal-clear images of the perp barging through the front door and slamming the poor homeowner with a bat before he looked directly into the camera and hit it with his Louisville slugger.

"Done!" Lionel tapped some keys and the screens went blank. He stood up. "I'll grab the camera if Marcus is done with it."

He was back in less than two minutes with the camera in its plastic evidence bag.

"Marcus has already pulled fingerprints and swabbed it for DNA." Lionel took the camera out of the bag and set it down on his desk, looking at the various output ports. He dug in a drawer that must have held a hundred different cables, finally choosing one and hooking the camera up to one of the computers on his desk.

"It has a couple of memory options. We'll see if it was recording directly to its internal memory or to a card."

"We want everything on the camera," I told him. Who knew what else we might find in the other interviews and background they had shot?

"I can record the last hour so we can view it now and record the rest later, if you want?"

"Perfect. I've never done well with delayed gratification."

Lionel grinned, then turned everything on. "There's not a memory card in the camera, so everything is on the internal memory."

Ten minutes later, we were watching the footage while he downloaded everything else on the camera.

"Seems more real when you watch it on a larger screen," I said as the murder scene played out in front of me again.

"There," I said, pointing out a few frames where there was a flash of a foot in the image. It looked as though the killer had thought about walking in front of the camera before changing their mind.

Lionel took a couple of different screenshots after we'd watched the scene several times.

"Great, we're looking for a person with a dark blur for a foot. Should be easy to find." I was disappointed, but not surprised. I'd never been as lucky as Julio to catch a criminal looking directly into the camera. "Email me the clip. I'll let

Darlene and Pete have their chance at interpreting the inkblot."

He sent it, along with the screenshots that he'd done his best to enhance.

"I'd say the footage is untouched," Lionel said. "Especially if he didn't have a chance to tamper with it after the murder."

"So the only possibility is if he faked the whole last scene."

"That's right. From the last cut to the point where it stopped recording after the murder, the sequence appears complete. Having the camera helps. He would have had to tamper with some of the identifying codes that the camera leaves on the film. It's possible, but it's more difficult since the footage was on the internal drive. The time stamp appears to be continuous."

He rattled off a lot of other technical jargon that went over my head, then said, "I can dig deeper, but that will mean doing things that will make it harder for someone to reconstruct the recording to its present state, if you know what I mean. It's like I would be analyzing a DNA sample, but I'd have to destroy it to do it."

"I see." Though I wasn't sure I really did.

"Better to wait. If it needs to be done, we can send it to a forensic lab that has the equipment to record every step they take, so that the process could be reexamined if someone like a defense attorney wanted to pick it apart."

"I get it. So the simple answer is that you believe there's a ninety or ninety-five percent chance that the footage is authentic."

"I'd say that's fair."

"Good enough."

I left his office feeling sure that Sly Harris either wasn't our man or was a criminal mastermind. I doubted the latter. When I got back to my desk, I called both Pete and Darlene to give them the scoop on the camera. We all agreed that Sly needed to be put on the back burner as a suspect of last resort.

"I want to search the house and grounds again. Finding the murder weapon has to be high on our list," I told Pete.

"With your dad giving it priority, we should be able to get a few deputies to help."

"We could get some of the firemen too. They certainly know what an axe looks like," I said, meaning no disrespect to our brothers in red.

"Good idea. I know the chief. I'll give him a call. He loves making his guys go out and do grunt work."

"I want to talk to Wells's parents again, and Bart Crenshaw. We must be missing something."

"I think we could come up with a motive for Sly if we can give him an opportunity."

"He'd need a means too. If we can't break his alibi, then we can't explain how he got rid of the axe," I reasoned.

"We either have to figure out how he fooled the camera or find a way to get another person into that locked house."

"Cara hit the nail on the head. We have the same problem that ol' Thaddeus had. How is someone getting into the Lynch house without disturbing the locks and bolts?"

"Good point. I'll go out on a limb and say it's not the same person breaking into the house now as it was ninety years ago."

"We can agree there. But if we figure out the riddle of the locked house, we might be able to exonerate Daniel Lynch of the original murders," I said.

"I'll organize the search for tomorrow morning," Pete said.

"Great. I'm going to visit Eugene and Miriam Wells again."

After I hung up with Pete, I got a text from Darzi's office letting me know that Vicky's autopsy would be held that afternoon. It would be perfect timing after my visit with the Wellses.

I used the forty-minute drive to Tallahassee to try to think the murders through. I still felt like there was a link missing between Wells's murder and Vicky's bludgeoning. They had met each other, so there was at least that one connection.

"We heard there was another murder at that house," Eugene Wells said as he walked me into their living room.

"There was. A young woman who was working on a documentary about the house's… reputation."

"You let them film there?" he asked, clearly enraged.

Miriam sat on the couch, looking tired and weary with loss. "We got a call from that man. Sly. He wanted to interview us. He wanted to talk about my son's problems."

"I'm sorry about that. But if the owner of the house was willing to let them be there, then we really couldn't do anything to stop them from filming," I explained.

"You saw how many people were at Gregory's funeral?" Miriam said with bitterness. "Only my niece came into town. No friends. None of our extended family. My brother told me that we're better off now that he's dead."

"Be fair, Miriam. He didn't exactly say that," Eugene told her.

"Same as," she hissed. "Now there are people who want to publicize all of Gregory's problems. They aren't interested in the twenty-nine years that he was brilliant and hard working. Just about his craziness, being homeless and dying on the front porch of an old house that's supposedly haunted."

"I don't think Sly Harris will be rushing to get this documentary done now," I said.

"We've had a dozen calls already from news stations and two different TV shows, one a true crime show and the other a ghost show," Eugene told me. He sounded as though he were close to a breaking point.

"I understand your exasperation with the… gawkers. If they start harassing you, call the Tallahassee Police Department and report them. Or if you want, you can call me and I'll talk to TPD about it." I felt bad for them, having had all the problems with their son while he was alive and now having to deal with the aftermath of his gruesome murder.

"It's just everything," Miriam said. "I thought I'd already dealt with the loss of my son when we'd refused to see him again. Now here I am. Some piece of me deep in my core must have longed for him to return. To come back to us the way he was—smart, healthy, loving Gregory. I must have believed that a miracle could happen. How laughable. How could any part of me be so stupid?" She began to cry for her son and for herself.

I felt helpless that I had nothing to offer these people.

"Funny," Eugene said. "We did get one card of condolence from his old company. I guess his social security number triggered something and the HR department sent it automatically. They also let us know that he had some money in a 401(k) that he must have forgot about or couldn't figure out how to raid. Fifteen thousand dollars." Mr. Wells had drifted over to the coffee table and picked up a corporate condolence card. "I didn't know that a car logo could be incorporated into a mourning wreath."

"You said that his mental illness came on when he was almost thirty, and that he held down a good job with U.S. Auto. Where was he living?"

"Nashville, where they had a large design and development office."

"Do you recognize this woman?" I showed them a picture of Vicky Bradford that Sly had texted to me. Vicky was five years younger than Gregory Wells. I wondered if they could have known each other earlier in their lives. Maybe when they'd met last week, something had been rekindled. Of course, that still didn't explain who killed them. I made a note to ask Sly and Vicky's family whether she'd also moved on from her marriage as her ex had apparently done. Maybe someone had seen Vicky and Wells together and had killed them as a result of a jealous rage.

Eugene looked closely at the photo. "No, I don't think

so. Was that the woman who was killed?"

"Yes. Her name was Vicky Bradford."

"No, I don't think Gregory ever mentioned anyone by that name."

"We have some emails from him," Miriam said, standing up. "I've got a nephew that's almost as clever as Gregory. He can probably get them all together somehow and send them to you."

"That would be very helpful." Learning more about Wells's past could help, though we had no way of knowing if his murder was related to something from ten days ago or ten years ago.

"I'll text you Martin's number and you can talk to him." Eugene took out his phone and I noticed that his hands shook as he tapped the screen. I called him to save him the time inputting my number.

We talked for a while longer, then I made my excuses and left them to their grief.

I made it to the autopsy as they were finishing the external examination of the body.

"Glad you could make it," Dr. Darzi said as I came in. Again, Andre was assisting with the autopsy.

"I'm dancing as fast as I can," I said, wincing at the sight of Vicky's body.

"This is savage. Worse than the other one."

"Escalation?"

"You're the detective," he said. "By my count, seventeen blows with a hatchet or small axe."

"Is it the same weapon as was used on Gregory Wells?"

"Nothing rules that out. The measurements I've taken here are consistent with those on Wells's forehead and back."

"Are there any signs of drug use?" I was thinking of Wells and his addictions.

"Nothing obvious. Her teeth and gums are in very good

condition. No track marks anywhere, including places where people typically inject if they are trying to hide their habit."

"Anything unusual?" I was willing to grasp at straws at this point.

"No. And no signs of recent sexual activity of any kind."

"Then I'm out of questions." I felt at a loss. Where was the evidence? Two brutal killings with nothing concrete on which to anchor the investigation. Maybe a ghost *did* kill them. *With a ghost hatchet*, I thought darkly.

"When I saw this body come in and heard on the news that the house was famous for another set of axe murders, I did a little research."

"I'm shocked," I joked. Dr. Darzi was the most curious individual I knew and well known for digging into esoterica.

"I haven't found any autopsy photos from the historical murders. However, I did find a dozen crime scene photos online. Two in particular had very high resolution." He clicked some keys on the laptop he used to display his notes and X-rays on monitors hung from the ceiling. Two sepia-toned pictures appeared. The first showed the body of a woman. Or I should say, it showed a body, and I assumed that it was a woman because it was in a nightgown. But it was certainly impossible to tell from the face, as the head was deformed from heavy blows. The second photo showed an axe covered in dark stains leaning against a wall, a sheriff's deputy standing beside it.

"That's the original murder weapon? Looks bigger than what was used here."

"Exactly. You are a better student than I thought," Darzi said with a smile. "You can see the size of the axe compared to the man in this photo. Also, you can see how much damage was done to the woman's head simply from the weight of this weapon." He paused. "What you're looking for is smaller. Here are several examples." He switched the images to three different hatchets. They were all slightly larger than a modern camping hatchet.

I made notes and took pictures to use for the search,

wondering about Mr. Tippets's missing hatchet. Then I excused myself before Darzi began retrieving and weighing the organs. I'd had my fill of blood and guts.

Coming back into town, I drove by the Lynch house. What I saw made me worry even more about Mr. and Mrs. Wells and the family of Vicky Bradford. There were three news trucks parked along the street with presenters standing on the lawn, trying to get shots without the others showing up in the background. All three were from stations within a hundred miles of Calhoun, but I was sure that some of the stories would be picked up by the national affiliates.

I had let several calls go to my voicemail that day from news organizations. Dad would field most of the interviews, though there were always those reporters who were a little hungrier and would try to find a peon like me to talk to, thinking that we might be stupid enough to say something that wasn't part of the company line. Not me. I didn't talk to reporters unless ordered to.

Later that night, I got a call from Pete.

"I want your thoughts on something," he said.

"Personal or professional?"

"It's this business with Terri Miller and Jessie seeing her on the security video."

"What about it?" I was dangling a toy mouse for Ghost as I talked.

"I brought in those two friends of Terri's. They each thought that it looked like Terri, but they couldn't be sure. Who could with what you can see on film? The problem is, I don't want to show that footage to her mother." I could tell how upset he was.

"I don't see how you can keep it from her."

"You know what it's going to do to the poor woman. We've both seen families on these emotional roller coasters," Pete said sadly.

"You're right. Even famous cases, like those pictures that were found down at Panacea that they thought were of a girl who'd gone missing out in Arizona. I remember they aired the case on *Unsolved Mysteries* and the mother said she'd looked at dozens of pictures that might or might not have been her daughter. I can't imagine what that would be like."

"That's my point. You saw the footage. Is there any way that Jessie could really be as sure as she says she is?"

"I don't see it. The video isn't great and there's that funky angle from the ceiling. All that said, I think the mother would want to know. I'm sure that mother out in Arizona would be willing to look at a hundred more photos if there was even a slim chance it would help her understand what happened to her daughter."

"I get that," Pete said. "I just hate to hurt her for what's probably a wild goose chase. Still, I guess I'll tell her. Besides, she'll probably hear about it anyway. I've asked everyone to keep this quiet, but eventually word will get out."

"You're right to keep it quiet for as long as you can. If that really is the missing Terri Miller, she might be hiding for a reason, and if she hears that someone recognized her, then she might do another runner and this time go farther away."

"That's another reason I doubt it could be her. We've carpeted this town with missing person flyers. How could she stay off the radar?"

"Best place to hide something is in plain sight."

"I'm not really buying that. If that is Terri, then she was probably just passing through. I'll get with her mother tomorrow. Speaking of tomorrow, I got a commitment for twenty firefighters and ten LEOs. I've told everyone to meet at nine o'clock at the Lynch house."

I thanked him and went back to entertaining Ghost. Then Cara came into the living room and immediately took over playing with the spastic kitten.

"Hey! I was playing with him," I protested.

"No, you weren't. You were talking to Pete." She waved a feather up and over the top of Ghost's head, causing the kitten to fall over backward.

"Ghost, did you see who killed Gregory Wells?" I asked,

attempting to lure him away from Cara's toy.

"You have your own cat."

"Ivy never played. Even when she was younger." I looked over to the chair where she was lying. She opened one eye as though she knew we were talking about her. "You could go play with Alvin."

"He's sound asleep. Eating and watching the kitten are the only things he's interested in. Are you any closer to a good suspect?"

"With the locked house problem, we don't have anyone who had the opportunity to kill Vicky. With Wells, it's the opposite problem. Anyone could have murdered him. On top of that, motives are thin for both. I just keep coming back to there being some big piece of the puzzle that's missing."

And that's where I was at three in the morning when my brain and bladder decided to wake me up. For the better part of an hour, I went back and forth on how the murders could be related. The idea that they could both be completely random was an unsatisfying answer. Could Vicky have been the main target and Wells the secondary? If so, how did it happen that his murder had occurred first?

Normally, if there are primary and secondary targets, the murders usually happen very close to each other. The secondary target has usually interfered with the killer reaching the primary, or the killer believes that the secondary can identify them, so it's a threat that needs to be eliminated. Could that have been the case here? Was Wells somehow blocking the killer from reaching Vicky? 'Round and 'round my brain went, getting absolutely nowhere.

CHAPTER TWENTY-TWO

I was up and out early so I could get to the office and clear out my emails, and any urgent business related to the other cases that were filling up my inbox, before I went out to join the search for the murder weapon.

When my phone said it was eight o'clock, I decided that it was late enough for me to call Gregory Wells's cousin, Martin.

"What time is it?" he growled, sounding like he was coming out of a deep sleep.

"A little after eight," I said, being helpful.

"That's not possible. It's still dark," he argued.

I cringed, realizing that I hadn't Googled the area code. *My bad*, I thought. "I guess you aren't in the Eastern Time zone."

"Who *is* this?"

"I'm Deputy Larry Macklin with the Adams County Sheriff's Office."

"Oh, right. Okay, give me a minute." I heard noises that suggested a trip to the bathroom, followed by a drink of water. "I'm in Portland, Oregon."

"Sorry. I just got it into my head that you weren't that far from Tallahassee."

"I travel a lot for my job, so I get by to see my aunt and uncle pretty regular. I wished I could have made it to my cousin's funeral. Business just didn't work out."

"Your aunt and uncle said you might be able to help with getting some of Gregory's old emails from the time when… I mean before he… had his problems."

"I'm glad you're taking his death seriously. I know you could just dismiss it as a homeless guy meeting a bad end. Gregory was so much more than that. I guess all homeless people are more than their homelessness, but Gregory was brilliant. Reading his emails will give you some idea. I just wish there was a way for you to go back and talk to him. I'm smart. He was *miles* above me. The first time I saw him after the onset of his mental illness was frankly terrifying. The man I knew was gone." He paused and it sounded like he was fighting back tears at the memory of his cousin.

"It was funny, though. He'd have moments, days, even weeks, when he would, like, come back and almost be himself. At first his parents would see those flashes of the old Gregory and it would give them hope that everything could go back to the way it was. In the end, it was all just fate's cruel joke on them."

I thought of Terri Miller's mother. How cruel was it of Jessie to insist that it was Terri in the video? I shook off that thought and said, "I'm particularly looking for any mention of a woman named Vicky Bradford. She was killed on Friday night in the same house where Gregory was killed."

"Wow! Yeah, sure. I archived all of his emails years ago when his parents wanted them as a way to remember the old Gregory. He never used email again after the disease took control. He had a whole set of conspiracy theories based on emails. Most of them were… well, crazy. Again, he was brilliant and a few of his theories weren't that off the wall. The long and short of it is, I can even do a name search through them. I'll send you everything tomorrow at the latest."

I thanked him and apologized again for waking him.

I had to rush to get to the Lynch house by nine. Pete had outdone himself by providing coffee and several dozen donuts for the helpers.

"I'll expect to be reimbursed from your first sergeant's paycheck," he told me.

"Stop it! I'm serious," I growled at him. I didn't understand why everyone seemed to think I was going to get the sergeant's position. I hoped that Cara wouldn't hear about it. I didn't want her thinking that there was a chance I'd get a promotion.

Just as we were getting ready to review the ground rules and what items we were searching for, I looked over and saw Dad being pulled toward the group by the largest sled dog in the world.

"I heard about the search and decided to bring him along."

"He is a rotten tracking dog," I said.

"The firemen love him," Dad said with a smile. Sure enough, every single one of the firemen knew Mauser by name and had to have their turn wrestling with him, including the two women.

"He's a bloody distraction," I pronounced.

We finally got everyone's attention and listed the items we were looking for, specifically a hatchet, a cell phone or a laptop. They were also to call one of us if they saw anything that could be evidence. At last we got everyone organized into several groups. Each one would form a line to sweep the grounds and surrounding areas.

Once the search started, I went inside and walked through the house again. Without any personal possessions, the house just wasn't that hard to search. I poked and prodded every bolt, knocked on the walls and looked hard at the two fireplaces. Nothing. Finally, I went upstairs and found the hatch that opened into the attic. It was ten feet up and there wasn't a ladder anywhere to be seen. I doubted the crawlspace was that big, and what would someone do once they were up there? Crawl out on the roof and leap down twenty-five feet?

I went back and joined the searchers. In three hours, we'd covered a thousand feet around the house.

"We found some items, but nothing that screams evidence," Pete said.

"I checked inside the house again. Did someone look underneath it?"

"Yeah, there wasn't anything."

"Then I guess we're done here."

I got back to the office and spent most of the day covering other work that was piling up. Around two, I saw Pete leading Mrs. Miller down the hall toward Lionel's office. I didn't envy him that experience. No matter what the outcome, it was going to be a nightmare for the mother until her child was found.

As proof that sometimes miracles *do* happen, Tommy Romano's lawyer called me back at four o'clock.

"I saw that you'd left a message," Kassim French said stiffly. There was a very refined European accent hidden in his English.

"Yes, we're investigating Mr. Romano's death."

"Mrs. Romano told me. She also asked me to cooperate with you in any way I can. Let me say that you can help us as well. If you uncover evidence that the truck driver was at fault, or that there was a failure to maintain the truck, we would be most interested."

"What about the car?"

"The car?"

"Mr. Romano's BMW. What if *it* failed in some way?"

"Of course. Though since I know that Tommy maintained his car in excellent condition, and with BMW's reputation..." I could almost hear him shrug over the phone.

"What I'm most interested in are the threats that Mr. Romano received from his business associates."

"Mrs. Romano mentioned that. I will say that the threats were of the general nature that one expects from… those with hotter blood and less education. Also, intimidation is a standard bartering practice in some parts of the world."

"Where did he do business?"

"Mostly small countries that had been a part of the Soviet Union. Cheap labor, but with a little touch of Old World tradition." French sounded like he was reciting a sales slogan. "There were also a few contacts in the Middle East."

"So you don't think that any of them would carry out their threats?"

"I don't see the profit in it. Particularly if they were going to disguise it as an accident. Don't get me wrong, these men can be very dangerous if pushed. However, if they kill you then they want the whole world, or at least their world, to know about it."

"As a message to others," I mused.

"Yes, exactly. Gun down a whole family, that's their type of thing. They also like bombs, but not in this country. They don't like to rouse the attention of the ATF and Homeland Security."

"I'd still like you to make a short list of the most dangerous ones," I said, then a thought occurred to me. "Did Tommy Romano ever threaten anyone?"

There was a long and telling silence at the other end of the call.

"Can I take that for a yes?"

"No comment." I didn't see any point in pressing him.

"How did he and his wife get along?" I realized that if I was going to look at the death as a possible homicide, then I should look at Mrs. Romano as a suspect too.

"Like any married couple, they had their fights. I will say that neither of them ever talked about divorce."

"If you would send me a list of the worst of the threats, I'd appreciate it."

"Of course," he said and I gave him my email.

That night I cooked burgers for dinner. They were made from deer meat provided by a friend who spent a good part of every fall sitting up in a tree.

"They're better grilled," I commented on my own cooking.

"It's too dark to grill out."

After I finished my second burger, I leaned back in my chair. "Tomorrow is Halloween," I blurted.

"Did you just now realize this?" Cara asked with raised eyebrows.

"My mind has been wrapped up in these murders."

"It's not like we're going to get any trick-or-treaters out here."

"No. I was thinking about the Lynch house. I probably need to do something to protect it. And make sure that our killer doesn't use the holiday to get number three."

"That's a creepy thought." Cara shuddered.

"One look at the bodies and you'd know that we aren't dealing with a sane person."

"Could it be someone that Wells met in the hospital?"

"Maybe. He was in several institutions and three or four rehabs. It's possible that he met someone crazier than him."

My phone rang before I could pursue that thought any further. I looked at the screen and saw that it was Julio. "What's up?"

"I just arrested a couple of perps you might want to talk to. If I'm right, they're the guys you're looking for in the Wells murder."

"Excellent. I'm on my way."

"Bye," Cara sighed good-naturedly as I got up from the table.

"I'm sorry about the dishes. If you leave them, I'll do them when I get home."

"You cooked. I'll clean up." She shooed me out the door.

I got to the jail just as Julio was finishing up the paperwork.

"I didn't know if they were your guys until I rounded them up. They've been busting into cars at night," Julio told me.

"Are you done with them?"

"They're all yours. They'll be arraigned in the morning. If you need them held any longer than that, just let me know. There are at least two or three more charges we could drop on them."

"Which one is the most likely to talk?"

Julio took the flyer I'd handed out to the all the deputies and pointed to a dark haired guy with narrow, haunted eyes. "His name is Benny Vasquez, AKA Speck. Twenty years old and a smart aleck who isn't too smart. As soon as I put a little bit of pressure on him, he started talking as fast as his lips could move."

I thanked him and arranged with the sergeant at the desk to have Benny brought up to an interview room.

"You look like you've had a hard night," I told Benny when we were both seated in the interview room.

He hurled a number of naughty words at me before looking down at the table.

"I'm actually here on a whole different matter. This one could have you wearing state-issued clothing for the rest of your life." That was enough to get him to look up at me. I thought for a minute that he was going to start cursing again until I looked into his eyes and saw real fear.

"What 'chu talkin' about? I never did nothin' but steal shit."

"We'll start with a question to which I already know the answer. If you lie, then we'll go down a very dark path which ends with you spending time at Raiford," I explained. He was back to studying the table. "Do you understand me?" That got a nod. "Good enough. Did you and your buddies beat up this man?" I showed him the best picture I had of Gregory Wells. It was one from when he had been booked into the Leon County jail several years earlier.

Benny looked at the picture, but there was no reaction.

"I need an answer."

Nothing.

"Remember what I said. I can see the road that leads to you being a permanent resident of the state prison." I pointed my finger at him.

"Maybe."

"Maybe what?"

"We beat up a few guys. Guys who wanted to buy drugs and bums. 'Specially bums."

"So many that you don't remember who you beat up?"

"They all look alike, the bums."

"Well, this particular bum is dead."

This caused his head to jerk up, his attention fully focused on me. "No! No way I killed someone!"

"Where were you on the evening of Thursday, October 19?"

"That wasn't when we beat him up."

"But that's when he was killed."

"Wasn't us. We didn't do nothin' else to him." Benny was shaking his head vigorously.

"Where were you that night?"

"We weren't here."

"Where were you? Remember, we're talking prison for a long, long time."

"We went down to Tampa. We were gone 'til, like, Saturday."

"You have any receipts?"

He put his head down on the table.

"I need proof," I told him.

"What do you think we were doing down there?" he said without lifting his head.

"Drugs?"

"Just a little something to set us up for a month or so. Not a big deal. Don't, man. I can't serve a long sentence."

"If I get some proof, I'll say that you cooperated with my investigation."

"What's that mean?"

"It means that the State Attorney and any judge you face won't be pissed off at you."

"Check my bags. They were in the car when we were arrested. I stuff shit in there. We ate out all the time. I even paid for the gas one time."

"We'll check it out." Then I showed him the picture of Vicky Bradford. "Do you recognize this woman?" His eyes were completely blank. I didn't have to have him hooked up to a polygraph to see that his heart rate didn't react. This kid was an open book, and he'd obviously never seen Vicky in his life.

"No."

"One more question. Have you ever seen your friends or anyone else with a hatchet?"

His face stayed blank. "A hatchet? No, man, not since I was a kid. I did the Boy Scout thing for a year." He seemed pleased with that remarkable accomplishment. I had to restrain myself from asking if he got a merit badge in dickhead.

"Okay." I stood up. "I'll be back if those receipts don't check out." I was sure they would. The odds were good that they were off the board as suspects.

I stopped by the Fast Mart and bought a pint of ice cream as a *mea culpa* to Cara for running out after dinner. I felt even worse since it had turned out to be a wild goose chase. *Not true. Eliminating suspects is almost as good as nailing them*, I reminded myself.

I got home before Cara had gone to bed, which gave us a chance to enjoy our frozen fat and calories out on the front porch under the stars.

"These cases are confusing. I feel like I'm working half blind with one hand tied behind my back."

"I think you're mixing your metaphors again."

"It's getting to be a habit. These cases are mixed up too," I grumbled.

We saved enough for all three of our furry housemates to get a spoonful of ice cream. As I watched Ghost play with his ice cream, half licking it and half batting it across the floor, a tiny bulb lit somewhere in the back of my brain.

What am I thinking about? Something to do with Ghost? With cats? With ice cream? I couldn't get a hook in it and hoped that I'd remember whatever I was hiding in the back of my mind sometime during the night, which happened frequently.

I slept intermittently, waking every couple of hours to spend time alternately trying to bring up from the depths of my mind whatever it was I thought I remembered, and trying to see what was missing from my two cases. I didn't get any answers, only a poor night's rest.

CHAPTER TWENTY-THREE

Sitting at my desk on the morning of Halloween, I felt at loose ends. I had this pot of ingredients that didn't make a meal. Two pots, if you counted the accident investigation. I decided that if I was going to continue with my cooking analogies, I needed some food. It was eleven o'clock when I decided to head down to records for no other reason than to see if Beth Miller had brought in any baked goods. She almost always had a plate of some kind of cookies or muffins.

Just as I came around the corner, I saw Dad stuffing the last bite of a raspberry muffin into his face.

"I hope that wasn't the last one," I said with a heavy dose of woe-is-me.

"You snooze, you lose," Dad said, winking one of his bright green eyes at Beth.

"See how he is? When I was a kid, if I was late for dinner I had to go to bed hungry," I told her and she smiled at me.

"If you're starving, I've got a few leftover cookies on my desk," Beth said.

"Yes, please."

"Such a polite boy," she said, heading for her desk.

"Only when he wants something," Dad quipped.

"The only thing I want today is a snack," I said. "And a break in a case."

"I'm going to guess that there hasn't been any progress on the Lynch house murders."

"I'd tell you if there was. I'd like to tell you that we're making progress, but I'm really just treading water."

"Cases can be like that. Seems like you aren't getting anywhere and then something comes along to break it wide open."

"Fingers crossed," I said, taking the sandwich bag of cookies that Beth handed to me. I was looking at them, imagining how good they would taste.

"They're chocolate-fudge-coconut-cinnamon cookies. I know that sounds like too much, but just try one," she urged.

I took one out of the bag and bit into it. "Amazing" would have been my one-word description. I was so absorbed in tasting the cookie that it barely registered when Dad asked me a question.

"…the accident," he said as I caught the last couple of words.

"The what?"

"The accident case. Toomey said you were working on it. Can we finally take that one out of the inbox?"

"Maybe," I said. "Probably. I think there's something there, I just don't think we're going to be able to track it down. His sister wants us to go after some guys in Eastern Europe or the Middle East who threatened him."

"We aren't Interpol." Dad frowned.

"Something bugs me about it. And I'm not just digging into it because I had a crush on the wife back in elementary school."

"What?" Dad's eyebrows lifted as far as they would go. "This is the first I'm hearing about this?"

"I told you… Well, maybe I didn't. Sherry Romano. I knew her back in sixth grade."

"Romano? What was her maiden name?"

"O'Neal."

"Sherry O'Neal?" Dad looked utterly shocked.

"Yeah, she moved away before sixth grade was over. I had big plans to ask her on a date, or whatever you do when you're in sixth grade." I was rambling on while Dad just stood two feet away, staring at me with his mouth hanging open. I stopped talking.

He chuckled. "You better be glad you never went out with that wildcat. Do you know why she moved away?"

"I don't remember," I said, trying to think back. *What is Dad talking about?* I wondered.

"You must have known back then. Everybody did. She stabbed a teacher."

"What?" As soon as he said it, some faint images stirred just below the surface of the murky pond that was my memory.

"She had to stay after school. I don't remember all the details. Something about her hating the feel of chalk on her hands and the teacher telling her that she couldn't leave until she'd done some equations on the blackboard. At some point, she picked up the knife he had brought with his lunch. It was just a table knife, but she managed to stick it all the way into his kidney. Damn near killed him. There was a plea deal. Moving to Tallahassee was part of the deal."

Now it was my turn to let my mouth hang open. Everything changed in that moment. "I guess there's no chance of seeing the case file?"

"It would have been sealed when she turned eighteen. There wouldn't be anything on her record," Dad confirmed.

"I wonder about any other offenses," I mumbled to myself.

"You didn't run her?"

"It was an accident! She wasn't even at the scene." I was having a hard time processing all of this new information. Could Sherry have been involved in the accident? Did a crazy act when she was in elementary school add up to a murder twenty-odd years later? When Dad had told me about the attack, it felt like a game changer, but was it really? Kids could do crazy things, which was why records got sealed when they were eighteen to protect them from having to live down a criminal act committed when they weren't fully responsible. I began to calm down, realizing that I needed to look at everything in a reasoned way. *No flying off the handle*, I told myself.

"I'd say you still have some work to do," Dad told me. "That said, don't let this distract you from the Lynch murders. I've had four calls from reporters this morning." He grabbed one of my cookies and left.

"Did you need something else?" Beth asked.

"No, I just came down for the cookies," I said over my shoulder as I headed back to my desk, my mind racing furiously through all the new information.

Pete was at his desk as I came by.

"Cookies?" He pointed to the bag. I took one and handed him the bag. Then I explained what I'd just learned.

"Seems a stretch from a child stabber to an adult brake-line cutter."

"The brakes weren't cut. Just the opposite."

Pete nodded, happy with a bag of cookies in his hand and with the knowledge that it wasn't his case.

"What happened yesterday with Terri Miller's mom?" I asked.

He set the cookies aside and sighed. "Exactly what I was afraid of. She couldn't be sure. Who could? But she felt like it was possible. I saw her get excited. More excited than the video warranted. I pushed the information out to all our deputies that there's been a possible sighting. They're to detain the woman for her health and welfare if she's seen again, then contact me immediately. This morning, I found myself driving through the neighborhoods around the Fast Mart like there was a chance I'd spot her."

"I'll keep my eyes out."

"Tell Jessie not to get herself too involved in this. Those neighborhoods aren't great."

"I'll tell her." He was right. Jessie had a tendency to go rolling out on her own if she didn't think everyone was taking her seriously. She'd gotten into trouble before.

I looked at my email and saw a file with attachments from Wells's cousin. Before I opened it, I ran a background check on Sherry Romano, finding a few minor violations. A couple of them looked like the type of offense that could represent a plea bargain. Minor assault, malicious damage, all five years old or older. Everything dealt with and clear. The Leon County Sheriff's Office had been the responding agency in the cases, so I sent them a records request, but it would be tomorrow at the earliest before I got those reports. I resolved to concentrate on the Wells and Bradford murders in the meantime.

I opened the email from Marvin and downloaded the attachments. After sorting through them, I knew that this was going to be time-consuming.

All of the emails were personal. The accompanying message from Marvin said that he hadn't found any mention of Vicky Bradford in any of the emails. He also said that he had not sent any emails that dealt specifically with U.S. Auto business, since Gregory had signed a confidentiality agreement when he was hired.

After going through a hundred of the thousands of emails, it was obvious that there were two kinds. There were those to family and friends who weren't tech savvy, and then there were those to his techie family and friends. The techie ones often talked in general terms about what he and the recipient were doing at work. From these, it was clear that Wells had been as smart as everyone said. Most, if not all, of the tech stuff went above my head. What I was surprised to learn was that he'd also been involved in network security. Some of the emails were warnings about hackers and malware. I wondered if that hadn't fed the paranoid part of his schizophrenia.

Like everyone's emails, they were mostly pleasantries mixed with personal business that must have seemed important at the time. I came across no bombshells that would blow the case wide open, or even push the door open a crack. At least none that I recognized at the moment.

I sat back in my chair and rubbed my eyes. After two hours of going through the emails, my eyes were sore and I just needed to get up and move around. It was past one and I decided to go out for lunch. I texted Darlene and asked her if she'd like to meet me at the taco stand. I got a thumbs-up emoji and: *10 min.*

I'd just ordered when she pulled up.

"I got your order, Chief," the cashier yelled out to Darlene.

"My man can bring it," she said, pointing to me while she took a seat at one of the picnic tables.

"Your man?" I frowned as I carried the food to the table.

"Don't get your tail ruffled. Pass me some of that good stuff." Darlene dug into her food.

I gave her a rundown of the information I'd gotten from the Wells emails.

Darlene stopped eating and put her taco down. "On my list of horrible things to happen to a family, that one makes the top ten. You say he was really smart?"

"Like super smart. Computers, electronics, all the high-tech stuff."

"I guess that explains the notes and all the odds and ends in his bags."

"You're right. There *were* some odd electronics in there. I might want to take another look at it. His cousin did say that he could have lucid moments, especially if he was on medication."

"Didn't Bart say that he fixed his cell phone?" Darlene asked, finishing her taco.

"That's right. Like I said, he must have still had some high-functioning moments."

After lunch, I headed back to the office. I decided to go straight back to the evidence room and ran into Pete on the way. "You want to come look through some of the stuff that we took out of Wells's nest?" I asked.

"Sure."

Shantel pulled out the boxes for us. She ran the evidence room with an iron fist when it came to access and organization, which was just the way it should be.

"This is funny." In his gloved hands, Pete was holding a plastic Supersave shopping bag with various food stuffs in it.

"What?"

"These crackers." He pulled a box out of the bag. "And these." He held up a box of S'mores Oreos.

"What about them?"

"They don't sell either of these at Supersave."

"So?"

"They don't sell them anywhere in this county. You have to go to a Publix in Tallahassee."

"How do you know that?"

He gave me a look. "One, these are my favorite captain's wafers. I make Sarah go out of her way to get them for me at Publix. Two, Jenny loves S'mores everything. Her birthday was a month ago. Sarah had seen these Oreos somewhere and asked me to pick some up for Jenny's party. I drove all over town, including asking at the Supersave, and found out that their distributor didn't think they'd sell here, so they don't carry them."

It slowly dawned on me where he was going with this. "So where did a homeless man get those Oreos and crackers? He couldn't just drive over to Tallahassee."

"Someone gave them to him." Pete looked at the expiration dates. "These must be fairly new. They don't expire for almost a year."

I pulled out my phone and called Reverend Tolliver. He told me that they just got items from the Supersave for their food bank and most of the time the expiration dates were approaching. He found Bart Crenshaw and put him on the phone.

"When can I get out of this joint?" Bart shouted into the phone.

"Soon. Did Gory get food from anyone?"

There was silence on Bart's end of the call.

"Hello?" I asked.

"I'm thinking," he groused. "He was hoarding some goodies. Sometimes he'd share with me, but he got real snippy when I wanted to know where he got the good stuff."

"Think, now. Did he say anything else about the food?"

"Just that he'd earned it."

"Earned it?"

"I figured he meant that he'd panhandled the money for it. That's how we got most of our cash."

I asked a few more questions that he wasn't able to answer. I was about to end the call when one more question came to mind. "Did you ever see him with a woman?"

"Gory?" Crenshaw gave a little snort of laughter, which I thought was all he was going to have to say on the subject, then he added, "No woman would go anywhere with him. Now, he did mention one that he got money from occasionally, but I never saw her. Happens that way sometimes. You get a regular mark. People make it personal. I've had a couple angels from time to time."

I hung up the phone and was left with a funny feeling in my gut. Had Sherry Romano been Wells's angel? Had she been the one bringing him food? And, if so, why had she been helping a homeless paranoid schizophrenic? A homeless paranoid schizophrenic who used to work for a car company as an expert on hacking?

I called Eugene Wells. "Does the name Sherry Romano or Sherry O'Neal sound familiar?"

"Maybe. Let me ask Miriam. She's got a lot better memory for names." I heard them talking in the background. "Miriam says that Gregory had a girlfriend in high school. Her name was Sherry O'Neal."

"Would you put your wife on?" Once she was on the phone, I asked, "Do you remember her?"

"I certainly do. I didn't like her. She was... manipulative. It was Gregory's first real girlfriend, which just made it worse. It took almost a year for him to wise up to her. I can tell you, I spent most of that time biting my tongue."

"Where did they go to high school?"

"Leon High here in Tallahassee."

I thanked her and hung up. Then I called Sergeant Toomey.

"I hope we still have the electronic control units from the BMW," I said, and went on to explain my suspicions

"I've heard they can be hacked," Toomey said thoughtfully.

"I'm going down to talk to Lionel."

I found Lionel in his office talking on the phone.

"It's an upgrade." Pause. "Everyone hates it." He looked at me and rolled his eyes. "I can't make it go back to the way it was." He hung the phone up and shook his head. "Major Parks isn't happy with Windows's latest upgrade."

"Is it possible for someone to hack into the computer system in a car?" I asked hurriedly.

"Absolutely. You can buy a device online that will let you make all kinds adjustments to your car, like make it so all your doors unlock on the first click of the remote, or turn off that constant buzzing nag about your seatbelt. Once they get access, a good hacker could do almost anything if he understood the coding."

I pulled up some of Gregory's emails to his tech buddies and let him scan through them.

"Yeah, this guy is smart enough. This was a few years ago, but what they are doing today is built on the foundation of what was being done ten years ago."

"Could a hacker make the brakes engage?"

"I would think so. Most new cars today have emergency braking systems that are run by the car's brain. Triggering that wouldn't be beyond a hacker. You think that's what happened with the bridge accident?"

I nodded. "Maybe. How would they time it?"

"A fancy car like that BMW, it was only a couple of years old. It would have a satellite uplink for navigation and sending information back to BMW." He paused. "Wait! A better idea would be through the driver's phone. He probably had his phone connected via Bluetooth, so if you hacked the systems, you might be able to remotely see what the forward and rear-facing cameras were seeing. Then, when the time is right, you trigger the brakes."

I looked at Lionel like he'd just told me there were rattlesnakes living in my car. "That's creepy as hell," I said.

"Modern technology is a double-edged sword. People have proven that cars can be hacked just like insulin pumps or pacemakers."

"Great. How do I prove it?"

"The guy's phone would show a trail and, of course, the car's control units could tell. But didn't you say they were damaged?"

"Yes. Big bucks to try and recover the data."

"And even if you recover the data and there are signs of hacking, a defense attorney could get an expert or two who would testify that the damage made any information retrieved unreliable."

I texted Darlene and Pete: *I think I know what happened. Not how everything happened, but why and who. Can we meet this afternoon?*

CHAPTER TWENTY-FOUR

We met at our office at three-thirty. Darlene and Pete both looked like they'd had a long day, but I was fully energized.

"Sherry Romano," I said when both of them were sitting down in the conference room.

"Who's Sherry Romano?" Darlene asked.

"She's the widow of the guy killed in the truck accident," Pete told her.

"Not an accident. The car's electronic control units were hacked by Gregory Wells."

They both leaned forward.

"The homeless guy?" Darlene asked.

"He worked for U.S. Auto in their research and development department, which at that time most certainly would have included electronic security."

"Why did he hack Romano's car?" Pete asked.

"He did it for Sherry Romano."

"She was having an affair with Wells? That doesn't seem likely," Darlene said.

"They were a couple back in high school."

This got both of them to raise their eyebrows.

"The food. She was buying him the food," Pete said.

"What food?" Darlene asked and Pete explained.

"So, for old time's sake and some cookies, he killed her husband." Darlene frowned. "I'm going to play devil's advocate on this one."

"We need that. There are a lot of moving parts and not a lot of evidence at this point. I wanted us to get together to discuss how to move forward," I said. Getting a warrant to search Sherry's house was going to be high on the agenda. Would she slip up and leave something incriminating in the house?

"I see where you're going. I guess she killed Vicky because of something she'd seen or heard?" Darlene asked.

"The copy of the interview with Wells was edited, which leads me to think that Vicky might have figured it out and was going to blackmail Sherry with something that they filmed. Something that Sly didn't see or didn't recognize for what it was."

"The Wells and Bradford murders were brutal. Do you think she's capable of hacking someone to death with a hatchet?"

"When she was in elementary school she almost killed her teacher with a table knife."

"Now you're talking," Darlene said.

I told them the rest of her history.

"I've got a call in to Romano's sister. I think that she suspects her sister-in-law."

"I thought she was pointing her finger at angry business associates," Pete said.

"She was scared. I don't think she'd have been that worried about faceless, nameless clients from halfway around the world who were upset at her brother."

"Anything else?" Darlene asked.

"Evidence? No."

"Did you say that the data on the car's computers could be recovered?" Pete said.

"Maybe, for a price."

"I think we're going to need that before a judge will issue a search warrant." Darlene was right.

"We know what we'd be looking for—the computer that was used to trigger the car to engage its emergency braking system."

"If there is any evidence from the car, you could get a warrant, but without that… Or maybe witnesses that saw Wells and Sherry together." Pete frowned.

"Or the evidence that Vicky had." I was frustrated. Sherry had done a good job of covering her tracks so far. Was it luck? Could we find where she'd made a mistake? If we couldn't, what would a judge let us do? A phone tap? I wasn't even sure what good that would do. She didn't appear to have any living accomplices.

"What's the motive?" Darlene asked.

"I ran a credit check on Tommy Romano. He's very solvent. I can ask his sister about the size of the estate when I talk to her."

"Any signs of trouble in the marriage?" Pete asked.

"Nothing that has come out so far. Again, the sister might be able to give us something."

"There's your way forward. Talk to the sister for motive and past history. Move forward with analyzing the car's ECUs and try to find some of the other evidence, like whatever Vicky knew," Darlene said.

"I hate to bring up a sore spot, but have you figured out how she had an opportunity to kill Vicky?" Pete asked.

"We talked about that. I think there is a tie-in with the original murders."

"What?" Darlene asked.

"Not the murderer, but the way access was gained to the house." I explained about the stolen money and the Lynch boy's possible innocence.

"Lucky for you, you don't have to even deal with the Vicky Bradford murder. As long as Sherry doesn't have an alibi for the time that Wells was murdered, then she'd have the opportunity. That porch was wide open to anyone coming by," Darlene said.

"If Wells and Sherry were in cahoots, then he would have

been comfortable enough with her so that she could walk up to him with a hatchet in her hand and hit him in the head with it."

"I guess her motive would have been so that he couldn't expose the murder plot against Romano," Pete said thoughtfully.

"By all accounts, Wells was a nice guy. Eaten up with paranoia and whatever other issues he had, but not the kind of guy who would want to be an accessory to murder."

"She might have talked him into hacking the BMW by telling him that it was a joke," Darlene suggested.

"Probably something like that. According to Wells's mother, who knew her when Wells and Sherry were dating in high school, Sherry was very manipulative. Once she heard some of his paranoid delusions, she could have just come up with a story that fit into his fears."

"We should keep this quiet for as long as we can. When Sherry learns that we're onto her, she'll call in the lawyers and shut us out," Pete said.

"I agree."

"I need to get home. It's Halloween and I love to scare the Dickens out of the kids." Pete chuckled.

"You aren't a nice man," Darlene said.

"If I scare the kids away, then I get all the candy," he said with a smile.

"You need more rocks and less candy in your bag, Charlie Brown." Darlene smiled.

"You're just jealous 'cause you've got to stay up and make sure none of the little rugrats burn anything down."

"Hush, now. Don't even talk about fires." Darlene wagged her finger at him.

We'd been lucky over the years that Halloween was still a fun holiday in Calhoun, and that even the bad guys seemed to give the night over to the young kids.

Back at my desk, I finally got through to Romano's sister at four-thirty.

"I said all I'm going to say. I never should have said

anything," Gloria told me.

"Who do you really suspect of killing your brother?"

"I told you. I don't have anyone specific in mind." She was a horrible liar.

"Do you have any idea how large your brother's estate is?"

"How would I know that?"

"Doesn't it all go to his wife?" I wanted to see what she would say.

There was silence.

"Take a guess at the amount." I pushed her.

"Millions. The company was worth twenty million when he forced the rest of us out. He sold off the assets and transitioned it into a name for importing shoddy European junk." She didn't spare the bitterness.

"You sound like you hated him."

"What I hate was that it was the right thing to do. That is, if all you looked at was the bottom line. He sent us checks regularly. If he hadn't forced us out, someone else would have taken us over before or after we declared bankruptcy. There just aren't enough people who will pay for true and honest craftsmanship anymore."

"Sherry will inherit millions."

There was a long pause. "Yes. My husband is on good terms with their lawyer, Kassim French. He used to represent all of us until Tommy went out on his own."

"You're scared of her."

"At a family get-together two years ago, she almost stabbed me because I told her she was being too rough on Tommy."

"What do you mean 'rough'?"

"I watch true crime TV shows and listen to podcasts. I know what can happen if you cross a psychopath. I don't want her coming after me."

"Don't you want her brought to justice if she killed your brother?"

"Tommy's dead. My family is alive. I want us to stay that

way. I tried to warn Tommy after she threatened me with the knife. He wouldn't listen. The woman had some kind of hold over him. Yes, I'd love to see her get what she deserves, but can you promise me that she'll get the death penalty?"

"No."

"I know how all this works. She has a lot of money at her disposal. After you arrest her, she'll get out on bail. That woman wouldn't hesitate to come after me. Do you remember that female astronaut? The one who drove across country wearing a diaper to kidnap her boyfriend? That's the type of determination I've seen in Sherry."

"I understand your fear, but…"

"No buts. Sorry." Gloria ended the call before I could say anything else. I didn't blame her. There were no guarantees, and with our current evidence I couldn't say for sure that Sherry would even be arrested on murder charges.

It was almost five. I went back to find Lionel.

"Would you look through Wells's possessions with me?" I asked him. "There were a number of electronic items that none of us could identify."

"You looking for something that might help him to hack into a car's ECU? I'm not too familiar with ECUs." He pulled up some images of a BMW's ECU on his computer and examined what the connectors looked like. "Okay, let's go check it out."

While we waited for Shantel to pull the boxes, Lionel looked at the clock.

"We got to make this quick. I'm taking my daughter trick-or-treating. Her mom bought her an Elsa costume." He saw my blank expression and pulled his phone out to scroll to a picture of his five-year-old in a princess outfit. "You know, from *Frozen*."

"Oh, yeah." I had seen a few thousand ads about a Disney movie by that name. I smiled at the picture. "She's cute." What else could I say? Especially since my first thought had been that she looked a little crazed, holding up her scepter menacingly.

We quickly went through the boxes until we came to a couple of small black plastic boxes held together with duct tape. One had an input connector that Lionel said matched what was used on the BMW.

"Looks like he jury-rigged this together so he could connect a keyboard or maybe a laptop to it."

"I think this is now exhibit A. We'll have to get someone from BMW to take a look at it," I said as much to myself as to Lionel.

I let him go so he could guide his princess from door to door, gathering chocolate and sugar. The box went back into the evidence room.

I called Cara to let her know that I was going to spend a little more time putting everything I knew about Sherry Romano and the murders into a single document. Soon we were going to have to present everything to a judge and the State Attorney. The challenge would be to do it in a way that made sense of acts committed by a crazy woman.

It was close to seven by the time I left the office. I was surprised to see Lt. Johnson coming in. Everyone had noticed that he'd been scarce around the office since word had gotten out that he was leaving.

"Macklin," he said by way of greeting.

"Lieutenant." He was ten feet away, walking toward the office as I was heading to my car. I could have let it go at that, but I felt like I needed to say something. "I'm sorry that you're leaving." I had searched my soul a bit to make sure that was true.

"Are you?" He turned, sounding surprised.

"You were willing to keep my feet to the fire, which I needed." I was sure that was the truth.

"As I've told you, you've got what it takes to be a great investigator. I don't think it does you any good to be working at an agency where your father is in charge."

"You're probably right." I had a moment when I didn't know if I wanted to take it any further, but then it seemed like the right thing to do. Johnson had always been honest with me. "Or maybe you aren't. I had my doubts at first, but you know what? I feel good about working here. I agree with you that there are pitfalls I have to watch out for, but knowing that the man at the top is going to do the right thing and that, not just me, but *anyone* can go to him if they think there's a problem or need help, that's a good thing. Not every department is like that. We may make mistakes, but it won't be because we didn't try to do the right thing."

Johnson's eyes were hard and his face firm as he stared at me. "I'm just moving down to Panama City. I'll be keeping an eye on you." He started to walk away, then stopped. "I'll expect you to live up to your ideals." Then he was gone.

The sun was low in the sky as I pulled out of the parking lot and started toward home. I stopped at a red light and looked over at the gas station that sat on the corner. To my surprise, I saw Sherry Romano leaning over at one of the gas pumps. At first I thought that she was filling up her sporty little Audi convertible. The odd thing was that the trunk was open. Then I watched her hang up the hose and pick up a red plastic gas can and put it into the trunk, where I realized there was already a second can.

The light had changed and the car behind me tapped their horn. Already past the turn into the station, I couldn't pull in behind her, so I went through the intersection to the first place I could turn around. Traffic seemed heavier than usual for this time on a weekday, most likely due to Halloween. By the time I got back to the station, Sherry was gone.

I drove as fast as I could without putting on my siren and lights. Being unmarked, people didn't get out of my way like they would have if I'd been driving aggressively in a patrol car. On top of that, I was being hypersensitive to the number of kids walking the streets. Some were in costume, some not. Still, I managed to get to the Romano house in only five minutes.

What I wasn't prepared for was Sherry Romano being prepared for me. She was out of her car, her head on a swivel and clearly highly alert, and she spotted me as soon as I was close to the house. A small group of children were heading up her drive as I neared the house.

Knowing that she'd seen me, I didn't have the option of being discreet anymore. Besides, I didn't like knowing that those cans of gasoline were in the back of her car. Clearly she was planning on burning something, though I had no idea if it was her house, the Lynch house, a pile of evidence, or even another body. Since her house had a circular driveway and I couldn't easily block her in, my plan was to pull in facing her car. If she wanted to make a run for it, she'd have to back out and I would have several options at that point, including a slow speed collision that would disable her car, hopefully without igniting the gas.

With her eyes glued on me, I thought she was going to get back into the car. Instead she shocked me by grabbing the smallest child in the group that had walked up the driveway. The child was dressed in a white costume with some sort of mask. Boy or girl, I couldn't tell, but before I could do anything, she had flipped the child into the open front seat of her car. The other children seemed stunned and just stood there as she climbed into the car.

I'd already nosed into the drive and managed to throw my car into reverse, but not fast enough to stop her from backing out. If she hadn't had the kid, I would have rammed her car. But my mind wouldn't let me even consider that with a child in the car and at least four gallons of gasoline in the trunk.

Sherry whipped the little Audi around before I could get turned the right way. The children had come running down the driveway, screaming about their abducted companion.

I hit the lights and siren and called dispatch. I requested that a car be sent to the Romano house to talk with and comfort the children. I assumed they'd be able to tell us who the child was and where the parents were. I also informed dispatch that we had an abducted child and to alert the watch commander and Dad of the situation, but that no one should attempt to stop Sherry at the moment.

I was following as fast as I dared. Any attempt to get close to Sherry just encouraged her to lay on more speed. I didn't want to see anyone get run over or incinerated, so I opted for keeping her in sight. I had a suspicion where she was going. Sure enough, we were making all the turns that would lead us to the Lynch house. I called Dad.

"I just heard."

"I'm following. But go ahead and move cars into position to block the roads leading out of town."

"I'm already doing that. What is your evaluation of Sherry Romano?"

"Unstable. Grabbing the kid was crazy. I don't trust her. At this point, I'm sure she's homicidal. I'm not sure about suicidal."

"We need to know when to move in."

"I think I've got a better chance on my own. Any more pressure on her and who knows how far she'll go."

My phone rang. I didn't recognize the number, so I put Dad on hold and switched over.

"Get back. If you don't, I swear I'll kill this boy," Sherry said when I answered.

"Whatever you say. Right now we aren't interested in you, we just want to get the boy back safe," I assured her. Every word was the truth. We could deal with Sherry Romano once the child wasn't in any danger.

"I don't want to see you behind me anymore." She had to half scream as she was driving with the top down.

"Okay." I slowed down. Feeling sure that she was headed to the Lynch house, I turned so that I could come up behind the house. This was a gamble. If I was wrong and we lost Sherry and the child, then it could turn into a statewide or even a multi-state search. "What I need to know is how I can get the child back," I told her.

"I'll leave him someplace and you can pick him up."

"Where?"

"I'll tell you where the kid is when I'm safe."

"Not good enough."

"Fine! I'm taking him to the Lynch house. I'll leave him there. But if I see any cops, I'll burn the place down with him in it. Understand?"

"Yes. Just leave the boy there. Listen, I'm not going to lie to you. You know we'll be chasing you. But I'll give you a head start if you leave the boy unhurt."

"You know, I thought you were kinda cute in a nerdy way back in elementary school," she said. "Now I know you're just a wuss. I'll call you when you can pick up the boy."

As the call disconnected, I thought it was odd that she'd told me that she was going to leave the boy at the Lynch house. Why had she given that away?

CHAPTER TWENTY-FIVE

I switched back to Dad and reported what Sherry had said.

"We can get eyes on the house without her knowing it," he responded.

Our SWAT team had several deputies who were very good at donning ghillie suits and crawling through the underbrush or hiding in a tree. I was also sure that Pete was on his way with his sniper rifle. He was the best shot on the team. Not the best at crawling through the underbrush, but with his rifle and scope he didn't need to get too close to have a shot at Sherry if she exposed herself and posed a threat to the boy.

I parked on a street behind the house and approached from the back. All of the surrounding properties were lots of at least two to five acres, so I had a little bit of country to cross. I wondered what Sherry could be up to. What was the point of all this? Grabbing the trick-or-treater had been a spur-of-the-moment decision, but she'd already bought the gasoline for some loony purpose of her own.

A few minutes later, I could just see the back of the Lynch house from a clump of blackberry brambles in the hundred yards of no man's land that separated the Lynch house from the Khans. My clothes weren't offering much protection from the brambles and I winced as I pushed through them. I could see the shed that Wells had holed up in and crept toward it, staying low and behind it so that the shed would provide some cover from the house.

At the shed, I settled down out of sight to watch. I didn't dare get any closer. I would have a hard time living with myself if an imprudent action on my part led to the death of a child.

I called Dad again.

"We've got the front covered and have stopped all traffic, both pedestrian and motorized," he told me.

"Has anyone seen her?"

"We've seen movement at one of the windows. The distance makes it difficult to be sure. We're losing light too. That'll let us move closer, but everything else will be more difficult."

"I'm going to call her," I told him, waiting for him to shoot the idea down.

"Do it. Try to get her to leave the boy. Who, by the way, is named Zander Washington."

"I wish I had two phones. I'm putting you on hold again." A second phone would have allowed Dad to listen in on my conversation with Sherry.

"You better be staying back." Her voice was full of menace.

"We're back. Can I speak with Zander?"

"The kid?"

"Please."

"Speak," I heard her say, her voice distant.

"Help me! She's nuts. I want my mom!" the poor kid shrieked.

"There, are you happy?" I could hear him still yelling in the background. "Thanks for getting him stirred up," she groused at me.

"Sherry, I know you didn't mean for everything to get this far out of control. We can work this all out. Start by letting the boy go. Just push him out the door and tell him to run down the street."

"I figured y'all would surround the place."

"You know that our primary concern is for the boy." I figured that she was thinking she could use the boy to distract us so she could escape, and at this point I wanted to encourage that way of thinking.

"I need time," she muttered. "Just give me some time."

What would time buy her other than full darkness? She had to know that the longer she held up in the house, the more law enforcement officers there would be around the place.

"How much time?" I pushed.

"Give me an hour." She hung up.

I got back on the phone with Dad.

"She can have an hour as long as we don't see or hear anything that suggests she's hurting the boy." There was grit in his voice. I knew that as soon as he thought that boy needed to be rescued, the cavalry would be set loose to charge the house with the intent of saving the child at any cost—to Sherry Romano or themselves.

I settled down to wait. The evening was warm for October and I had to keep wiping the sweat from my eyes. I was trying to make time pass faster with the power of my mind, but I wasn't having any luck. I sat there and strained my ears and eyes, hoping not to see or hear anything that would suggest that there was evil happening inside the Lynch house.

I got a text alert. It was Cara. I'd forgotten to tell her that I wasn't going to make it home anytime soon. I thought about ignoring the text until I looked at my watch and saw that we still had twenty minutes left in Sherry's hour. Taking the time to text Cara wouldn't hurt anything.

Her text read: *Where are you? Emergency? I just went out on the porch and your Ghost almost got out. I could just imagine the little idiot getting under the porch and us having to bring Mauser over here to entice him out.*

I remembered that there had been something about

Ghost in the back of my mind, but I still couldn't retrieve it. I answered: *Serious issues here. I'll be home when I can. Don't expect me anytime soon. Happy Halloween.*

She sent back: *Be safe – kisses!*

Time slipped on until Sherry's hour was up. It was now full dark. The moon wasn't up and the grounds around the house were shrouded in total blackness. I was just thinking about moving closer to the house when I suddenly remembered what had been nagging me about Ghost. While I'd been fumbling around under the house trying to catch him, I had turned and whammed my head on a support pillar. What I'd noticed then, but hadn't given any thought to at the time, was that the pillar wasn't in line with any of the others. It looked like all the others—same size, materials and age—but why was it there?

I stalked toward the house as a bright light suddenly pierced the night. A large fire had erupted on the top floor. At almost the same instant, I heard people shouting and my phone started to ring. I ignored it and moved faster. I was trying to remember exactly where to find the access panel to get under the house.

There was a loud crack as wood splintered somewhere toward the front of the house. I stumbled through the azaleas and camellias until I finally found the hatch. I opened it and saw a light shining back at me as the sounds of a dozen sirens wailed in the distance. I pointed my flashlight toward the light coming at me and saw a crazed woman with a bag and a hatchet scuttling toward me. I pulled my gun, but the awkward position slowed me down and she was on me before I could clear my holster. I rolled back into the bushes as she barreled into me, chopping at the air.

I was off balance and back on my haunches as she came at me. I tried to bring up my gun while grabbing at her hatchet arm with my other hand. She got a good whack on my left hand with the blunt end of the hatchet that shot pain all the way up my arm. I rolled and brought my gun hand down on the side of her face, trying to use my body to pin her hatchet arm.

I struggled to bring my gun to bear on her. I felt her hatchet arm getting away and I knew that if the weapon contacted with my head, things would take a very nasty turn. I did what I had to do. I leaned forward and bit down as hard as I could on her hand. She let out a shriek that I was certain could be heard over the sound of fire trucks screaming into the front yard.

She dropped the hatchet, but blood made her arm slippery and she managed to squirm out from under me. Up like a flash, she grabbed the bag she'd dropped and ran in the direction of the shed. I hesitated for just a moment. Should I go to help with the fire or give chase? The decision was easy—I wasn't going to give her a chance to escape. There were plenty of other responders to rescue the boy and put out the fire.

I ran after crazy Sherry as fast as I could. The firelight from the house made the shadows even darker. I tripped a couple of times, but she must have been having as difficult a time of navigating in the dark, because I was still managing to close the ground between us.

Sherry heard me coming up behind her. Suddenly she stopped and I saw the black shape of the bag coming back at me. It slammed into my shoulder as I managed to get my head out of the way. Something heavy fell to the ground as Sherry took off again.

I was right behind her as we reached the street where I'd parked. We both saw the patrol cars at the same time. Sherry started to turn back toward me, but I was in no mood for more field sports. I kicked her feet out from under her before dropping down hard on her back. Before I knew it, a state trooper was standing above me, cuffing her hands.

"We got her accomplice," he told me, leaving me to wonder who he was talking about.

"I need some water and maybe some alcohol," I told him as I got to my feet. At that moment, all I wanted to do was get the taste of her blood out of my mouth.

We walked Sherry to my car and locked her in the back.

"He's some lawyer," the trooper said, handing me a bottle of water. "Started shouting about his rights."

So Kassim French and Sherry Romano were in this together, I thought. After washing my mouth out, I drove around to the front of the house. Water cascaded down from the fire hoses as crews worked to get the flames under control.

"Are you okay?" Pete asked earnestly when I pulled up.

"Might want someone to look at this hand," I said, climbing out of the car. It was already starting to swell. Sherry ranted and cursed in the back seat. I slammed the door with my good hand, muffling her complaints.

Pete led me to an ambulance parked out at the curb. The traumatized Zander was sitting on a stretcher, snuffling and wiping at his eyes. Hondo was talking to him and trying to assure him that everything would be all right, but the boy was badly frightened.

Suddenly I heard a soft woof and turned to see Dad being pulled toward us by Mauser. The Dane's eyes were focused on the boy, not taking any notice of the riot of sound and activity around the house.

"Dad, I don't think—" I started, but the boy had already seen Mauser. He visibly straightened up and the tears quit flowing.

"Wow!" was all he had time to say before Mauser's big head collided with his legs. Mauser rubbed the boy with his head while Zander laughed and attempted to pet him.

"Zander! Oh thank God!" said another voice. We all turned to see a frantic woman jogging toward her son. She hugged him while he petted and laughed at Mauser, who stayed beside the boy and his mother, his tongue lolling happily.

"Zander met Mauser at our church's fall festival," his mother said, half crying and half laughing.

Finally, Dad pulled Mauser away from the happy reunion. The dog turned his full attention to me.

"Don't touch my hand," I warned, holding my arm in the

air as Mauser's head collided with my side. "Kittens and kids, huh? Maybe you have some uses after all," I begrudgingly told the big buffoon.

Five days after Halloween, I stood looking at the burned-out hulk of the Lynch house. Pete, Darlene, Lionel and Albert Griffin were with me. The fire department had managed to save about forty percent of the house.

"These old houses were made from heart of pine. They were lucky to have saved any of it." Mr. Griffin shook his head sadly.

"I'm glad they saved the most important part for our demonstration today," I said.

"I brought the drone and the pole." Lionel was pulling things out of a king-size duffel bag.

"First let's get a shot of the hole in the floor from the top," I told Lionel, who nodded and set up the drone. We were using the drone because no one with any sense would try walking into the ruins.

We watched on a laptop as the drone flew through the charred remains of the house.

"There," I pointed as the drone hovered near the corner of the interior walls of the dining room.

On the screen, we could see where pieces of the baseboards had been removed from two sides of the ninety-degree angle formed by the walls.

"That three-foot-by-three-foot piece of flooring was built so it could be removed from inside the house or from underneath. To lift it up from the inside, you'd have to remove the baseboards. I doubt it was removed from inside very often, if at all."

"You said the brother built the house?" Darlene asked.

"That's right," Mr. Griffin said. "Thaddeus had done much better financially than his younger brother. When he decided to build the new house, he contracted with Simon to do it."

"Simon must have been jealous of his brother's wealth, so he built a secret door in the floor so he could sneak in and rob Thaddeus." Pete nodded.

"Exactly," I said.

After everyone had a chance to get a look at the hole in the floor, and we were sure we had enough pictures to go with our evidence to the State Attorney, Lionel brought the drone back.

We moved to the side of the house and set up the laptop again. This time, Lionel used a telescoping pole that had a light and small camera attached to probe beneath the house.

"That is the pillar that was used to support the piece of flooring. There were several wooden wedges that had to be removed, and then there was enough give so that you could remove the top layer of bricks. After that, you just eased the piece of flooring down and out of the way. That left a hole big enough that most people could squeeze past the remaining pillar and up into the dining room," I explained.

"Which is what Simon must have done. At night, he'd sneak into the house, go to Thaddeus's office and steal money. Of course, Thaddeus wasn't able to figure out how someone was getting into the house and it drove him crazy," Mr. Griffin said.

"You have to wonder if that was part of the pleasure Simon got out of it," Darlene observed.

"Finally, on the last night, Simon must have been caught by Mrs. Lynch. When she saw Simon, she would have known right away that he was the one who had been stealing from them. She probably turned to run back upstairs. Simon knew he had to stop her, so he grabbed the axe from beside the back door and hit her as she reached the stairs." Mr. Griffin was enjoying telling the story.

"And when he saw what he had done, he gave his brother forty-one." Pete paraphrased the old ditty about Lizzie Borden.

Mr. Griffin nodded and continued the narrative. "His anger and jealousy must have taken over and he climbed the stairs, axe in hand, to kill his brother. Who knows why he killed the other children? I do think it was a conscious decision to leave Daniel alive. He knew that the older boy would be blamed for the hideous crimes."

"Why do you think the boy killed himself?" Darlene asked.

"I don't think we'll ever know. Maybe he was convinced he *had* killed his family. Remember, they had no other explanation for the crimes. Perhaps he felt guilty for having slept while his family was slaughtered. Then there's the fact that he was being accused of the crime. Being in jail for a terrible crime like that, and knowing that you were innocent but would probably be found guilty, would drive most people to the brink of despair."

"So as for the most recent murders, Sherry Romano killed her husband with the help of Gregory Wells," Darlene said, looking at me for confirmation.

I nodded. "Yeah. She'd heard through her real estate connections that Mr. Hinson was considering selling the house, so she came by one day to look at the property. While she was walking around, she bumped into Gregory Wells. They'd been sweethearts in high school and she knew he was brilliant. I don't know exactly when she hatched the plan to kill her husband, but I suspect she'd been thinking about it for a while. She'd been having an affair with their lawyer for over a year. Anyway, at some point she figured out that Wells could help her get rid of Tommy, so she manipulated him into hacking the BMW's electronic control units, which gave her the ability to slam his brakes on at the best possible moment for her plan."

"She wasn't stupid and knew that Wells had to be silenced," Pete said.

"Wells was a good guy. I don't know what she told him to convince him to hack the ECUs, but she knew that he wouldn't be on board when he learned that it had killed her husband, so she killed Wells first."

"Once it had been hacked, the BMW was a ticking time

bomb that she could set off anytime she wanted to," Darlene said.

"That's right." I nodded.

"And the other woman?" Mr. Griffin asked.

"Vicky and Sly interviewed Wells a couple of times," I said. "In one of them, he went off on a paranoid rant. If you assumed that he was just lost in his own fantasies, you might not pay any attention. He mentioned a car's being hacked and his secret love. He even gave her initials and the real estate agency where she worked. All of it was mixed up with a whole boat-load of crazy jabber, but Vicky figured it out. She was tired of working with Sly and needed money to go off on her own, so she made the mistake of blackmailing Sherry."

"Never a good idea to blackmail a psychopath," Pete interjected.

"No. Sherry figured out a way to get rid of Vicky with the added benefit that it would focus more attention on the axe murders, and hopefully divert us from the car accident."

"So she used a burner phone to lure Sly out of the house while she snuck in and killed Vicky," Darlene said knowingly.

"Precisely. She was pretty pissed at Vicky for trying to blackmail her, which is why we saw the overkill with Vicky that we didn't see with Wells. I don't think she had anything personal against Wells. He just needed to die as part of the plan," I explained.

"That's just sad," Pete said.

"That's evil, and with any luck a jury will give her what she deserves," I said.

"Okay. I see all that, but why did she come back to the Lynch house?" Albert asked.

"Two reasons. One: once she learned that she was the focus of the investigation, she needed to create time to get away."

"How did she know we suspected her?" Pete asked.

"That was my fault. I questioned Tommy's sister. She

was clearly scared and I guess she told her husband. He, in turn, called the lawyer, who had been a friend of the family. Of course, what the husband didn't know was that the lawyer was having an affair with Sherry and knew at least part of what she had done. He told her that the gig was up and they hatched this plan to get out of Dodge. That included her coming here and burning the house down to get rid of the evidence of the hole in the floor."

"About that. How did she even know the hole was there?" Mr. Griffin asked.

"On the day she came over to look at the property, she even looked in the crawlspace underneath. Remember, she was an architect as well as a real estate agent so, unlike me, she was immediately suspicious of a pillar that was out of sync with all the rest. She thought there might be something wrong with the house, so she inspected the pillar and discovered that it was a secret entranceway. It was pure luck, but she sure used it to her advantage."

"But I don't see how burning the house down would have helped her escape," Lionel said.

"I don't know what her original plan was, but I played into her hands when I chased her here. Probably she'd planned on getting one of the neighbors to see her. Anyway, somehow she planned to establish that she was inside the house. Once someone could swear that she was locked inside, she'd start the fire, sneak out through the hole, and then French could pick her up a few blocks away. She'd done searches on her computer for fires where people had died and they hadn't found any bones. Odds are, we'd have figured it out, but probably not quickly. Anyway, there would have been some confusion for a few days, during which she and the lawyer could fly off to Eastern Europe where he had a number of connections."

"You said there was another reason she came to the house," Mr. Griffin said.

"Yes, she wanted to retrieve the evidence that she'd stashed in the pillar."

"In the pillar?" Lionel looked confused.

"The false pillar is hollow inside. I don't know if Simon Lynch used it to store things, or if he just didn't see the point in making it out of solid brick. Either way, it left a handy spot for Sherry to stash the hatchet and the items she'd taken from Vicky. If the house burned down, she was afraid that the items would be found, and her plan rested on creating as much doubt about her guilt and her whereabouts as possible. So she had to come get everything."

"Where did the hatchet come from?" Pete asked.

"That was Mr. Tippets's from across the street. She'd talked to him once about selling his house, so she snuck over and stole it before she murdered Gregory Wells. I think she might have originally planned to leave it at the scene with the idea that everyone would think Wells had stolen it from Tippets and then someone used it on him. Maybe she changed her mind when she decided that the haunted house story could provide another layer of distraction to any investigation."

We left the house with evidence for Sherry Romano's trial, and for the book that Albert Griffin was going to write exonerating Daniel Lynch and naming Simon Lynch as the true killer of the Lynch family.

At home that evening, I was conducting my new nightly ritual of soaking my hand in ice. The X-rays had shown a few broken bones near my knuckles. Not wanting to be hampered by a cast, I'd opted for an Ace bandage, lots of ice and Ibuprofen, and time.

"So Ghost helped you to solve the murders," Cara said, smiling at me.

"I guess you could say that." The little menace was crawling up her arm to the back of the couch. Ivy watched him, the look on her face clearly saying that she wasn't having any part of the kitten and wouldn't stoop to solving crimes herself.

"And it put to rest the ghost of Daniel Lynch," I said. "When I told Alistair that Daniel hadn't killed the family, he was pleased that his mother had been vindicated in her belief that her cousin was innocent. Then when I told him that the real killer was Simon Lynch, he had to swallow the realization that his grandfather was a murderer. Still, I like the fact that it wasn't Daniel."

"Me too. The poor boy didn't have much of a life. It's nice that you've cleared his name." Cara snuggled against my side.

"I have one more thing to do."

"What's that?"

I pulled the P38 can opener out of my pocket. "Return this to its rightful owner."

We were quiet for a moment, then Cara asked, "What about Terri Miller?"

"Pete's put the case back on the front burner. But I don't know what the answer is." I wrapped my arm around Cara and pulled her close, thinking of all the ways that life could change in an instant.

Larry Macklin returns in:

Winter's Chill
A Larry Macklin Mystery—Book 16

ACKNOWLEDGMENTS

As always, thanks to my wife, Melanie, for her editing skills and support; to H. Y. Hanna for her inspiration, assistance and encouragement; and to all the fans of the series. Larry never would have come this far without all of you!

Original Cover Concept by H. Y. Hanna
Cover Design by Florida Girl Design, Inc.
www.gobookcoverdesign.com

ABOUT THE AUTHOR

A. E. Howe lives and writes on a farm in the wilds of North Florida with his wife, horses and more cats than he can count. He received a degree in English Education from the University of Georgia and is a produced screenwriter and playwright. His first published book was *Broken State*. The Larry Macklin Mysteries is his first series and he released a new series, the Baron Blasko Mysteries, in summer 2018. The first book in the Macklin series, *November's Past*, was awarded two silver medals in the 2017 President's Book Awards, presented by the Florida Authors & Publishers Association; the ninth book, *July's Trials*, was awarded two silver medals in 2018. Howe is a member of the Mystery Writers of America, and was co-host of the "Guns of Hollywood" podcast for four years on the Firearms Radio Network. When not writing, Howe enjoys riding, competitive shooting and working on the farm.